THE DEADLIES

DEFINITELY DEADLY

A. C. MILLER

iUniverse, Inc.
New York Bloomington

Definitely Deadly
The Deadlies

iUniverse books may be ordered through booksellers or by contacting:

iUniverse
1663 Liberty Drive
Bloomington, IN 47403
www.iuniverse.com
1-800-Authors (1-800-288-4677)

ISBN: 978-1-4502-7167-7 (sc)
ISBN: 978-1-4502-7169-1 (dj)
ISBN: 978-1-4502-7168-4 (ebook)

Printed in the United States of America

iUniverse rev. date: 11/10/2010

ACKNOWLEDGMENTS

I would like to extend a special thank you to the following people:

To my husband who ordered me to *"Go write!"* when my fidgeting during TV-watching finally got on his last nerve.

To my two daughters; Cady who is following in her mother's footsteps and writing her own stories, and Lexie who could care less about my stories but loves me just the same.

To my parents who encouraged me even though this isn't their kind of book.

To my co-workers at The Road who kindly overlooked my anti-social scribbling during lunch hour in the staff room.

To Susan who always listened to my rants during the writing and publishing of this book and who always took my side.

To Sally Brooks who was my very first editor and the Deadlies' first fan, and who threatened to hold hostage the edited chapters until I gave her the last three chapters...I promise it is worth the wait.

CHAPTER ONE

VILE FIENDS.
    Satan's spawn.
    Unclean creatures.
Evil minions.
Demons.

Those are just a few of the *kinder* names that the humans have called us over the years. It is rather insulting but I have found that when confronted with something out of the ordinary, humans tend to overreact just a tiny bit. But, let me tell you, the last person that called Demon an evil minion and threw holy water on him ended up going through a stained glass window. I hear that he still can't walk past a church without curling into the fetal position and weeping like a baby.

We are the Deadlies. You know…the Seven Deadly Sins. We are daemons that feed off the sins of humanity. Sounds totally evil, doesn't it? But, if we didn't drain away some of that crap, you would soon notice it. You think it is bad now. This is nothing. I bet that makes us seem a little less evil now, doesn't it?

We are the assassins of the supernatural world and it is our job is to execute supernatural criminals. Any vampire, shapeshifter, goblin, ogre, etc. that commits a violent crime is turned over to us. We make sure he or she no longer exists. They call us the Enforcers. That is probably all you need to know.

Only four of us are full-blooded daemons. The others are half daemon mixed with some other supernatural being—except for me. I am half-human and half-daemon. My father was a human and my mother is a daemon, a succubus to be exact. There is a race of daemons whose only purpose in life is to… well, perhaps we can just say they enjoy intimacy with others and leave it at that. The succubus is the female of the race and the incubus is the male counterpart. They are the only daemons that can shapeshift and thereby become whatever or whoever the human wants them to be. It is not a bad deal really. Some of the children of succubae and incubi can shapeshift too. I am not one of them.

Anyway, when I was born it was immediately obvious to both parents that they were not going to be able to pass me off as a human. I had my father's blondish brown hair, brown eyes, and pale skin, but the black wings rather ruined the illusion of humanness. In the daemon world, only the Deadlies and the Graces have wings. All of the Deadlies have black wings. If they had been white, we would have been Graces. I shudder to think of it. However, I can't help thinking that if my wings had been white perhaps my father wouldn't have reacted as disagreeably as he did. To be perfectly frank, he went ballistic. He passed away over five hundred years ago.

Though I am now several hundred years old, I look about twenty-five years old. Daemons stop aging physically at that point. I may have my father's colouring but I have my mother's facial features. I have a lean build, made for speed not strength. Fortunately, I have daemon strength anyway. Not every daemon-human hybrid does. It is very important in my line of work since I am the least threatening looking person on the planet. I just look too human. Our supernatural criminals tend not to take me seriously. That is a big mistake and it is usually their *last* mistake.

When I was fourteen years old, I went to live with the other Deadlies in their home, which is outside a city called Blackridge. It wasn't that big when the Deadlies first set up shop there, and you wouldn't believe that so much supernatural crime could happen in such a small area but Blackridge was definitely a hot spot. Things haven't changed much over the years. There are still criminals and we still perform executions daily, but for the most part our lives are somewhat tame.

Then one night, it all went to hell.

It was past two when Kaz and I left the last bar of the evening. The bar was still crowded with humans, drinking, flirting, and dancing. They would probably be at it for two hours more, but we had been in six bars so far, and I had had enough. Even Kaz Shade who was Gluttony was ready to call it quits and that is saying something. Besides, when you have just downed fourteen martinis in four hours and you're still standing, people look at you funny.

Kaz is one of my best friends among the Deadlies. He is tall with broad-shoulders and lots of hard muscle. He is dark and his black hair nearly reaches his waist. It's done up in a bunch of little braids and he has all these coloured beads through it. It takes hours to do it, but when you are immortal, you have all the time in the world. A few hours doesn't amount to much. His eyes are black and when he is pissed off; his face is very stern and forbidding like one of those guys who you would say you wouldn't want to meet in a dark alley, although *most* of the time he's not dangerous.

It was a cool night. Though temperature has no effect on us, we were wearing long black coats to hide certain supernatural aspects of our bodies. The wings tend to freak out the humans. We were both shirtless beneath our coats. The "no shoes, no shirt, no service" policy didn't apply to us because we'd kept our coats closed until we were safely inside the bar. What they didn't know wouldn't hurt us and besides, everyone inside was too drunk to care. I suppose we could have followed the rules and worn shirts but hell, *you* try stuffing six-foot wings into a t-shirt. Not only will you look like some kind of mutant; you'll be damned uncomfortable while you're at it. Kaz had added a dark hat to his ensemble to hide the black horns jutting out of his forehead.

"Going home alone again," Kaz sighed heavily and adjusted the hat lower on his forehead as we stepped out of the bar into the night. "Wish Riot had come with us."

I snorted. "It didn't look to me as though you were suffering for attention." Women seem to like my friend's tall, dark, and scary appearance. "Besides, if he had come with us, you wouldn't have stood a chance. Those women in there would have been chasing *him* down the street, not us."

Kaz grinned. His teeth were a flash white against his dark, dark skin. "We could have scooped up the slow ones."

"Thinking of adding another Deadly to your list?"

He shrugged. "It's not like there's a limit on these things."

I rolled my eyes. "I'm not surprised that you're Gluttony. What would Rowan have to say about your lecherous tendencies?"

Kaz winced at the thought of his girlfriend's reaction. "Is that before or after she turns me into a toad?"

"Look at it this way," I said sympathetically. "Now you can tell Rowan how you virtuously fought off all those women for her sake. Brownie points, man, brownie points."

Kaz' laugh echoed off the walls of the surrounding buildings, which is probably why we didn't hear them coming.

Now, I'm six-foot one in stocking feet. In my black boots, I'm about two inches taller. Kaz is three inches taller than I am. That puts him at six-foot six in boots. We're not exactly ideal prey if you know what I mean. So, you could have knocked me over with one of my own feathers when we found ourselves suddenly surrounded by a flock of vampires that decided that we looked like lunch. This surprised me. Vampires are not supposed to come after unwilling partners and those that do, usually don't choose people who look like they can fight back.

One of the vampires, a tall, scrawny man with ash gray skin stepped forward, grinning and flashing fang at us. That was also unusual. Vampires are usually more discreet when they approach a potential partner or victim. A stealthy attack doesn't give the other person a chance to raise the alarm and the vampire doesn't get a stake through the heart. Something was definitely wrong with this picture.

"Well, well." The vampire tried to chuckle but it came out in more of a strangled hiss. "Look what we have here, boys. It's a midnight snack." He chuckled again. He sounded like a sick snake, but I guess it's hard to laugh through fangs. The others laughed along with him, nudging each other.

"What the hell is this?" Kaz demanded.

"Bloodsuckers," I said.

Okay, okay. I know. But, I was shocked. I wasn't expecting a vampire ambush. So sue me. It was out of my mouth before I realized what I was saying. Just between you and me, that happens to me a lot.

The tall skinny vampire narrowed his eyes at me. "What did you call us?" He seemed annoyed that we didn't properly appreciate the fact that we were in deep shit.

Shock was quickly wearing off and now I was just offended that we had been marked as easy prey. I mean, damn it, if Demon had been with us, they wouldn't have come within fifty feet of us. His Deadly is Wrath and he looks like it. "Bloodsuckers," I repeated flatly. "And not very smart ones either."

Snake paused, taken aback by our obvious lack of fear. He glared at me. "You're awful mouthy for someone who is about to become food."

"It's one of my many charms." I snapped back. "And you're awful cocky for someone who is hunting people four times your size with a pack of dried up corpses at your back."

"Dev!" Kaz choked out. To anyone else he might have sounded worried. Actually, we were both trying very hard not to laugh. I didn't think the bloodsuckers would appreciate it if their targets suddenly got a fit of the giggles, so I ground my teeth trying to keep a straight face.

The vampires sucked in their breath and turned to their leader, waiting for him to react. The skinny bloodsucker looked at us doubtfully, but he couldn't back down now. It would make him look bad in front of his pals. He glided up to me until we were nose to nose. "Do you know what I am?"

I shrugged. "I think we covered that already though I have to tell you, dude, you really look like a snake."

His yellow eyes narrowed to slits. So did mine. Looking back on it now, I realize that I probably shouldn't have said what I did next, not aloud anyway. "Do you suppose he has a forked tongue too?" I said in an audible aside to Kaz, keeping my eyes on the little bloodsucker. "Wonder if it's a pierced forked tongue. He looks like the type."

Kaz couldn't hold back any longer. He burst into laughter. The bloodsuckers were not amused. "You are *dead*, human!" Snake snarled and stepped back from me as the others moved forward to join him. "But first, I'm going to enjoy kicking your ass!"

Kaz and I exchanged looks. Human? Well, it was reasonable of them to think so. With the hat on, Kaz could pass for human easily. However, since we weren't human, the vampires had just made a big boo-boo.

Snake began to strip off his black coat, slowly and methodically, the way you do when you want to intimidate your opponent. He flung his shirt off over his head and tried to stare me down. I looked at Kaz. He shrugged and gave a slight nod. That was good enough for me. We returned the favour, removing our coats and tossing them on the ground. Our six-foot wings sprang free, a bit ruffled, but imposing, nonetheless. Kaz flung aside the hat for good measure. There was no mistaking what we were now.

For a moment, they only stared at us in shock. Finally, one of the other vampires found his voice and cursed. "I know who you are!" he whispered. Everyone looked at him. He swallowed hard. "*Enforcers.*"

"And you just threatened to kill us." Kaz said in a soft, deadly "Wrath" voice.

I glanced at him. "Hey, that's pretty good."

"Thank you," Kaz said glancing at me. "I've been practicing."

"I can tell. But you know, technically Snake just threatened to kill *me*."

"You do tend to have that effect on people."

I widened my eyes and pretended to be shocked. "Who, me?"

We looked back at Snake. He was staring at us, frozen in terror. "I didn't know that you were Enforcers!"

"No, you thought we were human." I told him, all mockery gone from my tone. "And you didn't even care if we were willing humans or not."

"That puts you boys at the top of the execution list." Kaz added.

I think Snake cursed. It was hard to tell through all that choking and gasping and the sound of his friends running the other way. "You—you sh—should have identified yourself!" he stammered.

Kaz stepped forward. "And *you* should have been more careful about who you and your goons decided to pick on." he growled.

"You really ought to make some new friends," I suggested. "You should have seen them scrambling over each other to get out of here when they saw the wings."

Snake glanced back over his shoulder quickly and realized that his posse had indeed abandoned him. He hissed something that sounded like "bastards." I had to agree with him. My friends would never have turned tail and run off on me if we had been in Snake's situation.

"This just isn't your night, Snake." I said trying to sound sympathetic.

He glared at me, terror fleeing for the moment in a wave of anger. "You really are an asshole."

"Not everyone appreciates my honesty." I admitted cheerfully.

He smiled in spite of his predicament. Even as he inched backward, we were advancing slowly. I could feel his fear but I didn't savour it the way Wrath would have. When he felt he was at a safe enough distance, Snake tensed, ready to bolt if we even breathed funny.

"Well, then," he said carefully as if he expected us to charge him like rabid dogs. "I guess I'll be going."

"No." Kaz said softly as we drew our blades from the sheaths on our backs. "I think not."

Snake was fast, but we were just a bit faster. He didn't know what hit him. I promise.

We live in a large country house several miles outside of Blackridge, surrounded by bush and farmers' fields. The closest neighbour was on the next country block. The place is difficult to spot from the road unless you know what you're looking for. The isolation and desolate appearance of the house seems to discourage people from coming over on a regular basis to borrow a cup of sugar, or eye of newt, or whatever the hell humans borrow from their neighbours.

The house is white with black shutters. It is three storeys with a large wraparound wooden porch also painted white. The inside of the house isn't anything special. It is much larger on the inside than it appears on the outside. There are seven bedrooms and three guest rooms on the second floor. The third floor is actually a large attic. All of the carpets and panelled walls are dark colours just in case we ever have to perform an execution inside the house. It is much easier to hide the bloodstains. To date, we have never had to perform an execution on the main level of the house, but anything can happen in this line of work.

Kaz and I returned home about an hour after we had our run-in with Snake and his crew. There wasn't a drop of blood on us because it looked as though Snake hadn't had a chance to feed. We must have been his first hit of the night. It was a complete surprise when Riot met us in the front entryway, looked us up and down, and said, "Hope you hid the body."

"How did you know?" I gasped.

He smirked.

Riot's Deadly is Lust and he is an incubus. His parents were not incubus and succubus, so I am not sure how Riot ended up being one, but he is not just any incubus; he is *the* Incubus, able to inspire lust in anyone, no matter whether a human inspires that lust or more material things. It doesn't really matter what kind of lust he feeds from, though being an incubus, he prefers sexual lust to say, blood lust. In fact, blood lust is his least favourite. He explained it was kind of like eating lima beans. I could sympathize. I hate lima beans.

Riot is about Kaz' height and has very straight, waist-length, white-blond hair which he prefers to wear loose. There are black horns jutting out of his forehead. His skin is the colour of gold and his eyes are a shade or two darker. His appearance in public tends to cause women (and some men) to climb over each other to get to him

"Where is Demon?" I asked Riot.

He pointed. "Library."

We made a quick right and turned into the open door of the library. There were two men sitting on one of the dark red sofas. They appeared to be in a deep discussion but the conversation stopped and they looked up when we came in.

One of the men was Onyx Hellcurse, Riot's younger brother. Superficially, he does resemble Riot. He has white-blond hair, though his is shorter and curly, and black horns. That is where the resemblance ends. Onyx is shorter and younger than I am. He has green eyes and a permanent pout. He also has red daemon skin. His black horns are short, nothing more than a pair of stubs. His Deadly is Envy. Well, it seems only fitting that Envy should be Lust's brother.

Demon was leaning back on the sofa, his feet propped up on the coffee table, crossed at the ankle. It had a low back to accommodate his wings and how he could sit like that without falling on his ass, I don't know. His serious expression gave way to a big grin and his flame-blue eyes lit up as we entered. Demon Hellblazer and his brother, Bane, are the oldest of the Deadlies. They have been around for over 1000 years. Their mother was a succubus like mine, but their father must have been something human because, other than the wings, the twins don't look anything like a daemon. You wouldn't have even known that they were Deadlies if it were not for the black wings. Demon is also a vampire, the only one in existence that can walk in the sunlight without frying to a crisp. The Deadlies' symbol is a raven, the harbinger of death. Demon and Bane had been bringing death to supernatural criminals for centuries before the rest of us Deadlies were born. Between the jet-black hair and the black wings, they really do look like ravens.

"Hey, Demon," I greeted him as I strolled into the library.

"How was the bar?" he asked.

"Crowded."

"Aren't they always?"

"Kaz wished Riot was there. He was ready to commit another Deadly."

Riot laughed; a low chuckle designed to tickle one's fancy, so to speak. "Sorry I missed it," he said to Kaz. "Anyone in particular catch your eye?"

Kaz shrugged. "I was kind of leaning toward a petite blonde in a tight red t-shirt and having you there probably wouldn't have helped my cause."

Demon smiled. "What happened?"

"She scared me."

I raised an eyebrow at him. "Kaz, you're more than a foot taller than she was and outweighed her by about a hundred pounds."

Kaz raised his eyebrow back at me. "She was also drunker than a skunk and in between heaving up her guts on the sidewalk; she was having a deep and meaningful conversation with a lamppost."

Riot started to laugh. Demon gave us a small, knowing smile. "So, what did you do with the body?"

I know he's Wrath, but what the hell? Were we wearing a damned sign?

"It's hidden!" I said, annoyed.

"Where?" Riot demanded from the doorway.

"We tossed him in a dumpster in the alleyway."

Riot rolled his eyes. "Oh, that is just perfect. That will confuse the humans. Who has ever heard of a body in a dumpster?"

His sarcasm was starting to irritate me. "Look," I snarled. "It's hidden until garbage day at least, okay?"

Probably.

Demon winced. He closed his eyes for a second while he struggled to keep his cool in the face of our glaring lack of common sense. He opened them again. "Please tell me you're kidding," he said in a reasonably calm tone.

I bit my lip and looked at Kaz. He was gazing about the room, looking everywhere except at Demon. Nah, we didn't look at all guilty.

"I can't believe you guys dumped a body right out in the open!" Demon groaned.

"What were we supposed to do with it?" I demanded.

"You want that list alphabetically?"

"You could have sunk it in the river." Riot suggested. "At least the humans would have blamed it on the Mafia."

"Where the hell do you suggest we hide the bag of cement, smartass?" I threw open my coat to prove my point.

Riot opened his mouth to tell me just where I could shove the bag of cement, but Demon interrupted him hastily. "Forget it. It doesn't matter. Our priority now is to go back and dispose of the body properly before someone finds it. Where did you say it was?" he asked.

I told him.

Demon sighed. "All right, let's get rid of it before someone opens that dumpster." He frowned. "May I ask why you killed this man? Was he on our execution list?"

"Not that we know of." Kaz admitted. "To tell the truth, we really weren't expecting to off a vampire tonight on our way home."

Demon stared at us. "You executed a vampire?"

"Yes. Though, there were actually about ten of them." Kaz said.

"Thirty." I corrected.

Everyone ignored me.

"They stopped us in the middle of an open street." Kaz went on. "They were real bold, not at all worried about stealth."

"Ten bloodsuckers attacked you on a busy street?" Demon asked.

"They get real pissy if you call them bloodsuckers." I told him. "They were all at least six-foot nine, three hundred pound weightlifters—"

Kaz snarled at me. "Will you shut up?" He turned back to Demon and quickly explained what had happened earlier, including all my witty remarks, which he made sound as if I was being a smartass.

"It wasn't as bad as it sounds!" I protested as everyone glared at me.

I was relieved when Bane entered the room and everyone's attention turned to him and away from me. Next to Demon, Bane is my other best friend. We get along well because he is nearly as big a smartass as I am. Demon and Bane are identical twins. His Deadly is Vanity, but there isn't a vain bone in his body. Bane is able to shapeshift, but Demon does not have that ability.

Bane dropped onto the sofa beside his brother and propped his feet on the table next to Demon's. He stared at Kaz and me, and then rolled his eyes. "What did they do with the body?"

"For pity sake," I yelled. "We got rid of it!"

"In a garbage can," Onyx tittered maliciously.

I glared at him. "Hey, Jealousy, bite me."

Onyx' smirk turned to a scowl in an instant. He hates it when I call him "Jealousy" which was reason enough for me to do it. I didn't get along with Onyx.

"That's enough, both of you!" Demon snapped before he could say something back. Onyx slunk into a corner to sulk.

Riot sat on the sofa on the other side of Demon. "It sounds like we'd better go hunting."

"Not immediately." Demon said.

"I thought time was of the essence." Kaz frowned.

"It is, but now we also have nine little vampires to hunt down and execute before morning." Demon pointed out. "I'm going to call Daedalus first and see if he has heard anything about these rogue vampires. He should also know that there has been an execution, just in case someone reports the body before we get to it."

Daedalus is the chief of the local Satana, the police force of the supernaturals. We are sort of under Daedalus' supervision, though he has no control over us. He certainly has no control over Demon. No one does. Wrath needs no execution order from anyone. He does what he wants, when he wants. It is the Satana's job to uphold the law and make sure that the other supernaturals behave. However, when the supernaturals turn nasty, and require termination, that is *our* job.

Demon went to the desk and dialled a number we all knew by heart—666. "I'll ask him to loan us a couple of officers too." He went on while he waited for the chief to answer. "The more eyes and ears we've got out there, the better our chances of finding the vampires before dawn."

At last, Daedalus picked up and Demon put him on speakerphone. "This is Chief Hellcurse." Daedalus' gruff voice came over the line.

"Daedalus, this is Fechín." Demon said.

There was a pause and then, Daedalus sighed. "Go ahead, Fechín."

Demon quickly explained what had occurred and, thankfully, he omitted my smartass remarks. "Do you think they belong to the Blackridge kiss?" Daedalus asked.

"If so then the stapan will probably know who they are." Demon said. "If they are not, then he will want to assist us just so we don't scrutinize his people too closely."

"So, you'll visit the stapan and find out."

"There will not be enough time tonight." Demon said. "We need to dispose of the body and find the rest of the rogue vampires. What I need from you are some of your people to help us search."

There was silence on the other end of the line and then Chief Hellcurse said curtly, "I'll have Medea and a couple of officers meet you outside the bar."

Demon didn't thank him or even say good-bye. He just hung up. "Okay, let's work."

"I'll take Dev." Riot and Demon spoke at the same time and then grimaced at each other. It isn't because I'm so popular and they were both so eager for my company, but they knew that one or the other of them would be able to keep me in line.

"I can take him." Bane offered.

"Hell, no!" Demon exclaimed. "I would never be so heartless as to set the two of you loose on Blackridge together!"

Bane scowled. *"Excuse me?"*

Though I like Bane, I was affronted too. Demon was assuming that we were going to cause trouble. We would, of course, but that was beside the point. I was getting ready to dig in and be difficult when Demon said, "I'll take him, Riot. He'll just make you nuts."

"Maybe I'll drive you nuts too." I said to him.

Demon raised a black eyebrow at me. "You don't scare me."

Ah, a challenge. "Oh, yeah?" I snapped.

Riot rolled his eyes. "He's all yours, Fechín. Good luck."

Sometimes I feel so unappreciated.

CHAPTER TWO

DEMON DROVE THE VAN. He is the only one of us who truly likes motor vehicles. He collects them the way some people collect stamps. Since Demon chooses all of our vehicles, they are all black. He claims it is because it makes them less conspicuous. I think he just likes it because they look cool. The van's shiny bumpers were flat black and with the windows blacked out, it was like riding in a moving shadow.

We could have simply flown to the city, as Kaz and I had done earlier that evening, but there were no clouds to block the moon's light and Demon pointed out that six large, winged men flying through the air were going to attract attention. Apparently, we didn't want that.

"We'll split up at the City Square," he informed us as he turned from our dirt road onto the highway.

When we reached our destination, Medea and two Satana officers were waiting for us. I groaned when I realized that one of them was Darkfist Hellcurse, the Chief's son. He considered himself a lone wolf and referred to himself as "The Fist of Justice." He wanted to be an Enforcer, but if you aren't a Deadly, then you cannot be an Enforcer. Since we are immortal, it means that the bad guys can't kill us and believe me, when they know they are inches away from execution, they will try like hell to kill us. The average daemon is an Eternal. They can live forever unless someone kills them. It takes a lot to kill a daemon, but they can still die. Darkfist couldn't quite grasp the concept.

"Medea," Demon said as they approached us.

Her yellow eyes gleamed as they raked over him lustfully. "Demon, it has been a long time." Medea purred with a sizzling hot smile— literally. Flames shot from her mouth as her lips parted. She was hot for him. I think it had something to do with the danger associated with him being Wrath.

"Yes, I suppose it has," he said.

"I would love to see more of you," she told him.

I coughed and Riot nudged me. Whether he was agreeing with me or telling me to behave, I don't know, but when I looked up at him, he was grinning.

Medea walked over to Demon, her hips swaying, and pressed her small, muscular body against his. Her breasts strained against the tight leather vest and we were all watching her, wondering if they were going to spring free. Medea was a good foot shorter than Demon was, even with the three-inch heels on her black leather boots, and had to tilt her head back to meet his gaze. "What's up?" she purred.

He smiled at her, more amused than aroused. "What did the chief tell you?" Demon asked in a bland tone.

Medea sighed and stepped back from him. "You're no fun." She pouted and he laughed. She smiled back. "All he told me was that you were in charge of this little adventure. So, what's the deal?"

"We're looking for nine vampires. They have gone rogue."

"So this is an execution?" Medea asked. "We don't usually assist in executions."

"I know, but daylight is coming and I want to find them before they get home for the day. The more people we have looking for them, the faster we'll find them."

Medea nodded. "Okay. What do you want us to do?"

"We are going to split up into teams. That way we can cover more ground, faster. We have reason to believe that as of an hour and a half ago they had not yet fed. They may still be looking for food or they may have simply run home since they know Enforcers are in the area. Do not," he glared at Darkfist. "*Do not* execute any vampires unless Dev, Kaz, or I verify that they are rogues."

Darkfist scowled at him but said nothing. He was stupid but not suicidal.

Satisfied that he had made his point, Demon turned to the rest of us. "Riot, you and Kaz can take the van. That will limit the number of lecherous humans you'll run into." Demon glanced over at the other female officer that had been standing quietly off to the side up to this point. "Jordis can go with you."

Riot's smile disappeared and he looked away as Jordis Shadowmoon came to stand on the other side of Kaz. Jordis is a very beautiful woman with turquoise eyes and long black hair, so it seemed strange to me that Riot wouldn't enjoy her company. He likes everyone.

"Medea, you and Darkfist can be one of the ground teams. Bane, you and Onyx will be the air team."

Onyx and Bane looked at each other. It was a catch-22. The only reason Onyx was getting to fly was so that Bane wouldn't have to listen to him bellyaching about having to walk. The down side, of course, was that Bane had to work with Onyx. Suddenly, I was glad that Demon opted to take me with him if only to keep me from causing further trouble with the bloodsuckers. Hell, I could have been stuck with Onyx.

"Thanks so much." Bane growled at his brother.

Demon handed the van keys to Jordis. "You can drive."

Kaz opened his mouth to protest and then shook his head, obviously thinking the better of it. Jordis slid in behind the wheel of the van. Kaz and Riot both headed for the back seat, then stopped and looked at each other. While Riot was still considering whether he wanted the front or the back seat, Kaz got into the back and slid the door shut. Riot gaped at the closed door and then, slowly looked over his shoulder at us. Aware that we were all watching him, he finally got into the front passenger seat. The van started up and slowly pulled away from the curb.

Bane turned to Onyx with an air of reluctance. "Well, let's go," he muttered, spreading his wings and taking off. Onyx hastily spread his wings too and soared after Bane who seemed intent on losing his partner.

"It seems Bane isn't well pleased with his team mate for the night. I know just how he feels." Medea commented, glancing back at Darkfist who was sulking. She looked at me. "Sure you don't want to trade, Dev?"

"Not a bloody chance." I replied.

She sighed. "I didn't think so." She glared back at Darkfist. "Come on." She walked away with Darkfist trailing behind her still sulking.

Demon and I watched them until they turned the corner at the end of the street. "Why didn't you send him with Riot and Kaz? You know he's going to ditch Medea as soon as he gets the chance." I remarked to Demon. "Wouldn't it be easier to contain him in the van?"

He smiled slightly. "Don't underestimate Medea. She isn't about to give him the opportunity to lose her. There is a good reason why she is the team leader and he is not."

I wasn't inclined to agree, convinced that eventually she would have to summon one of us to rein him in for her. However, if Demon had that kind of confidence in Medea's ability to control the idiot who was I to contradict him?

"Okay, now where exactly is this body?" Demon asked.

I led him into the alleyway beside the bar Kaz and I had visited earlier in the evening. He opened the dumpster and looked inside. He shoved aside a garbage bag to find the corpse. I felt a flash of guilt since that meant that someone had come out and opened the dumpster after we had deposited the body in it. Since the alley wasn't crawling with cops, I guess they hadn't found it. That was a relief. Eight dollars an hour is not enough for some hapless dishwasher to discover bodies in dumpsters.

Demon glanced back at me. "Good execution, nice and clean. You must have hit him fast. He wouldn't have felt a thing."

"Gee, I feel so much better knowing that he didn't suffer." I said. "I've been in anguish over it. Now I'll be able to sleep at night."

"Now, now. Don't be sarcastic."

"So, any ideas about what we are going to do with it?"

"I'm fresh out of cement too."

I laughed. Demon grinned as he drew cell phone out of his pocket. "I have an idea."

"Who are you calling? Body Snatchers R Us?" I asked.

"Same thing. The Clean-Up Crew." he said.

"Oh no," I protested. "Not the Boogeys, Fechín!"

The Boogey Men are large humanoid creatures, covered from head to foot in long, brownish-red hair. The only way to tell the males from the females of the species is that males' bodies have enough hair to obscure most of their private bits. The females, on the other hand, let it all hang out. You may recognize the Boogeys under the name Big Foot.

The smell of them is appalling. Well, if you hung out in a closet with some kid's rotten gym shoes, I doubt you would smell like roses either, but the other reason for the stench was in the dumpster. Boogeys eat the corpses of our supernatural kills. They are the reason why you never find a dead werewolf or vampire in your backyard. You would think that, being Sloth, this wouldn't bother me so much, but my nose was already twitching and I feared it might just detach itself from my face and flee in terror.

I was still protesting summoning the Boogeys when Demon hung up and glared at me. "Got any better ideas, genius?"

Since I didn't, I shut up. Ten minutes later, four large Boogeys were entering the mouth of the alleyway. The largest Boogey led the way with the other three trailing behind him at a respectful distance. My nose wrinkled as they approached. I glanced at Demon. He appeared unaffected by the stench.

"Thanks for coming, Nightscare." he greeted the tallest of the Boogeys. "Did you have any trouble?"

"Nah," Nightscare said blasting us with his rancid breath. "We just came through the Robinson kid's closet. Kid sleeps like the dead so we didn't have to worry about someone seeing us. We took the sewers from there."

Ah. That explained the particularly revolting odour emanating from the Boogeys.

"Where is it?" Nightscare growled in a voice so deep and gravelly that it was hard to understand him unless you knew him well.

"They hid it in the dumpster." Demon told him.

Nightscare licked his lips. "Extra flavour. Yummy."

"Aw, gross!" I muttered to Demon.

Nightscare brushed past us and I held my breath. I tried not to be obvious about it, but I think I was turning blue. I looked over at the other male Boogey in the alley as he sauntered toward us. It was Nightscare's son and from the look of him, he had been bathing in the sewer water as they came along. There were things stuck in his long brown hair that I did not want to identify. The two females trailed after him gazing at him in obvious adoration. Apparently, sewer water is the Boogeys' aphrodisiac.

The Boogey grinned at me, showing the sharp teeth of a predator. "Yo, Sloth!" he bellowed, apparently unconcerned if the humans heard him.

"Yo, Beetlespaz!" I called back and promptly gagged as I inhaled the smell of Nightscare. I caught a glimpse of Demon's amused smile and scowled at him.

Nightscare lifted the lid of the dumpster and leaned down to peer in. "Humph," he grunted. "He's kind of scrawny."

"He didn't have a chance to feed yet." Demon explained. "But, that could just be his natural build."

Nightscare studied the corpse more carefully. "It's a vampire?" he asked surprised.

"Yes."

"An execution?"

"Of sorts."

Nightscare looked at Demon, sharply. "Does Daedalus know about this?"

"Yes." Demon replied impatiently. "Look, we don't have all night. Do you want him or not?"

Nightscare nodded his shaggy head. "Well, there's not a lot of meat on him. I got a large family to feed. Is this all you got?"

Demon's cell phone beeped. He flipped it open and looked at the text message. He flipped it closed and tucked it back in his pocket. "I think we can help you."

The text message was from Riot. They had found three of the nine missing vampires. Kaz had confirmed their identity and from questioning them, they had uncovered the whereabouts of at least five others. Demon gave permission to proceed with execution. Nightscare gave Snake's body to one of the females and sent her home. Then, he sent Beetlespaz and the other female to Riot's location pick up the three executed vampires while he accompanied Demon and me to hunt down the other five.

By the time we finally tracked them down, I realized, too late, that Demon hadn't taken in blood in a while. He can survive on wrath alone, but when he doesn't have blood, well, the outcome isn't pretty. Unfortunately, Nightscare ended up feeling a bit let down by the small amount that was left of the vampires after Demon was through with them. "Who the hell am I supposed to feed with that?" he had demanded. "That won't even satisfy a youngling!"

An hour later, we returned to the same spot where we had split from the others. They were all there waiting for us. Riot was leaning against the wall of a building. Onyx was beside him trying to imitate his brother's easy stance. Riot made it look sexy. Onyx made it look uncomfortable. Bane was sitting on the steps with Kaz, out of strangling distance of his partner. I wondered if that was Bane's idea or if Riot and Kaz had made him sit over there to protect Onyx.

Medea and Jordis stood slightly apart from the other Enforcers. Darkfist was leaning against the van, still sulking. I guess that Medea was better at keeping him under control than I gave her credit for.

"Get your ass off my van!" Demon snapped as we approached. Darkfist started and bolted upright.

"Did you find the others?" Riot called out.

I glared at him incredulously. How he could look at Demon and ask such a stupid question? "Are your taste buds out of whack?" I demanded.

Kaz rose from the stairs, watching Demon warily. "You found them?"

I'm sure I must have looked a bit green. "Oh, you could say that."

"How many did you find?" Bane asked as he approached cautiously.

"Only five," I told him wearily with a glance at Demon. He was beginning to calm, the excitement draining away. "They weren't at the same location you'd told us about. They had moved on to a club on La Clare Street. They were waiting in an alley to ambush someone. Boy, were *they* in for a shock."

"Did you get a chance to question them?" Bane asked.

I glared at him. "What do *you* think?" I demanded.

"So, there is still one unaccounted for." Riot said.

"He could still be out there looking for fresh meat." Bane suggested.

Images of Demon shredding the rogue vampires flashed through my mind. "Please," I groaned, passing a hand over my face. My skin felt clammy. "Don't say meat."

"Sorry." Bane said sympathetically.

I glared at Bane and pointed at his brother. "Why didn't you tell me that he hadn't fed yet?"

Bane winced. "I didn't know, Dev, or I never would have let you go with him."

"Next time, Bane," I told him. "*You* go with Demon."

He nodded. "Deal."

"So," Riot interrupted. "Are we going to continue to search for the other guy or do we go home?"

"We think he's already fed." I replied. "He'll have gone home. We may have found his victim. We found a woman in the park under a bench. From her wounds, we think she tried to fight him so it was probably our rogue that attacked her."

"Dead?" Kaz asked.

"Not yet." Demon answered softly. "We took her to the hospital. Dev left her with an orderly and then disappeared into the night like all good Samaritans. I'll call my contact at the hospital later to see if she made it."

We all fell silent for a moment. If she didn't make it, her family would be making funeral arrangements. If she lived, she would believe that a human had attacked her with a weapon. Demon had taken care of that before we dropped her off. After all, we couldn't have her going around claiming that a vampire attacked her. People would think she was nuts.

We said goodbye to Medea and Jordis. Darkfist ignored us. No one bothered to say good night to him. They left and we all piled into the van, Demon behind the steering wheel again. Bane got into the front passenger seat. "Will you be all right to drive?" he asked his brother.

"I'd rather ride with Demon in his most dangerous mood than with you in your best." I remarked from the back seat.

Bane turned to glare at me over his shoulder. "My driving isn't that bad."

Demon snorted. "In what universe?"

Onyx leaned forward over Demon's shoulder. "What did *you* do with the bodies?" he sneered.

Demon glanced back at him, eyes hard and ruthless. "What bodies?" he growled, his fangs flashing in the darkness.

Onyx sat there with his mouth hanging open for a moment and then sat back. He looked so green that I almost felt sorry for him.

CHAPTER THREE

WE RETURNED HOME. IT wasn't until we got inside the house that we realized that Demon was covered in blood and other bits of bodily matter. It was disgusting and I was glad I hadn't known beforehand because it would have really cheesed me off.

Morgana met us at the front door of the house. She took one look at Demon and stumbled back out of his way, quickly. He stalked past her with a wicked grin, his eyes still glowing, and went straight up the stairs without speaking. "What the hell have you guys been doing?" she gasped, her eyes following Demon.

Bane told her about our evening. "One vampire is still at large," he explained. "Riot and Kaz found three. Demon and Dev found the other five."

"Actually, only Fechín found them," I explained. "I was throwing up in the gutter. It wouldn't have been so bad if a couple of them hadn't found time to feed between the time Kaz and I lost them and Demon caught up to them."

"I'm glad I missed it then." Morgana said with a look of sympathy. She is the only female of the Seven Deadlies. Her Deadly is Greed. She has a big crush on Demon. Unfortunately, Demon had no interest in her as a lover.

Bane placed a hand on my shoulder. "If I had known that Demon was going to go Wrath, I would have gone with him instead."

To "Go Wrath" meant that Demon hadn't bothered to use his sword. It meant he used his bare hands and his fangs. As I said, it was not a pretty sight.

"It's okay." I shrugged and tried to sound nonchalant. "I've seen him in action before. I think because there were five of them there was just more...well, *more*. You know?"

Bane nodded. He was used to dealing with his brother's episodes and typically, he accompanied Demon on executions. We stood around for a few minutes, each of us reminiscing about a time when he had seen Demon do his thing and trying to gross each other out with the stories. Kaz was telling one particularly gruesome (and I'm sure highly exaggerated) story when Demon returned.

"I'm glad you're back." Morgana tossed her long black hair over one shoulder as Demon came down the stairs. "You had a phone call..." Morgana trailed off, distracted by Demon's bare chest. His hair was wet so he had obviously had a quick shower. I didn't know where her mind was going with this and I didn't want to know either.

I waved my hand in front of her face. "Morgana!" I sang out. She blinked slowly as if coming out of a trance. Her green, cat's eyes had yellow flecks in them, as if she had just been thinking a greedy thought. She glared at me.

Demon raised an eyebrow at her. "The phone call?" he prompted.

She turned her back on me in an obvious snub. I stuck my tongue out at her back. "Actually, there have been a couple of phone calls since I got home." she said in a business-like tone. "I received a message about an hour ago from Hadrian. It came through Maia."

Maia Severn is a werewolf and our liaison with all things gruesome. She keeps us up-to-date on who is doing what, when, where, how and to whom.

"Did she say what Hadrian wanted?" Demon asked.

"No, but here is the message," Morgana went to the small telephone table and held up a piece of paper. "I wrote it down for you."

Morgana handed the message to him and he read it aloud.

Maia got a message from Hadrian. He wants a meet with the Deadlies and wants me to set it up so call ASAP. Maia also needs to talk to Dev so she says to tell him to haul his sexy ass to the phone and call her.

I glared at Morgana. "You probably could have left that part out."

She grinned. They say that revenge is sweet and Morgana was thoroughly enjoying this moment. "What, and miss seeing you blush?" she teased.

I scowled at Morgana as the others' eyes turn toward me. I tried to keep my expression bland and indifferent, but I'm sure the others were well aware that Maia and I were attracted to each other. Unfortunately, she had a human boyfriend and I deemed it best to maintain some distance.

Demon handed the message to me. "Was that the only call?" he asked Morgana.

She shook her head. "Serkan called too," she said.

Demon frowned. "What did he want?"

"He didn't say." Morgana said. "He just said that it was important and that he would call back."

"Do you want to call him first?" I asked Demon. "I can call Maia later."

He shook his head. "No, call Maia. Finding out what Hadrian knows about these rogue vampires is more important right now."

"Since Serkan is our liaison with the vampires, I thought you would want to inform him about the rogues."

"There is no sense in calling him until we have a meeting scheduled." Demon pointed out. "Have Maia set up the meeting for us tomorrow night as soon as the sun sets."

"No way," Riot shook his head grimly. "Hadrian is not going to agree to meet with us before he feeds. He'll be at his weakest then."

"If he is not feeding from the unwilling then he has nothing to fear from us."

"So this is a test?"

Demon gave Riot a small smile. "You could call it that."

"Oh come on," I protested. "Ten of his followers came after Kaz and me because they thought we were human. Do you think their stapan is doing anything different?"

"We don't know for certain that they were Hadrian's people." Demon pointed out. "If he is being a good boy, he will meet us at dusk and if he is following the rules, everything will be fine."

"And if he is not following the rules?"

The blue flames in Demon's eyes flared and his mouth curved into a deadly smile. "Well, we are the Enforcers." he said softly.

Damn. Sometimes he scares the hell out of me.

CHAPTER FOUR

I FORCED MYSELF TO walk and not run for the phone in the library. I could have called from the hall phone but to be honest, if I was going to make an ass of myself over a woman, I didn't want any witnesses. I sure as hell didn't want to give my friends any ammo to use to tease me.

I dialled Maia's cell phone number after pretending to look it up in the address book, just in case anyone was spying, but I could have recited her number by heart. She answered on the first ring. "Hello?"

"I especially liked the part about my sexy ass." I greeted her.

Maia laughed. "Hi, Dev."

"Tell me what you have from Hadrian." I prompted.

"Apparently, a few of his people didn't make it home tonight and the Clean-Up Crew was seen in the area." Maia paused. "You wouldn't know anything about that, would you?"

"Hadrian wants to meet us about the Crew?" I asked surprised. "How did he find out so fast?"

"He isn't the one who mentioned the Crew. As far as I know, he doesn't know about that. I heard about them from another source." Maia said. Her sources—whoever they were—were usually quite reliable. "But, Hadrian said that he's missing ten vampires. He wanted me to find out if you went hunting tonight and if you executed anyone."

"Like ten of his people, for instance?" I suggested. "Why would he believe that we would execute them? Does he have reason to believe that they were doing something wrong?"

Maia chuckled. "He's too cagey to admit to anything like that. He does seem a bit paranoid about Fechín after their last run-in." She spoke carefully, using Demon's human name as if she had almost forgotten. Using daemon names like Demon or Bane over the phone was a no-no.

"He should be. He threatened Serkan."

"Serkan is a sovereign vampire." Maia reminded me. "Hadrian would have a hard time killing him."

"Fechín doesn't allow that sort of thing to slide. A threat is a threat, no matter how indirect, and can quickly lead to someone trying something stupid. Hadrian is lucky that Fechín didn't kill him outright."

"Wait a minute." I frowned as something she said sank in. "Hadrian said that he was missing *ten* vampires?" Daylight was beginning to peek in through the library windows. "Sunrise. So the tenth bloodsucker never made it home."

"Dev." she said, reprovingly.

I rolled my eyes. "Sorry. The tenth *vampire*, I mean. Your source was right about the Crew, but they only took nine bodies."

"So where is the tenth?" she asked.

"I don't know. We didn't find him, just his victim."

"Fechín?" she suggested.

I shook my head. "No, I was with him the whole time. He didn't—" I hesitated, remembering that chattering away about executions and vampires over the phone was also a no-no. If Demon caught me, he would freak. "I only saw him take five of them." I finished.

I must have sounded nauseous again because Maia made a sympathetic sound. "Poor Dev," she said. "What you're telling me is Fechín lost it."

"Fechín never loses it." I replied. "He's always in control. That is what makes him so frightening."

She sighed. "I suppose you would have to have nerves of steel to be who he is."

"His Deadly is the worst." I agreed. "You've never seen him lose control. I have. I wouldn't trade Deadlies with him for all the money in the world."

"I don't blame you."

"Listen, Fechín has a message for you to take to Hadrian. He wants to meet tonight at dusk." I said. I gave her Demon's message about not feeding first.

Maia expressed the same doubt that Riot had.

"Hadrian does not want to try sneaking anything past Fechín tonight. He is so not in the mood."

"Okay, but I still don't think he'll go for it," she said.

"This is not a request. This is an order and you can deliver it as such. Fechín doesn't play games. Hadrian should know that by now. Those rogues stopped Kaz and me on the street thinking we were humans. They weren't looking for willing partners and they didn't intend for us to walk out of that alley alive."

Demon entered at that moment and saw me still on the phone. "I'm almost done." I told him.

"Put her on speaker," he said.

I floundered for a minute trying to figure out which button to push. Demon sighed and moved around to the other side of the desk, gently nudging me aside. He hit a button. The phone beeped. I leaned against the desk with my arms folded across my chest and let him do the talking. "Maia, this is Fechín. Dev told you when we want the meet with Hadrian."

"Yes," Maia's voice sounded hollow coming through the speaker. "But, I still don't think he'll agree to it. Hadrian is not stupid. He won't face you without feeding first."

Demon's eyes narrowed and he began to pace in front of the desk. "Hadrian has just admitted that the rogues were his people. If that is true, it means one of two things. He doesn't know what they were doing, which makes him a bad stapan, or he did know which makes him our next target." Demon's fangs flashed as he grinned and his voice came out in a low growl. "Tell him that if it makes him feel any better, I will not feed either."

"That would not make *me* feel any better." I announced.

"I don't think Hadrian will find it very reassuring either." Maia agreed.

"If Hadrian does know about this, he'll lie through his teeth if he knows what's good for him." I said.

"There is that." Maia said.

"So, he gets to live another night." Demon said. "Oh, and tell him to come prepared to give up the tenth man."

"He *says* that he doesn't know where he is." Maia told him. "Apparently, this particular person is still on the missing in action list."

"Number ten is holed up somewhere then." Demon said thoughtfully.

"Or got caught in the daylight." she suggested.

Demon looked at me. "Was he that young and stupid?"

What he was really asking was if this vampire was a recent one or had he been around a while? Sometimes the new ones laboured under the mistaken belief that they were invincible. That was why they had to be under the protection of an older, more experienced vampire like a stapan or another sovereign vampire at the very least.

"Snake wasn't fresh," I told him. "Possibly Kaz' age and the others with him had to be within the last fifty years at least. No one was younger than that."

"So they should have all known enough to avoid sunrise." Demon said.

I nodded. "Hadrian's missing man wouldn't be out in sunlight trying to find his way home. He would go to one of Hadrian's boltholes."

Hadrian had hideaways around the city for vampires who, for whatever reason, couldn't manage to make it home before sunrise. The older vampires knew better than wander around the city after a certain time. They usually knew when sunrise would begin and made sure that they were home in plenty of time. Some of the younger, less experienced vampires sometimes tried to push the envelope a bit. When that happened, Hadrian's human servant, Simmons, would call us in a panic and ask us to find the vampire, alive or otherwise, before some poor unsuspecting human did. If the vampire made it to a hiding spot, we would let him remain there and guard the place until it was safe for him to come out. Then Demon would give the vampire a biting lecture on getting his or her ass home before the sun came up. No pun intended. If the vampire didn't make it to a bolthole, we would be looking for a vampire flambé.

Demon frowned thoughtfully at the desktop then he looked up at me, the flames in his eyes leaping, as if he had an idea. "Maia," he said. "Tell Hadrian that all ten rogues are accounted for and dispatched. Tell him to meet us at dusk at the Black Candle Pub and tell him to come without feeding. If he or anyone he brings with him has fed before the meeting, I'll execute him on the spot."

He hung up abruptly and turned to me. "I can't believe you said execute on the phone." I gaped at him.

Demon shrugged. "It isn't as if you haven't said it ten times or more by now so anyone who may be eavesdropping has already had an earful." He gave me a stern look. "Am I right?"

I nodded sheepishly. "Sorry." I said. "But, you know, we haven't executed the tenth vampire."

"We are about to do so." Demon replied. His eyes gleamed with excitement as he went into hunting mode. "After all, we know where all of Hadrian's boltholes are, don't we?"

CHAPTER FIVE

D EMON TOOK KAZ AND me with him, not only because we were more human looking than the others were, but also because we could identify the rogue. It saved us the extra step of having to verify the vampire's identity before execution. Usually we wait for Demon's go-ahead. However, if he wanted to execute someone he could make a judgment call and no one was going to slap him on the wrist for it. That is a good way to lose a hand.

I wasn't eager to watch Demon do his thing again, but I wasn't going to complain either. It would just give Kaz ammo to use to rag me. Still, it was a great relief when Demon said we would each take a different area to search. Whoever found the vampire first was to dispatch him and text-message the other two. We piled into the van and drove into Blackridge. We dropped Kaz off on a street corner near some ramshackle old apartment buildings and then Demon dropped me off on the beach. He was going to check the warehouses further down the lake.

Blackridge Beach is a long strip of sand, about ten miles long, where people come to enjoy the warmth and the water. The weather was extremely hot that day so the beach was busy. I stopped for a minute to watch the swimmers splashing and screaming in the lake and shook my head. They really would scream if they knew what was swimming in that lake with them. The Deadlies only swim in that water when we absolutely have to.

A small stream at the top of Blackridge Mountain winds its way down to a heavily wooded area and into a basin, which then widens into the Lishannon River. From there the river flows through the city and out into the Blackridge Lake. The lake connects to a chain of other lakes and eventually dumps into the ocean somewhere in the eastern part of the country. All this means that the water that carries things out to the ocean can also carry them into the lake. When you add in whatever might come down from the mountain or out of the basin and the river—on top of what already lives in the lake—well, you can see why I dislike swimming in it.

The beach was not my destination. It is somewhat difficult to have a bolthole right on the beach. I mean, what would you do? Bury yourself like a pirate's treasure chest? Instead, I walked along the boardwalk, casually making my way to an old fishing shack that had a hidey-hole in the attic. The shack was at the far end of the beach where the sand ended and it turned into pebbles. Most people would not have ventured this far. That is what made it such a perfect hiding spot. That, and the fact that the place looked like it would fall down on your head if you breathed on it too hard.

As I walked toward the house, I noticed a man standing on one of the piers. He had a fishing pole in his hands. A little boy standing beside him was eagerly casting his line into the water. "Look, Daddy!" he crowed. "Look how far I got it!"

The man smiled at the boy and then glanced at me with pride in his eyes as if to say, "Isn't my boy a genius?" I smiled politely as I passed by. I couldn't help thinking that the kid was lucky to be able to go fishing with his dad. My father took me fishing once when I was about four. I still remember how he wrapped me up in a coat to hide my wings. He was terrified that someone would see my "deformity" but he was determined that he was going to take his son fishing. It is the only good memory I have of him.

I pushed the memory away as the man and his son went back to their fishing. I walked on to the little shack. It was standing out further into the lake on tall wooden posts. I crossed the long bridge that led to its small front porch. I tried the door. It was locked and I didn't have a key to the shack. There was no sense in knocking because the vampire, if he was in there, was dead to the world and would be unable answer. It would certainly look suspicious if I kicked the door in. Fishing Dad would be on his cell phone to the cops and Demon would never forgive me if he had to come and bail me out of jail.

I glanced around at the man. He was more concerned with his little boy than what I was up to, but just in case, I used my body to block his sight as I pulled a small lock pick set from my pocket. This way, it would appear as though I had used a key. He would think that I owned the place or at least that I had a right to be there. In a few minutes, I had the door unlocked.

I stepped inside the shack and closed the door behind me quietly, trying not to step too heavily on any one spot on the floor. The floor had rotted in places and left large holes through which I could see the lake lapping at the posts. I didn't trust the rest of the floor. I wasn't in the mood to go swimming. I looked up and saw the trapdoor in the ceiling above my head that led to a storage area. I had checked this particular shack many times and it always amazed me that anyone could fit into the tiny attic. I grabbed a nearby chair and gingerly stepped on it. It looked as rotten and unstable as the rest of the place. Carefully, I pried open the trapdoor and pulled a flashlight out of my pocket. I turned it on and stuck my head into the opening.

Suddenly, something greyish flashed past my head and I jumped back, nearly falling off the chair. There was a loud thud as a solid body hit the floor. Before I could make out exactly what it was, the floor gave way beneath it and it fell into the lake with a splash.

Cautiously, I got down from the chair and went to see what had come out of the attic. We regularly find other supernatural creatures who have taken refuge in Hadrian's hideouts. Most supernaturals prefer dark, out of the way places to hide. I peeked over the edge of the gaping hole. Floating in the water was a lizard like creature with leathery grey skin and red eyes. It looked up and hissed at me, displaying two sharp little fangs in the upper part of its mouth. I recognized it at once.

"Sonofabitch!" I exclaimed and I grabbed my cell phone, dialling as the creature dove under the water and began to swim away.

"This is Fechín." Demon answered his phone.

"Fechín, this is Dev."

"Did you find him?"

"No. What I found was almost as bad."

"What is it?"

"I am pretty sure that it was a Chupacabra."

"In the attic of the fishing shack?" he asked amazed. I understood why he was surprised. We don't get many Chupacabras around here.

Chupacabras take on different appearances, depending on where they live. Some look like the offspring between a lizard and a dog. They walk on all fours and have long, thin spines along their backs. They are usually about the size of an adult black bear. Others, like the one that had flown out at me, are purely reptilian with sharp spines all over them and webbed claws. They walk on two legs like a human.

"How big was it?" he asked.

"This one was pretty small," I told him. "I would say about the size of an adult raccoon."

"So it was a baby?"

"Well, it was young anyway."

"No sign of an adult?'

"No. But then, I wasn't going to stick my head in there to check either."

"You wouldn't have to. An adult would have come after you to give its offspring a chance to escape."

I eyed the opening warily.

"We'll keep an eye open for an adult just in case." Demon went on. "I doubt Baby is here all by himself."

"Wonderful." I said.

Demon sighed. "Do you want help killing it?"

"No. I should be able to handle this. It went through the floor into the water. Do Chupacabras swim?"

"Not the ones that come from this area."

"Well, this one did."

There was a brief pause on the other end of the line. "He is a very long way from home then."

I sighed. "I guess I'm going swimming."

"I am afraid so."

"I hate swimming with creepy crawlies." I heard something on the other end of the line that sounded suspiciously like a snicker. My eyes narrowed. "I don't see what's so damned amusing about this."

"You wouldn't." he replied and hung up.

I placed the cell phone on the table and shed my jacket. I unsheathed my blade, took a deep breath, and plunged into the lake after the Chupacabra.

Twenty minutes later, I found and executed the little beast as it tried to eat the bait that was hooked on the line the little boy had cast out. It was fortunate that I had caught up with it when I did. It may have been a baby, but it was strong enough to pull that little boy into the water and it might have found him more palatable than the worm.

I dragged the body over to one of the cement blocks surrounding the small dock. There was an old rope, once used to anchor a boat to the pier, attached to one of the blocks. I tied the body to the block. With any luck, by the time the body came free of the rope, it would have decomposed enough to make identifying it impossible. As I started to swim away, I felt the water stir behind me. I looked over my shoulder in time to see a large, dark shape glide through the water toward the dead creature. A large mouth opened and swallowed the whole thing with one gulp. Then it gave one big yank and the rope holding the Chupacabra's body snapped. Slowly, the beast swam away again toward the open lake taking its prize with it.

I gaped after it. Well...that could work too.

I swam back to the shack, levered myself back up through the hole which I then covered with a piece of plywood that I found leaning against one wall. I looked up at the opening to the attic. I had not actually checked inside and, knowing that Demon would ask, I retrieved my flashlight from the small wooden kitchen table and grabbed a chair. I stood on it again and took a quick look inside the attic. The vampire wasn't there, but something with eyes was. I gagged and nearly fell off the chair again. Apparently, I had disturbed the Chupacabra during lunch.

I climbed down again and I pulled my coat back on, grimacing at the feel of wet feathers dripping water down the inside of my jacket and into my boots. I grabbed my cell phone and dialled Demon again.

"One Chupacabra terminated." I told him when he answered.

"Good," he said. "I'm coming to get you. Kaz found the target."

I stepped out of the shack and managed to re-lock the door without the key. In my line of work, we have skills that no human could attain. Daedalus always says that he is relieved that we're on the good guys' team because we would have been terrifying as criminals and we're scary enough as it is. I don't think he is joking.

I walked past the man and his son, pausing to watch them. They had pulled in the line and were staring at it in disappointment. The bait was gone. No doubt, they assumed that a fish had managed to carry it away. They had come very close to having a much nastier surprise at the end of their fishing line. Well, at least they would live to fish another day. I thought of the large creature that had eaten the Chupacabra and decided that it might be a good idea to mention it to Demon. If it was something that he could reason with, he might be able to convince it to stay away from the beach. If not, then he would execute it. We couldn't have sea monsters appearing in Blackridge Lake and eating the good citizens.

A few minutes later, I was sitting in the passenger seat of the van trying to dry out as we cruised down Lawrence Street toward the neighbourhood that Kaz had been searching. This was not one of the better neighbourhoods of Blackridge. The city should have condemned the buildings, as worn out as they were, but there were still people living in them. These are the humans' throwaways. They are easy marks for the supernatural predators too because no one cares about them. Well, except us. We protect them when the human police are not able. After all, we are better equipped to deal with vampires and Chupacabras.

Demon pulled up to the curb outside an apartment building that was in comparatively good shape. It was one of the few places on the street that didn't look like it was about to collapse into rubble at any second. Kaz was standing on the top step of the apartment building stoop, coolly surveying a group of angry young men blocking his exit. Great. Kaz had somehow managed to piss off a street gang. So much for keeping a low profile.

Kaz glanced up at the van and pulled his hat lower on his forehead. He could have easily jumped over the gang's heads and landed safely beside the van, but such a feat might have led to some awkward questions. The last thing we needed was for someone to call up the local police and report a man who could jump small gangs in a single bound.

"Well, this could be a problem. What do we do now?" I murmured to Demon.

He opened the van door with a sigh. "Follow me."

I exited the van and came around to the driver's side. I waited patiently while Demon took a moment to assess the situation. Then he glanced at me. "Come on."

Demon and I crossed the street, moving slowly but with confidence. No one in the gang noticed us, but several of the people watching from their windows did. They peeked out, half hidden by their curtains. If the cops showed up, they would claim to have seen nothing, but not one of them was going to miss a thing, not with the promise of a fight in the air. I could smell their excitement. If Demon and Kaz did too, they didn't show it.

"Hey, Kaz," Demon said as we drew near. He didn't yell but Kaz heard him even over the kids who were taunting him and trying to goad him into a fight.

"Hey, Fechín," Kaz responded, keeping his eyes on the kid in front of him. This kid was the loudest and most belligerent of the group so I assumed that he was the ringleader. He was around eighteen years old. He was much shorter than Kaz was and Kaz probably outweighed him by more than a hundred pounds. It was like a Chihuahua trying to take on a wolf. He had a knife that he was tossing from hand to hand. Kaz had his blade hidden beneath his coat. If he had pulled that out the kid might have questioned the wisdom of tangling with Kaz.

The other boys moved aside as we approached. "Is there a problem here?" Demon continued in a quiet voice. He didn't even glance at the kid with the knife.

"It's nothing worth getting concerned about," Kaz answered with a bored drawl. "I'm just waiting to see how long this kid can keep fooling with that knife before he drops it and lops off one of his own balls."

I choked back a laugh since it had been exactly what I had been thinking. I struggled to keep a straight face since the slightest smirk would probably enrage the kid and incite him to do something foolish. He was already scowling at us.

"You dissing me?" the kid demanded.

Demon and I looked at each other. "I don't even know what the hell that means." Demon said to me.

"He thinks we are being disrespectful to him." I explained.

Demon scowled. "Then why didn't he say so?"

It is hard to explain slang to someone over 1000 years old.

The kid's eyes had moved to Demon and I during this exchange. Taking his attention off Kaz was a mistake. As soon as he was distracted, Kaz was on him. He disarmed the kid and tossed him backward into his friends, knocking the lot of them over like bowling pins. Okay, Kaz may have overdone it a bit. It was a show of strength beyond human capability but the kid had it coming.

At this point, a smart human would have taken the opportunity to run like hell for his van while the rest of the boys were still trying to figure out what happened. Kaz sauntered toward us with a casual, unhurried stride. As soon as he joined us, we turned our backs on the gang and started toward the van.

Our self-possession pissed the kid off even more. He untangled himself from his friends, cursing at us the whole time. He was not terribly original. The other kids scattered to give their ringleader a clear shot at us while the rest of the street continued watching from behind the anonymity of their curtains. They were still expecting a fight. Frankly, I was too.

The kid didn't have his knife anymore, but he wasn't ready to give up just yet. He hollered after us and when I looked back, I saw that he was brandishing a gun. Instantly, all of the curtains closed and every apartment on the street suddenly had volume troubles with their TVs.

"Oh, for pity sake," I muttered as we turned back to face him. "The kid's carrying an arsenal in his pants."

"That's why the waistband is at his ankles." Kaz muttered back.

I choked back a laugh. I thought I was the only one who turned into a smartass under stress.

Demon sighed. "Why can't this ever be easy?" he asked.

"Easy is boring." I told him.

Demon eyed the kid sternly. "You have been disarmed once," he said. "Do you really want us to do it again?"

The kid snarled something and pointed the gun at Demon.

"Well, that wasn't very nice." I told the kid. In an aside to Kaz, I added, "What an extensive vocabulary he has."

Kaz snorted. "To go with the arsenal."

"I guess his intelligence is at his ankles too." I remarked.

"You shut up!" The kid gestured at me with the gun.

"Drop the gun." Demon said coldly.

The kid snickered. "I don't think so, asshole." He took aim at Demon. In the next second, that he would pull the trigger.

"That would be a really, really bad idea." I warned the kid. He snarled a few choice words at me, so it was obvious that he wasn't going to take my advice.

It was too late anyway. The flames in Demon's eyes had already blazed up. I shook my head. "You should have listened to me." I sang out.

Moving like lightning, Demon shot across the street, grabbing the kid by the throat. The kid barely had time to gasp and in the next second, the punk was flat on his back with Demon on top of him and his gun skittering across the pavement.

"*You will not shoot me.*" Demon's voice dropped to a low growl.

The kid gaped at him. Demon's hands gripped the front of the kid's shirt and he hauled him to his feet, staring deeply into the kid's dark eyes.

"*You will do as I say.*" His voice seemed to ooze from the walls.

The kid's face went slack and he relaxed in Demon's grip. It was damned eerie. At this point, had he been any other vampire, Demon could have fed on the kid, but that was not Demon's intention. He released the boy who continued to stare at him with air of a waiting dog. Demon held his gaze.

"Is everyone gone?" he asked.

"Oh hell yeah," I told him. "The other boys bailed as soon as they saw the gun. Their pal upped the ante and they didn't want to play anymore."

"Good," Demon said, still holding the boy's gaze steadily. "Now, will someone go and pick up that damned gun?"

"Say please." I chided.

Demon was not amused. Rather than risk ticking him off any more, I walked over, scooped the gun up, and tucked it in my coat pocket.

"What are we going to do about the rest of the neighbours?" Kaz remarked, pointing at the closed curtains.

"I don't think that I can do mass hypnotism but I doubt anyone in this neighbourhood will be calling the police anyway." Demon said.

The kid was still staring vacantly at Demon. "I'm surprised he's not drooling." I remarked. Demon glanced at me over his shoulder and out of the corner of my eye, I saw him reach up and wipe something off the kid's chin. I grinned.

"Shouldn't we be getting the heck out of here?" Kaz demanded. "Those other punks could be returning with reinforcements any second now. You won't be able to hypnotize them all before they try to kill us. I'll be damned if I'm going home riddled with bullet holes."

Demon's shoulders relaxed and he grinned. The flames had abated somewhat but his eyes were still gleaming. "Where is your faith, Kaz? Give me that piece, Dev." I handed it over.

Demon turned the gun over in his hands, eyes narrowed thoughtfully on the boy. "I wonder how many people he has held up with this little gun of his."

"Probably more than he can count." I said. "I don't think he's got enough fingers and toes."

Demon slipped the weapon into his coat pocket. "Well, I believe that we'll just relieve him of this, in the interest of public safety. Find the knife too. After all," he said with a sly smile. "We wouldn't want him to accidentally lop off one of his balls."

Kaz and I laughed. "Maybe we should frisk him in case he has any more dangerous weapons on him." I suggested.

"Good idea." Demon said.

Kaz and I searched him while Demon kept him in the trance. We found a second gun and a switchblade. I made a tsk sound. "What *has* your mama been about letting you play with such dangerous toys?"

"Hey!" Demon snapped at Kaz, giving his hand a light slap when he tried to extract some money from the kid's pocket. "No pickpocketing, Glutton."

"You said it, Fechín." Kaz grinned and shrugged. "It was worth a shot."

"Get in the van." Demon said to Kaz and me. "Let's get out of here before someone suffers a pang of conscience and calls the cops."

Kaz and I walked back toward the van, while Demon covered us, keeping his eyes open for the other gang members. Once we were safely inside the van, Demon started backing up, still holding the kid's gaze. He reached around behind him, groping for the door handle. Kaz was in the front passenger seat. He leaned across to open the door for him.

Then, Demon gave the boy his final command. *"We were never here."* He turned, breaking the trance, and got into the van. We had already driven away before the boy had finished shaking the cobwebs from his mind.

We did our debriefing in the van. Kaz explained that he had found the vampire hidden in a closet in what was supposed to have been an abandoned apartment. He had just finished calling Demon and was replacing the body in the closet for the Crew to pick up later, when someone came in and saw him with the body. Kaz thought that she was probably a nosy neighbour who was just coming over to see what was going on. She hadn't bothered to knock and he hadn't heard her come in. Before Kaz knew it, she was standing there gaping at him and the dead body.

Naturally, the woman freaked out. She had run out of the building, screaming, while Kaz tried to shove the body back into the closet. Unfortunately, the body would not cooperate and kept getting its fingers stuck under the door. By the time Kaz had wedged it in and got out of the apartment, the gang was already waiting for him in the street.

"They thought that I had ripped off some drug dealer that lives in the building and that I was loaded down with money." Kaz said mournfully.

"Were you?" I asked.

Demon gave a short laugh. "Would he look so miserable if he was?"

Kaz scowled at us. "I didn't even get time to call the Crew let alone search the apartment for cash before she took off screaming like a banshee and that gang showed up. I told them that I didn't have any money, but they didn't believe me and I couldn't let them search me or go inside and find the body."

"The body is still in the closet then?" Demon sighed.

"Sorry, Demon." Kaz said.

Demon was already on the cell. "Nightscare, this is Fechín. I have a body for you."

Nightscare didn't like the idea of picking the corpse up in the daytime, but finally agreed because it was now of the utmost importance to get that body out of the apartment. If someone decided to investigate the apartment, he might just find the body and call the cops. We weren't worried that someone could identify Kaz, the black hat had obscured his face, but we could not afford to have a human medical examiner perform an autopsy on that body.

"Be quick and call me when you've got it." Demon told the Boogey. He hung up and glanced at Kaz. "It's all taken care of."

"Thanks." Kaz said leaning back with a sigh.

"Why didn't you lock the apartment door so no one would bust in on you?" I asked.

"Are you kidding me?" Kaz demanded, turning to look at me. "Did you see the state of that building, Dev? Do you think those people have working locks? They don't even have working toilets." He leaned back in his seat again. "Besides, no one was supposed to come in. It was an abandoned apartment."

"And you know that because…" I prompted.

"We were there a couple of months ago." Demon answered.

I was surprised. "We were?"

"Darkmoon's human servant used to live there," he reminded me.

Darkmoon was Hadrian's vampire mate and she was a verified psycho, but Hadrian kept her on a tight leash so we had no reason to execute her…yet.

"That was Efram's place." I said, snapping my fingers as I remembered.

The Satana had raided Efram's place a while back and we went with them because we believed that he had been hiding one of our targets there. While the Satana drug unit had found nothing to interest them in the apartment, we found our target and performed our execution. We turned the body over to the Crew and left, but not before Demon gave Efram one final warning. "The Clean-Up Crew now knows where you live…and so do we." I don't know which of us frightened him more. I figure it had more to do with Demon knowing where he lived than anything else. He must have abandoned the apartment soon after. In his shoes, I would have done the same thing.

"Let's head home." Demon said, turning the van in that direction. "We've caused enough chaos for one day."

"Yeah," I said, leaning back in my seat with a grin. "Good times."

CHAPTER SIX

WE ARRIVED BACK AT the house a little later than we had intended. We had to make a detour when another one of our targets ran out in front of us on a busy street. Demon slammed on the brakes, tossing Kaz and me around the van because we weren't wearing seatbelts. I know. Bad us. Unfortunately, our wings tend to interfere with many human contraptions like seatbelts. The woman was inches away from the front bumper when Demon leaned out of the window to yell at her for being so careless. He recognized her at the same moment as she recognized him. She ran and the game was on.

We caught her trying to escape down the toilet drain in the women's washroom in a department store. Fortunately, the washroom was empty so we were able to execute her quickly and leave her locked in a stall until the Clean-Up Crew could come and collect her. Nightscare was still on his way to the apartment building, but he promised to send Beetlespaz over to claim the body.

"How the hell is a ten-foot Boogey going to get into the women's washroom without being noticed?" I demanded when Demon told us what was happening.

"There is a janitor's closet right next to the washroom," he told me. "I left one of those "closed" signs at the entrance of the hallway. The Boogey can get in to the store through the closet and slip into the washroom to get the body."

"What if someone sees him leaving with it?" Kaz demanded.

Demon shrugged. "Even if the cops believed the person who called it in, they wouldn't know where to begin to look for a Boogey."

Kaz rolled his eyes. "Good point."

We arrived home still jazzed from the chase as we walked through the front door. I went in first and was so busy crowing over our successful execution that I didn't notice the scene going on in the foyer.

"*Veronica is down!*" I called out raising my fist in the air in victory. "One murderous hydra terminated!" I stopped dead in my tracks.

Kaz nearly slammed into my back. "Dev, what the hell are you doing?"

Morgana was waiting for us in the foyer, arms crossed over her chest. She was furious, literally smouldering. Smoke poured out of her ears and her eyes were emitting red sparks. Poor Riot was standing helplessly beside her with a harried look on his face and it was apparent to me that he had been trying, unsuccessfully, to keep her from wrecking the place. She had overturned one of the hall tables along with the vase that had been sitting on it. Flowers were scattered on the floor in a puddle of water next to the table. The vase itself was in tiny pieces all over the hallway. Judging from Riot's wet hair and the slight cut on his forehead, I figured that she had smashed the vase over his head. This was no way to treat Lust.

"Congratulations." Morgana greeted us dryly. She glared at Demon as he came through the door. "Is there any particular reason that I have been left out of the last two hunts?"

Demon stood in the doorway, surveying the damage with cool eyes. "I beg your pardon?" he asked in a cold tone.

"It's about time you came home!" Riot gasped.

"What happened to your head?" Demon asked, frowning at him.

Before Riot could answer, Morgana uncrossed her arms and strode toward Demon. "You went on the hunt for the vampires last night and didn't take me along."

"Did you hit Riot?" Demon asked her, incredulously. He looked at Riot again. "Are you okay?"

"Yeah, I'm fine." Riot shrugged and then he grinned wickedly. "With anyone else, I would have considered that foreplay."

Demon rolled his eyes. Morgana ignored the exchange and jabbed her finger into his chest. "You left to hunt this last vampire without including me. I *am* a part of this team, am I not, Demon?"

"Are you challenging the decisions I make as leader of this team?" Demon snapped, blue flames flaring in his eyes.

"I am questioning why you are constantly leaving me out of the hunts!" The red sparks in Morgana's eyes responded in kind.

"Last night you were out and this morning I took the only two Deadlies who could identify the last rogue. In case you did not notice, Morgana, you are not the only Enforcer who was left behind today!"

Kaz, Riot, and I moved well out of the range of the two combatants, looking from Morgana to Demon as they spoke. Though Demon has no interest in her, it doesn't stop Morgana from coming on to him. As a result, he tends to keep her at arm's length and if he doesn't need the entire team to go somewhere, he usually opts to leave her.

"I have a cell phone, you know, and I *was* in Blackridge last night. You could have called me," she pointed out.

Demon started to speak and then, suddenly remembering that they had an audience, he stopped himself. "Morgana, we will discuss this in the library," he said stiffly.

Morgana spun around and stomped across the hall. There was an eager gleam in her eyes as she flung the door to the library open. She stepped inside, slamming the door behind her. The possibility of an explosion Wrath-style didn't intimidate her. I would say that she was looking forward to it. This was *her* idea of foreplay.

He didn't follow her immediately. He had one more detail to take care of before he did. He checked the messages on the phone pad. There was only one. He picked it up, read it, and looked up at Riot. "Serkan didn't call?" he asked.

Riot shook his head. "If he did, I didn't talk to him."

"What about Bane?"

"He went down to the basement to work out and I haven't seen him since."

Demon looked so worried that I became alarmed. "Is something wrong?" I asked.

He looked up at me. "Serkan said this was important. He isn't the type of man to make that kind of claim without a damned good reason. It is even more unusual that he has not followed up."

"Yes, but it is still daylight." I pointed out. "He'll be sleeping."

Demon nodded doubtfully. Kaz picked up the phone and started dialling. "If it will make you feel better, I'll just give him a call and leave him a message to call us as soon as he wakes up."

"Thank you." Demon said. He went into the library with a grim expression, closing the door firmly behind him.

I shook my head. "I don't know who I pity more right now, Demon or Morgana."

"Relationships are hard." Kaz agreed.

I snorted. "Oh, right! You and Rowan are so head over heels in love with each other it makes the rest of us gag!"

Kaz and Riot laughed.

"Speaking of head over heels in love," Riot said with a sly grin. "That message was for you from Maia. She needs a ride over here."

I groaned. I hated driving and worse, I hated having to try to convince Demon to loan me one of his precious vehicles. It usually ended in an impromptu demonstration in car mechanics and a driving lesson.

Riot smiled his best come-hither smile. "Do you want to pick her up or shall I?" he purred.

Even though I knew Riot only thought of Maia as a friend and not a potential lover, I still felt jealous. Women melted over Riot without any effort on his part at all. It is unfair.

I glared at him and held out my hand. "Give me the damn keys!"

Riot laughed and dropped a set of keys into my hand. Then just as quickly, he changed his mind and snatched them back. "On second thought, the idea of turning you loose on city streets with a three thousand pound weapon scares the hell out of me. I'll drive."

"What?" I sputtered. "I can drive circles around you!"

Riot laughed and gave me a friendly shove through the open front door. "Not today you aren't."

We screeched to a halt in front of Maia's apartment building. I gripped the dashboard and stared blindly through the windshield, terrified out of my mind. Now I remembered why Demon refused to let Riot drive his vehicles. I pried my stiff fingers from the dashboard and turned to him. The bastard was grinning at me. Slowly I held out my hand. It was trembling slightly. "Give...me...the... keys." I ordered hoarsely.

Riot dropped them into my hand, still grinning. Clutching the keys tightly, I pointed my finger at him. "Never *ever* drive again!"

"Chicken shit." Riot responded cheerfully and turned to open his door.

I debated beating the hell out of him right then and there, but decided that there were too many witnesses. Instead, I turned away from him and flung open the door of the van. I lowered myself to the ground. My legs collapsed under me like jelly. Riot came around the back, still grinning smugly.

"I'm telling Demon how you abused his baby." I told him.

"Spoilsport."

We walked into the front foyer of the apartment building. There was a woman in the foyer, retrieving her mail from a cubby on the wall. She looked up as we came in. She was gorgeous. Her hair was long, straight, and dark. She had a neat, slender figure. She could have been a supermodel if she had been just a little taller. I don't know many five-foot supermodels.

She glanced up from her mail as I pushed open the door and stepped inside. Her dark eyes passed over me with indifference. I may not be the best-looking man around, but I'm not exactly hideous. Still, I am fully aware that I am nothing next to Riot. He came in right behind me and her face lit up when her eyes settled on him. He had covered the horns with a hat, but I was waiting to see if she would freak at the sight of the golden skin and eyes. Instead, she smiled, perfect white teeth flashing against her mocha-coloured skin. I should have known better. No one, except for the other Deadlies, can see Riot as he truly is.

"Hi." she purred turning on the charm.

I rolled my eyes. Oh, brother. I was trying not to be jealous but damn, that man couldn't turn around without tripping over some lust-struck woman.

Riot barely glanced at her. "Hello." he said in a polite perfunctory manner. He started to walk past her without another word, his mind intent on going to the apartment to get Maia. I shook my head. For a guy who is Lust he can be damned clueless sometimes.

The young woman reached out and caught his sleeve. Riot looked down at her in surprise and she blushed, but she wasn't giving up that easily. "Um," she stammered while trying to come up with something to say that would keep him in the foyer with her. "Do you, um, live here?" she asked.

Riot looked puzzled. "No. We're just here to pick up a friend."

The woman's face fell and her hand slid away from his arm. "A girlfriend?" she asked.

"Well, Maia's definitely a girl." Riot answered, smiling when the reason for her disappointment finally sunk in.

"Really, man," I muttered. "You should see a doctor. There is definitely something wrong with your taste buds."

"Oh." she said with regret thick in her voice as Riot glared over her head at me. "Are you Dev?"

Riot and I looked at each other startled. He recovered before I did. Riot smirked. "Dev?" he repeated. "She has mentioned Dev to you, has she?"

"Yes, several times. Actually, I thought at first that Dev was her boyfriend because she talked about him so much. I mean, *you*, so much." She stopped, looking from Riot's broad grin to my red face, puzzled.

I helped her out. "He isn't Dev. I'm Dev." I told her.

Her obvious relief made me smile in spite of my embarrassment. "Oh, *you're* Dev. Well, she did say that you were cute." she told me and while I was busy blushing and stammering incoherently, she directed her dazzling smile back at Riot. "So you're a friend of Maia's? Well, you guys are here not a moment too soon."

"Oh?" Riot stopped snickering at me and directed his attention to her again. She gave a melting sigh and I pretended to gag behind her back. Riot shook his head, warning me to behave. Good luck with that.

"Her idiot of a boyfriend is up there yelling and tossing her stuff into the hallway," the girl explained. She paused and held her hand out to Riot, moving in closer as he took it. "I'm Megan by the way."

I sank to my knees, with my hands on my throat and my tongue hanging out. Riot gritted his teeth. I wasn't sure whether he was going to laugh or kick me.

"Nice to meet you," Riot said, trying to ignore my antics. "You say Mike is tossing Maia's stuff around and yelling?"

Megan actually batted her eyelashes at Riot. I was lying on the floor behind her, going through my mock death throes. She still hadn't noticed me. Riot was shaking his head desperately; worried that Megan would turn and catch me. No problem there. She wasn't in the least bit interested in what I was doing. She found Riot far more fascinating. "Yes, and he's yelling about Dev." Megan told Riot and started to turn toward me.

Uh oh. I shot to my feet quickly before Megan turned and caught me acting like an idiot. I met Riot's gaze guiltily met over Megan's dark head. "I'd better get up there." I muttered.

"No!" Riot exclaimed. "*I'll* go. You'll just cause more trouble."

"I will not!" I protested. Riot raised an eyebrow at me and I sighed. He was right. I would cause more trouble. It's what I do best. "All right, but if you get to kick Scarletti's head in before I do, I'll be really pissed off."

I remained in the front foyer with Megan while Riot went up to face Mike Scarletti and be Maia's knight in shining armour if she needed it. This sucked. Megan was watching Riot as he walked up the flight of stairs to Maia's floor. "Is he married?" she asked dreamily.

Royally sucked.

"No." I answered sulkily.

"Does he have a girlfriend?"

"No."

"Is he gay?"

I pretended to consider that but she looked so disappointed that I decided to be generous and shook my head. "No." I admitted.

Megan sighed happily. "Thank god."

I had to laugh. People just don't see the golden skin or horns when they look at Riot. He can't shapeshift physically, but people just seem to see in him whatever or whomever they most desire. The shapeshifting appears to happen in the other person's mind. I wondered who Megan saw when she looked at Riot.

Megan was still dazed enough that she had forgotten that she was carrying her newspaper. It started to slip from her hand and I reached out to take it from her before it hit the floor. Suddenly, water splashed in my face blinding me. I gasped and attempted to wipe my eyes. Then, a semi, or something like it, hit me from the side and I went down with Mike Scarletti on top of me, throwing punches. He managed to land one or two while I was still trying to pull myself together and figure out what had just happened. Once I realized that I had been ambushed and by whom, I began throwing punches back, gleefully pounding the shit out of Maia's boyfriend. Megan stood over us, screaming.

"Scarletti, knock it off!" Riot yelled, racing down the stairs as Mike and I rolled on the floor trying our best to kill one another. "Dev, stop it! You're going to kill him!"

Since neither of us was listening to him, Riot plunged into the fray, grabbing me by the scruff of my neck and tossing me aside like a rag doll. I hit the wall, taking out a chunk of plaster. Then he grasped Scarletti under the armpits and hauled him to his feet. Mike tried to fight Riot off, but wasn't big enough or tough enough to shake the other man. He might have stood a chance if he had been supernatural, but I doubt it. He was looking rather unsteady.

"Lemme go, goddamn it!" Mike protested taking a half-hearted swipe at Riot.

Riot released him and Mike started to sink to the ground. Riot caught him by his shirt collar and eyed him with antipathy. "Damn it, Dev! I think you really hurt him!"

"Oh, *darn*." I said.

"Fechín is going to *freak*." Riot said pointedly.

Oops. I had forgotten about that part. I winced. "Okay, okay. I'm sorry." I said, reluctantly.

"Devil! Monster!" Mike snarled at me through a swollen lip.

Riot and I looked at each other. "Okay, maybe I'm not sorry after all." I told him.

"Don't understand… water shoulda worked…" Mike slurred as he swayed in Riot's grasp. He stared at the vial that was lying on the floor. It's amazing that it had survived with us rolling around on it like that.

I realized then that Scarletti had thrown holy water at me. He was pissed off because I didn't melt into an evil puddle on the floor. I started to laugh. I couldn't help it. There was Scarletti with his nose was almost twice its normal size, gaping in bewilderment at an empty vial of holy water. I caught sight of myself in the reflection of the windows of the door. There wasn't a scratch on me. This was getting better and better.

"Goddamn you, Mike!" We looked up. Maia was standing at the top of the stairs. She strode down them and paused in front of Riot, Mike, and a wide-eyed Megan.

Maia and Megan looked similar. They had the same hair colour, but Maia's hair has a bit of curl to it giving her that tousled, just rolled out of bed look. She was also taller than Megan was. Her skin was the same colour as Megan's and, though she is pretty, she is not supermodel gorgeous. Of course, to me she is beautiful, especially right then when she was angry and her big brown eyes were snapping. She was smokin' hot.

"What is *wrong* with you?" Maia hissed at Mike through gritted teeth. "You can't go around attacking people. You're a police officer!"

"They are not *people*! They don't count!" Scarletti waved at me.

She made a sound of disgust and pushed past Riot and Scarletti roughly. She couldn't meet my eyes as she reached for the door.

"Where do you think you're going?" Scarletti demanded.

Her hand was on the door handle, but she didn't turn around. "I am going to do my job, Michael." she replied, stiffly.

"If you leave now, you don't come back."

The scathing look that she gave him over her shoulder said it all. She shoved open the door and walked out without another word. I grinned at Scarletti. "Hey, Scarletti," I said gleefully. "I gave you a black eye."

Mike lunged at me, swinging wildly, but Riot held him firmly by the back of his shirt. He snatched the newspaper that Megan was clutching to her chest and smacked Mike over the head with it. "Behave, damn it, or I'll let Dev blacken your other eye!" Riot glared and pointed at me with the newspaper. "You behave, too! Go and wait in the van."

As I turned away, I had to get in one last shot. "I broke your nose, too."

"Dev, I said *get out!*" Riot roared as Mike struggled to escape him to come after me.

I left the building, laughing. I jumped down the steps and strode toward the van. Abruptly, I stopped laughing. Maia was sitting in the van with the side door open. She had her face buried in her hands. I think she was crying.

"Damn." I said softly. In my eagerness to beat the tar out of Mike Scarletti, I had forgotten that I was beating up the man Maia loved.

I approached the van cautiously. I hate it when Maia cries. She doesn't do it often, but the few times I witnessed it, I felt completely helpless. It was even more difficult to bear because I suspected that this time, it was my fault.

"Maia?" I said softly as I leaned against the doorframe. "I'm so sorry about—well, I'm not *sorry* but—" I stopped talking. What could I say? I couldn't lie to her. I couldn't apologize for beating up Mike because I would probably do it again given the opportunity.

"I'm sorry that I made you cry." I said at last.

Maia lifted her head to look at me. Her eyes were bright, but that was the only sign of tears. Still, it did nothing to lessen my alarm. "It's over between Mike and me," she said softly. "This is the last straw."

If only.

"Don't say that. Mike says that, but he always takes you back in the end." I reminded her, trying hard to keep the bitterness out of my voice.

"I don't want that, Dev," she said, staring down at her hands. She met my gaze. "I just don't want to be with him anymore. He had no reason, no right, to attack you like that. It isn't just you and the other Deadlies that he thinks are not people. It's anyone who is supernatural. That includes me."

"I'm sure that isn't true."

She shook her head. "It is and I don't care anymore. It's too stressful. I can't deal with this."

I wasn't sure that I believed her. I wanted to believe that the relationship was really over, but they had done this up and down thing so many times they were practically a yo-yo. I didn't want to be the damned string, caught in between and yanked along with them. Even so, I still wanted to comfort her.

I reached up, skimming my fingertips lightly across her cheek and brushing back her soft dark curls. "Maia." I began. Her expression softened. My gaze dropped to her mouth. Her lips parted slightly and we leaned toward each other...

"Let's go."

I jumped at the sound of Riot's voice right behind me. Maia gasped and pulled away from me. I spun around to glare at him. He was grinning. I wondered how long the asshole had been standing there.

"What did you do with Mike?" Maia asked him.

"I took him back to his apartment," he said.

"Is he okay?" I asked grudgingly.

"He'll live. Let's get going. Fechín will be wondering where we are. I'll drive." Riot announced displaying the set of van keys in his hand.

My hand went to my pocket. "You bastard!" I exclaimed on finding it empty. "You picked my pocket!"

"It wouldn't have been so easy if you and Maia weren't so *involved*," he told us, grinning wickedly. "The waves of lust coming off you two were *yummy*." He licked his lips.

I chose to ignore that and snatched the keys back from him while he was laughing his ass off. "Hey!" he protested, frowning.

"I'm not getting into that van with you behind the wheel again!" I told him firmly. "I'll drive!"

"Oh god, no," Maia's hand reached out to snatch the keys away from me. "*I'll* drive! You're worse than Riot!" She shook her head. "How the two of you managed to get licenses I'll never know."

Riot and I looked at each other. "Licenses?" we repeated blankly.

Maia groaned and started the engine. "Oh my god, I don't want to hear this. Just get in."

CHAPTER SEVEN

AS WE CAME DOWN the long driveway toward the house, Demon was standing on the front porch waiting for us, hands on his hips and glaring. Bane leaned against the railing next to him with his arms crossed over his chest, grinning broadly and enjoying the prospect of watching Demon rake Riot and me over the coals.

"Uh oh," Riot said from the back seat.

Maia looked over her shoulder at him. "What? What's "uh oh?" She looked back at Demon and, suddenly, it hit her. "You guys took Fechín's van *without permission?*" Her voice grew higher and squeakier at the end of the sentence. "Oh my god, he is going to *kill* you!"

Maia may have been exaggerating. Demon certainly looked frustrated but I figured that it probably had less to do with our taking the van than with the fight he had just had with Morgana. Still, I wasn't keen on facing him while he was in this mood.

"What are we going to do?" Riot muttered, leaning forward over my shoulder.

I looked over at Maia. "How about turning this thing around and taking us straight to the airport? We'll get on a plane and head for Australia." I suggested.

Riot shook his head, not taking his eyes off Demon. "It isn't far enough away.

He would find us in about ten seconds," he said. "Let's go to the Antarctic. The snow and ice might slow him down a bit."

"How about you two get out there and take your lumps?" Maia suggested.

I scowled at her. "Look, if you're not going to come up with anything helpful..."

Demon leaned one hand against the post next to Bane and yelled out, "Are you two going to get out the damned van on your own or do I have to come over there, rip the doors off and drag you out by your—" Insert appropriate body part here.

"Oh, shit." Riot whispered. "Which would be worse?"

"Well, if we wait for him to come and get us, he may just *remove* said body part. I say we take our chances and maybe we can win him over with our charm." I suggested.

Riot and I looked at each other. "Nah."

We got out of the van and approached Demon and Bane warily. Demon had a cigarette in his hand. This was not a good sign. Demon rarely smokes. It is something that he only does when he is especially upset. You would think that Wrath would be angry all the time, but it wasn't so. Demon is usually quite reasonable. I was counting on this being one of those reasonable times.

"You took my van." Demon growled.

My conscience, the little voice that tries to keep me out of shit, suggested that this *might* be a bad time to be a smartass, and I should just humbly apologize and swear never to do it again. It was good advice, but when have I ever listened to advice, good or otherwise?

"We had to go and pick up Maia." I told him. "How would you have proposed we do that? Click our heels together and chant there's no place like home?"

Riot sucked in his breath and I heard his strangled voice hiss, "Dev, this is *not* the way to calm him down!"

Demon's eyes shifted to Riot briefly and then to Maia. "I see she was driving."

"She insisted." I told him. "She said I was a worse driver than Riot."

That made him smile a little, but there was still an unhappy expression in his eyes. Being *almost* certain that I wasn't about to get my ass kicked, I said, "Maia, go on inside. I think Demon needs a little man-to-man talk."

Maia walked up the front steps. He opened the door and held it for her. She laid her hand lightly on his arm and kissed his cheek. She slipped past him into the house. Once she was inside, Riot and I joined Demon and Bane. The four of us sat side by side on the front steps. Wordlessly, Demon handed me his cigarette.

"Was it a rough scene with Morgana?" I asked. I took a drag off the cigarette and I handed it to Bane. I amused myself by making smoke squares instead of rings. It's a talent.

"It started out that way," he replied dryly. "And it just got worse."

"She tried to jump you, didn't she?' I asked.

Demon darted a look at me but didn't answer. I sighed. "I'm sorrier for her than I can say, but this is her problem and not yours."

"It becomes my problem when it interferes with my ability to lead this team."

"Has it?" Riot asked curiously. He waved the cigarette away when Bane offered it. Bane handed it to Demon instead.

He took the cigarette and flicked the ashes off the end. "Her persistence certainly makes it hard to keep our relationship on friendly terms." He took a drag.

"Seeing your boss walking around in his jammies would make it hard to preserve that, yes." I agreed.

Demon blew out a steady stream of smoke. "I'm not her boss and I don't wear jammies," he growled.

I opened my mouth and then closed it, shaking my head. Poor Morgana. She didn't stand a chance in hell. However, to be fair, Demon doesn't exactly parade around the house with his assets hanging out.

"I've tried to tell her that I am not interested in a sexual relationship." he went on. "She is my friend, but she will never be my lover. She won't accept that."

"She can't accept it." Riot told him. "She doesn't want to believe that you don't feel the same way about her so she figures that if she keeps at you, you'll eventually come around."

"I have tried being nice to her. I have tried being firm. I just don't know what the hell else to do." Demon muttered. "I care about her, but she is like my little sister." He put his head in his hands.

We all sat staring at him, uncertain how to comfort him. It was not often that he required our reassurance.

"Well, maybe someday her real Mr. Right will come along and she'll fall madly in love with him and forget all about you." Bane said, patting him on the shoulder, encouragingly.

"I hope it is sooner rather than later." Demon sighed. "I can't take much more of this. The tension is unbearable."

"Yeah, it sucks." I said sympathetically. Just for a second, though, I felt a flash of jealousy. Why can't stuff like this happen to me? I imagined what would happen if another woman showed interest in me and then, suddenly, Maia realized that she had been in love with me the whole time. The resulting catfight would be colossal.

Yeah, right. Women don't fight over guys like me.

Demon rose and flicked the rest of the cigarette into the air. It burst into a small flame in mid-air and disintegrated. "Anyway, it's time to get ready for the meeting with Hadrian."

"Dressed to kill?" Bane asked as we went into the house. That was the twins' code for "are we going into this ready to execute Hadrian's candy ass?"

Demon nodded. "Dressed to kill."

Kaz and I came down the stairs together about half an hour later to find that Demon, Riot, and Bane were already there. They were wearing the same clothes that we were, black leather pants and no shirt. We sheathed our knives in the black leather armbands across our biceps. Two leather straps crossed over our chests held a larger sword sheath in place on our backs. Demon and Bane's long hair was braided and held in place with a silver clasp. Kaz and Riot had pulled their hair back into a ponytail. My hair was short enough that I didn't have to worry about interference. The reason for the minimal clothing and hair was to make certain that everyone saw the weapons. It was just our not so subtle way of reminding Hadrian and company who we are and what we do.

Demon nodded in approval as we came down the stairs. "Where is Onyx?" he asked Riot.

Riot shrugged. "He's still getting ready, I suppose."

"And Morgana, damn it." Demon muttered.

"She wasted all that time trying to convince you to let her braid your hair." Kaz said, trying for stoicism and failing miserably. He couldn't quite keep the grin off his face.

Morgana had offered to do more than braid Demon's hair. We had all been in the hallway debating how much hardware to take with us when Demon opened the door to his bedroom and found Morgana lying on his bed, half dressed. You have to give the girl credit for having brass balls. She was nothing if not determined.

She was surprised when she saw the rest of us there, but it didn't deter her from making her offer in front of us. Demon had demanded that she remove herself from his room. He had not been too polite about it either.

Demon glared at Kaz and started to growl something equally impolite to him. "Do you want me to go and get them moving?" Bane interrupted his brother.

"Would you?"

Bane flashed him a grin. "Yes, I would. I'll be back in a minute so don't kill Kaz while I'm gone."

He reached the bottom of the stairs and stopped, looking up as Maia came down. She also stopped and surveyed us, sucking in her breath sharply. Then she sighed. "Wow. It has obviously been a long time since I went on one of these meetings with you. I'd forgotten how impressive you guys look when you're dressed to kill," she murmured.

Riot grinned at her. "Impressive?" he purred suggestively.

Her gaze wandered over us appreciatively until she got to me, then she smiled. "Hot. Definitely hot. And dangerous." she said in a low, seductive tone.

Leave it to Riot to sense Maia's desire and to her to be so damned honest about it. Silently, I ordered myself to pull it together and tried to act nonchalant. I opened my mouth to make a smartass remark and nothing came out except a pathetic little squeak. I heard a snort of laughter behind me and turned to glare accusingly at Bane and Kaz.

"Would you all mind if we went to the library so we actually might make it to this meeting with Hadrian on time?" Demon asked with deliberate politeness.

We all looked at him. He was not smiling. Bane hastily excused himself and ran up the stairs to fetch Onyx and Morgana.

Demon threw open the library door with a bang and stalked into the room. Okay, he was seriously pissed. I was glad we were going to find some vampires for him to take it out on.

CHAPTER EIGHT

B ANE RETURNED WITH MORGANA and Onyx a short time later and we all sat down before Demon went over the details of the meeting with Hadrian. "Maia arranged the meet at the Black Candle." He turned to her. "He agreed to meet at sunset?"

"Yes." she replied. "Simmons didn't like it, but I gave him your message and he said he would pass it on to Hadrian."

"He had better." Demon said grimly. He glanced up at the clock on the mantelpiece above the fireplace. "We have about an hour and a half until the meeting. Daedalus is going to meet us there with the Crew."

We all started talking at once.

"Why is the chief coming?"

"The Clean-Up Crew?" someone groaned.

"Bring your nose clips."

"I thought Hadrian wanted to meet with *us* not the Satana."

"Is the Crew really necessary?"

Demon glared us into silence. I don't know anyone else who can do it as effectively. "Daedalus is coming to make this an official warning," he explained. "We want Hadrian to know that the Satana are watching his people too. The Crew is coming to make the same point that we are. A reminder of what the end result will be for him or anyone else breaking the law."

"Boogey shit." I remarked.

"Yes. Thank you, Dev." Demon said pointedly.

"So, what do we do for the next hour and a half?" Kaz asked.

"We go to the Black Candle and meet up with Daedalus and the others." Demon explained. "We'll debrief and wait for Hadrian. I want him to think he has walked into his worst nightmare. It'll throw him off balance."

"Is it really necessary to go this early?" Onyx wrinkled his nose. "I mean, we're going to be stuck in the Black Candle with the Crew for almost *two hours*."

"That's cruel and unusual punishment." I added, agreeing with Onyx for once.

"Rowan isn't going to like this." Kaz said. "The Crew is bad for business but we're worse."

"We aren't going to be sitting out in the bar." Demon pointed out. "And besides, Maia already gave her the heads up that we're coming."

"Oh."

"Now if you're all done whining, we have a meeting to get to before our meeting."

The door opened and our housekeeper walked in. Hex is an imp. She is about four feet tall and has pinkish skin. She would look like a tiny human if not for her blood-red eyes. Her dark brown hair has streaks of grey through it. She keeps it pulled back in a tight bun.

"Tea time!" Hex sang out. Bane held the door for her as she carried in a silver tray with a large silver teapot, several china teacups and saucers, and a large platter of cookies. The tray itself was almost as big as she was. It teetered precariously in her arms. She never quite got the message that we are not tea drinkers and her tea is horrible. It does resemble tea only in that it is brown and hot. That is where the resemblance ends. The tea is so strong that it could walk into the room by itself. It is terribly bitter and tea isn't supposed to have texture, is it? Since none of us has the heart to tell her outright, every day we suffered through Tea Time.

Hex set the tray on the desk. "By the way, Demon, you had a phone call."

"Serkan?" Demon asked.

"No, it was a woman. She said that she had to speak to you immediately."

Demon's dark eyebrows shot up in surprise. "Are you sure she didn't ask for Riot?"

Hex gave him a scornful look. "I may be old but I think I can tell the difference between Demon and Arkane."

Riot winced. Arkane is his real name and he hates it. "Hex, please. If you can't call me Riot, then at least call me Kane."

"Okay, okay." Hex soothed him down. "I am sorry. I will try to remember."

"Thank you."

"What did she want?" Demon asked Hex.

"She didn't tell me, but she was most insistent that she had to talk to you. I finally had to tell her that she would either have to give me her name and number and you would call her back when you had time or she could call back tomorrow."

"Did she give you her name?"

"No, she hung up. Shall I pour out, sir?" she asked Demon. She folded her hands in front of her demurely, trying to look like an old-fashioned housekeeper. We didn't dare laugh, we didn't want to hurt her feelings, but only Demon managed to keep a straight face.

"Actually, Hex, we're just on our way out." Demon told her.

"Oh, well." she said. "I can heat it up again when you come back."

"Please don't bother." Demon said hastily. "We may be very late."

Hex curtsied (another habit we couldn't break her of) and left the room.

Demon frowned. "Who the hell would be calling me?" he murmured, puzzled. Then he shook his head. "Okay, one problem at a time. If it is important, she will call back."

He turned to us with a grim expression. "Okay, Deadlies, let's work."

We arrived at the Black Candle with a little more than an hour to spare. Demon insisted on flying since we needed the extra time to meet with Daedalus and the Crew. It was cloudy enough to block the moon and as long as we stayed above the clouds, we were able to fly over Blackridge undetected.

Dillon Drakazar who is the nighttime bouncer at the Black Candle was waiting for us at the back door. He is a sárkány; a dragon that can take human form. They also call themselves the Drakakin. As a human, he is tall and slender with bright red hair, reddish-brown skin and green eyes. In dragon form, he is long and slender with bright red scales and green eyes. He has wings, but because it would be impossible for dragons to fly around Blackridge unnoticed, he rarely gets the chance to fly. There was a look of envy on his face when we landed in front him.

I had carried Maia and it was hard to fly, holding her tight against my body.

She cuddled in, her face pressed against my neck, her lips brushing across my skin. It was all very distracting. I landed on the sidewalk and held her for a minute, her face still buried in the curve of my neck. I released her, reluctantly. "All ashore for Black Candle pub," I said lightly.

She sighed, disappointed that the flight was over, and let her body press against mine as I lowered to her feet. She paused, her mouth an inch from mine and then she slowly backed away letting her fingers glide down my bare chest to my waistband before she turned to enter the bar.

Had she done that on purpose? Dillon held the door for her. She gave me a sexy smile over her shoulder. I guess the answer was hell, yeah.

"I could feed off the lust the two of you are emitting for a *month*." Riot hissed in my ear.

"Don't you dare!" I hissed back.

Riot laughed and steered me into the office where Daedalus, Medea, Nightscare, Beetlespaz, and a couple of other male Boogeys were waiting. The smell was intense and I tried to hold my breath.

"Leave the door open." Nightscare growled when he saw our reactions.

It wasn't going to help but it was nice of him to offer.

After Rowan's server brought drinks to everyone, we got down to business. The plan was simple. Daedalus would take the lead, making this a formal warning. Fechín gave him a list of some questions that he wanted answered. The rest of us were muscle, a threat to make Hadrian toe the line and encourage him to convince his little bloodsuckers do the same.

About fifteen minutes into the discussion, Rowan appeared in the doorway of the office. She is the type that never loses her cool no matter what is happening, but now her auburn hair was coming loose from its ponytail so that strands of it were trailing down her neck and shoulders. Her face was flushed with frustration. "Hello, gorgeous." Kaz said greeting her with a kiss.

She kissed him back hard, making him stagger, and then turned abruptly to Demon. "Fechín," she said, her usually calm brown eyes showing signs of being seriously irritated. "Please tell me that you have some goblins on your execution list."

Demon looked up at her. "Sorry, no. Are you having goblin problems, Rowan?"

"You could say that." she replied dryly. "Two of Xerxes' idiotic spawn are getting ready to tear my place apart!"

"Which two idiots?" Demon asked. It was a good question because the goblin had twenty children and "idiot" could describe any of them.

"Fenriz and Ragnar."

Demon frowned. "They come in here all the time. Why would they be ripping up your place today?" he asked.

Rowan waved her hands helplessly. "Ogres."

That was explanation enough. Ogres and goblins were not friends. Bluntly put, they were mortal enemies. Having ogres and goblins in the same bar was a bad idea. I was surprised that Dillon had let them in.

Rowan read my mind (she is a witch after all). "Rex, the daytime bouncer, let in the ogres. Dillon let in Xerxes and his pair of twits," she explained. "I think Rex left without telling Dillon that the ogres were already in here."

That was no surprise. Rex is a hobgoblin. Hobgoblins are not actually goblins at all. They are an offshoot of faeries except that they are taller and more human-like. They are also shit disturbers...so long as they are out of range of the shit. If goblins, stupid and mean as they are, are going to cause shit, they are going to hang around to wallow in it.

"Who are the ogres?" Demon sighed.

"Mordred and Mayhem," Rowan told him. She gave Kaz a sympathetic look. "Pain is out there with them."

Kaz winced. Mordred and Mayhem are his cousins and two of the worst ogres for looking for a fight. Fenriz and Ragnar would be more than happy to oblige them. The problem was that someone else might get hurt during the brawl and knowing Pain, Kaz' father, he was probably egging them all on. Though ogres are aggressive and violent by nature, Pain was over the top even by ogre standards. Kaz joined the Deadlies when he was sixteen, just to get away from his father. Now, he had as little to do with his family as possible. The odd time, however, we ended up running into them in the course of our work. So far, they hadn't been targets, but that could change at any time.

"You could leave this to the Satana." Daedalus offered. "After all, dealing with drunk and disorderly supernaturals is our job."

"Rowan didn't ask for you. She asked for the Enforcers. Maia, wait here." Demon got to his feet.

Daedalus shrugged. "Suit yourself." He flashed us a grin. "This just means that I don't have to waste time and energy on a bunch of drunk and obnoxious idiots." We daemons are very practical that way.

Daedalus remained in the office sipping his drink complacently while we followed Rowan down the narrow hallway to the pub area.

"Why the hell isn't Xerxes putting a stop to this?" Demon whispered to Rowan as they squeezed down the hallway side by side. "It isn't like him to let his sons cause trouble in a public place. He prefers to cause shit when there is no chance of getting caught."

"Xerxes headed for the washroom the minute the arguing started." I heard her whisper back. "I think the sonofabitch figures that if he doesn't see it happen, he can't be held responsible for his sons' actions!"

"Well, he's wrong." Demon said grimly.

"Too bad Pain didn't join him." Kaz muttered.

"Then the two of them would be tearing up my washrooms." Rowan pointed out.

"I doubt my father can even stand upright on his own right now let alone fight with Xerxes." Kaz replied cynically.

Rowan laid a hand on his arm. "I haven't been serving him, Kaz."

Kaz shook his head. "Mordred and Mayhem are probably buying them for him."

She smiled. "I thought they might be so I watered down every drink they bought."

"It doesn't matter," he said bitterly. "He's a sonofabitch drunk or sober."

"I'm sorry."

"It isn't your fault." He pulled her into his arms. "Don't look so worried, babe. Just because he's my father doesn't mean that he should get away with destroying your place." He lifted her chin and kissed her.

She still looked worried. "Yes, but maybe it shouldn't be *the Enforcers* dealing with him."

"Rowan may be right." I said thoughtfully. "Under the circumstances, maybe we should have let Daedalus take it."

We stepped through the swinging door into the pub.

Well, perhaps not.

Mordred and Mayhem had grown since we last saw them. They were probably over two hundred years old but in ogre years they were still very young. Mordred was about eight feet tall now, his brother was about six inches shorter, and they were still growing. Pain, on the other hand, was about twelve feet tall. Kaz was short by ogre standards.

Ogres are humanoid in appearance. They are not as hairy as a Boogey and their arms are so long that they drag on the ground. Their ears are small and flat, close to their head. Their foreheads come down low over their eyes, which bug out a bit so they always look as though someone just scared the hell out of them. Their skin comes in as many shades as a human's does, but the ogres' skin has a greenish tinge to it.

Though goblins are humanoid too, goblin males aren't like anything human I've ever seen. Goblin women are drop dead gorgeous but Fenriz and Ragnar look like someone sneezed and left two short, fat green boogers with big red eyes on the floor. They had short flabby arms and legs. They were certainly not handsome, except maybe to another goblin.

The other supernaturals gave the combatants a wide berth, but they were eagerly watching to see the outcome of the impending brawl. Suddenly, one of the spectators noticed us and I saw his eyes widen. He nudged his friend and nodded at us. In a few seconds, a surge of panic was running through the room. That is the usual reaction to our arrival. Ogres and goblins are mean, but we are far more dangerous.

We approached the rivals at an unhurried, but determined, pace. Pain had not yet seen us. He was laughing, half falling off his barstool, egging on his nephews and taunting the goblins. Ophelia, Mordred's girlfriend, was also there watching it all with eager eyes. She is a witch and one of the biggest troublemakers I've ever met, but she always managed to avoid being on the execution list, though just barely. She is not one of Rowan's favourite people and so I was amazed that she was still there. Rowan would have loved to throw her out, but I guess she had bigger problems right now.

Ophelia saw us first. Her green eyes fell on Riot and she smiled at him like a cat that has spotted a mouse. She may have been Mordred's girlfriend, but it didn't stop her from cheating with other men. She had never had an affair with Riot, but whenever she saw him, she never failed to try to tempt him. If she started that crap now it would make the situation worse.

"Mayhem," Demon quietly addressed the ogre closest to him.

He turned to glare at us. Mayhem is as dark as Kaz is and the dim lighting of the bar made it appear as though his yellow eyes were just hovering in the air by themselves. He didn't seem surprised to see us. "What do *you* want, Enforcers?" he snapped.

"I want you to sit down and behave yourselves or leave." Demon said. "It is your choice."

"Says *you*, Wrath?" Fenriz sneered.

"We will fight where we have been insulted." Mayhem's brother, Mordred, snarled at Fenriz. The goblin was making faces at him. It was childish, but provoking to the ogre nevertheless.

"Just remember that if you kill someone, you go on the List." Demon said firmly. "Now, decide what you are going to do or we'll decide for you."

Instantly, the rest of us surrounded the ogres. It was a strategic move. While the goblins would have thoroughly enjoyed getting into a brawl with us, ogres are more rational and fighting with the Enforcers would not appeal to them. They were more likely to back down. This also blocked their view of the goblins.

Ophelia took advantage of the fact that now her boyfriend couldn't see what *she* was up to either. She reached out and caressed Riot's ass, finishing with a little squeeze. Riot didn't even flinch. In fact, he ignored her. She frowned, irritated by his indifference, and she wasn't about to let him get away with it. Ophelia reached between Riot's legs to cup his balls. I have to give him credit, he didn't even yelp. His eyes got wide and he shifted away from her but that was it. Me, I would have jumped out of my skin. Fortunately, neither of the ogres noticed Ophelia and her wandering hands. Better, the goblins hadn't seen it or they would have been sure to point it out and the situation would have gone downhill very fast.

Mayhem looked at his brother. "Mordred, Father would be most displeased if we got entangled with the Enforcers."

"To hell with the old man," Pain slurred cheerfully as he toasted us. "And to hell with the Enforcers!"

"But, Uncle," Mordred frowned. "You know what Father said after the last time. He was very angry."

Fenriz hooted, gleefully. "Daddy might be *mad* at them!" he said a quavering voice, mocking the ogres. "You hear that, Ragnar? Their daddy wouldn't like it!"

"Oooh!" His brother joined in. The two goblins pretended that their knees were knocking.

Mayhem scowled and started to take a step forward as if he were going to push past us, but Demon had had enough. Without taking his eyes off the ogres, Demon backhanded the goblin with a careless swipe that sent Fenriz reeling backward and crashing into several tables.

"Demon!" Rowan wailed. "You were supposed to prevent my pub from being destroyed, not trash it yourself!"

Demon didn't look at her. His eyes focused on someone behind her. I turned my head and there was Xerxes slinking out of the washrooms with a look of guilt on his ugly face. "Xerxes will be more than happy to pay for any damages before he leaves and takes his sons with him." Demon said coldly.

Xerxes opened his mouth as if to argue and then, seeing the expression on Demon's face, thought the better of it. He nodded. "All right, Fechín, all right." He glared at Fenriz and Ragnar. "You two would have to pick a fight on the night when there are Enforcers around!"

Xerxes backhanded Ragnar who sailed across the room smashing a second table and landing in a heap next to his brother. Before Rowan could protest, Xerxes handed her several gold coins. "I'm sure you can find some leprechaun to change it to paper money for you."

A tiny man seated at the bar, turned eagerly at the mention of gold. He had red hair and a red beard. He was dressed in a green shirt and green pants with yellow suspenders. His matching green coat and hat lay on the stool next to him. "Sure, and I just happen to have some paper money with me, Rowan me darlin'." he said in a high-pitched squeak.

"I am not your darlin', Seamus." Rowan snapped as she moved behind the bar to transact business with the leprechaun.

Xerxes and his dimwit duo left. Riot escaped from Ophelia as the ogres sat down again. She turned to Mordred as he took the stool next to hers. She draped her arm over his shoulder and played with his ear. "Baby, you were *so* brave," she cooed.

Demon, Bane, Morgana and Onyx had already started back toward the office while Rowan squabbled with the leprechaun over the value of the coins in human currency. Kaz, Riot, and I stopped as Pain staggered to his feet directly in our path.

Kaz does not resemble his father much. He looks more like a daemon than an ogre. Pain is not as dark as Kaz is and his skin has more of the green tinge in it than Kaz' does.

Pain swayed unsteadily as he peered at us through bleary yellow eyes. "Kazang?" he slurred, staggering toward his son.

Kaz' hands clenched. "What the hell are you doing here?" he demanded in a low hiss.

Pain's chin jutted out defiantly. "I can be here if I want. My nephews like hanging out with me unlike my own *son*."

"How dare you come into Rowan's place and start fights?" Kaz snapped. He glared at his cousins who quickly turned away. "What the hell is wrong with you?"

"My son is a damned *Enforcer*, that's the only problem I have." Pain sneered. "You always were a pathetic excuse for an ogre."

"That's the nicest thing you've ever said to me." Kaz shot back and stepped around his father. He went on, his voice cold. "Just remember what I told you and don't kill anyone."

"I can't believe you would allow such a thing!" Pain whined. "Your own father—"

Abruptly, Kaz turned his back on Pain and stalked away without another word. Riot and I hurried to catch up to him. "I'm sorry about that, Kaz." Riot said.

"What's to be sorry about?" Kaz said fiercely, stopping short. "He's an asshole. He has always been an asshole and he will be a thorn in my side until the day he dies! My only consolation is that I know I'm going to live to see him die."

It was a harsh thing to say about one's father, but Pain has given Kaz little reason to love him. "What did he mean when he asked how could you allow such a thing?" I asked. "What did you do to him?"

"Nothing yet," Kaz said, staring straight ahead grimly. Then he glanced at us. We waited patiently for an explanation. He sighed. "When he's drunk he tends to get out of hand and those two," He jerked his head indicating his cousins. "They can't control him. They're good kids when they aren't under his influence. I'm surprised my uncle let them go out with Pain." He shook his head. "Anyway, that was just a reminder of what the penalty is for killing a human or anyone else."

Suddenly I understood. "He would go on the execution list."

Kaz nodded. "That's what I told him."

"I think I'd have a hard time killing your dad, no matter how big an asshole he is." Riot frowned.

Kaz smiled slightly. He started moving again. "So would I. He is my father after all, which is why I have an understanding with Demon."

"Oh?"

"If my father should end up on the execution list, it will be Wrath hunting him."

I gaped. "Oh, shit."

"That's what Pain said." Kaz said. "I'm hoping the threat of Demon will be enough to keep him in order."

We reached the office door where Demon and Bane waited for us. The other two had gone in. "Are you going to be okay?" Demon asked Kaz.

"Hell, yeah," Kaz told him with a grin. "There's no better warm up than kicking goblin ass."

Demon's smile hardened. "Then get ready for the main event. Hadrian's here."

"So let's go kick some vampire ass." I said as I pushed open the office door.

CHAPTER NINE

"IHOPE, *SLOTH*, THAT your remark was not directed at us." Hadrian's cool, soft voice actually had some heat in it when he addressed me. I could tell by the way that he said my name that he was intending to insult me.

"After all we've been through together, Hadrian," I drawled and shook my head. "I am shocked and disappointed that you don't know me better than that. That was pretty lame as far as insults go." Hadrian stared at me for a minute. I think he was a bit disconcerted when instead of getting angry and throwing a tantrum, I smiled back pleasantly.

Usually Hadrian has an entourage of at least twenty other vampires with him to show what a powerful stapan he is. Maybe he just likes all the flattery and adoration. However, he had only Simmons and Douglas, his vampire bodyguard, with him. Looking at Hadrian, you would not suppose that he was that powerful. He is not very scary looking. He is about a foot shorter than I am, skinny and pale with big innocent looking blue eyes and a mop of blond curls. He looked about thirteen though he had become a vampire at the age of twenty-seven. I wouldn't want you to get the wrong idea here, Hadrian is still a vampire and therefore dangerous, but I wasn't afraid of him. After all, I have dealt with supernaturals that would make your hair stand on end.

"Traveling light this evening, Hadrian?" I asked.

Hadrian tipped his chin slightly into the air and glared down his haughty nose at me. "Really, Fechín," he said coldly. "Would you please control your minions?"

"Since you asked so nicely, no," Demon said flatly.

Douglas shifted slightly, drawing our attention to him. He was Kaz' height and though his skin wasn't nearly as dark as Kaz' was, he was still quite dark. His eyes were black too. His dark hair was in a buzz-cut except for one long braid at the base of his skull that hung to the middle of his back. He wore no shirt, his arms crossed over his broad chest so that the muscles in his arms bunched. I'd never considered Douglas to be particularly arrogant, but tonight he was showing us that not only did he have just as much muscle as we did, but that he wasn't concerned about the odds. Well, we could change that.

Simmons was Hadrian's human servant. He was slightly taller than Hadrian was and was the great-great-great grandson of Hadrian's best friend and first human servant. If Simmons had a first name, I had never heard it. He looked from Hadrian to us, completely terrified and he didn't have any qualms about us knowing it. It showed unexpected intelligence on his part. After all, he was the only non-supernatural in the room. If things went south, he was definitely going to be a casualty. He was outgunned and knew it.

There was an empty chair next to Maia for Demon, but he chose to stand behind it rather than sit down. The rest of us stood just behind Demon, hands at our sides, ready to draw our weapons. The Boogeys stood by the door, which remained open. Someone had brought in a fan and it was blowing directly on the three Boogeys, carrying away some of their intense aroma.

"I am surprised to see you here, Chief Hellcurse," Hadrian began. Though he spoke to Daedalus, he was keeping a wary eye on Demon the whole time. "I understood that I would be meeting with the Deadlies alone."

"Fechín and I discussed this at length and decided that the Satana should be involved since we will be working closely with the Enforcers on this rogue vampire case." Daedalus said.

Hadrian inclined his head slightly as if graciously accepting Daedalus' presence, but he was probably relieved as hell. With Daedalus here, he knew that we did not plan to execute him immediately. "Indeed." he said haughtily.

"The rogue vampires were your people." Demon said.

Hadrian's eyes turned to him and he inclined his head again. "So I have been informed, and just let me say that I am shocked. Shocked and appalled that anyone of my people would feed from unwilling humans, especially when there are so many willing humans available. I do not and never have condoned feeding from the unwilling."

Hadrian's speech sounded like a PR person had prepared it. I opened my mouth to say so and felt someone punch me in the leg hard. I stifled a gasp of pain and glared at Riot. He was still staring at Douglas steadily as if nothing had happened, but I knew that the bastard was laughing his ass off inside.

"You should take your own advice, Hadrian, and take control of your people." Demon said. Then he paused. "That was an order, in case you were wondering. Explain to your people that immediate execution is the penalty for this particular transgression. There are *no* exceptions."

Hadrian smirked. "Naturally I will convey your message to my people, Fechín, and I will make it quite clear that rogue behaviour is unacceptable," he said. He placed his hands on the table and started to stand, his voice oozing with sarcasm. "Is that all?"

"No." Demon told him in a tone that made Hadrian drop back down into his chair hastily. "I want to know who the sovereign is that gave them permission to do this."

"I beg your pardon?" Hadrian said politely.

Demon smirked. "Come on, Hadrian. Those vampires would not have been out attacking humans without a higher power egging them on. Who was it?"

That had never occurred to me, but then I wasn't up on all the vampire stuff either. That is Demon's domain. A sovereign vampire is someone that has enough power to rule over the lower ranks. There were four sovereign vampires currently in Blackridge. Naturally, Hadrian, as stapan, was one. His mate, Darkmoon, was another. Douglas was a minor sovereign. He didn't have much power, but he had more than the average vampire did. The fourth was Serkan.

I frowned, wondering where Serkan was tonight. It was strange that he had not returned our phone call yet and usually Hadrian wouldn't meet with us without him. Serkan was the only person in existence who would have a chance in hell of stopping Demon from killing Hadrian.

Oh, wait. There were five sovereigns if you counted Demon.

"No one gave them permission." Hadrian said. "They were acting of their own free will."

Demon gave him a look of cool disbelief. "*Free will?* Please do not insult my intelligence. I may not be part of a kiss, but I know well enough that the lesser vampires are always under the control of a sovereign whether it is their stapan or another. Your people must have had permission from a sovereign to go rogue. I think we can safely cross Serkan off our list so that leaves three of you."

Apparently, Demon wasn't counting himself.

"I did not give anyone permission do such a thing!" Hadrian gasped. "And I am shocked that you would believe that I would do so!"

Demon didn't look as though he believed that, but he moved on. "What about your mate?"

"I am certain Darkmoon would not do so either!"

There was silence for a heartbeat and then Demon's eyes turned to Douglas. "Then that would leave you, Douglas."

Douglas frowned. "I did not give anyone permission to attack humans."

"Leaving me aside, there are only four of you who could have that kind of authority." Demon told him. "We agree that Serkan cannot be one because that is not in his nature. He does not feed from unwilling humans, period. Hadrian says he did not give permission and he also vouches for Darkmoon."

Douglas seemed unable to grasp that his stapan, who was supposed to protect him, had just fed him to the big bad wolf. I felt sorry for him in a way. I didn't believe for a second that Douglas would have given anyone permission to do anything, even blow his nose, without Hadrian's say-so. He may have been powerful enough to take charge of one or two vampires at the most, but not ten.

"Do you not understand yet, Douglas?" Demon said softly. "Hadrian did not vouch for *you*."

Douglas' complexion turned ash-grey and his mouth fell open. "B-But, I didn't do it!"

"Someone did." Demon pointed out.

Douglas was in a tight spot. If he said that Hadrian was lying then the other vampires would kick him out of the kiss if they didn't kill him for treason first. If he couldn't prove that he wasn't the culprit, he would face us. No matter what he did now, he was as good as dead. Douglas was starting to sweat.

"What's it going to be, Douglas?" Demon asked.

"I did not—"

"Yes?"

Douglas glanced at Hadrian looking for help. The stapan's placid, indifferent expression said it all. Douglas was expendable. His gaze dropped to the floor. "I will say nothing more." he said quietly. In Demon's cool expression, there was a flicker of compassion for Douglas. I hoped that meant that Demon would opt for a quick merciful execution.

"Hadrian," Demon said quietly. "You and Simmons may go. Remember to repeat my message to your people. This will not happen again. If it does, we will come knocking on *your* door and next time there will be no bullshitting your way out of it."

"No, no. Of course not," Hadrian turned to leave. "Come, Simmons."

Douglas did not look toward Hadrian. His breathing came faster but he did not flinch. I felt a flash of sympathy with a touch of respect for him, but that wasn't going to save him when Demon gave the word.

Hadrian paused at the door but he did not turn around. "I am sorry, Douglas."

The door closed behind them.

We returned home, exhausted and feeling rather angry about the way things had turned out. However, Demon was certain that Hadrian would be more diligent in ensuring that his people were following the rules from now on.

"We thought he was being diligent before." Bane pointed out.

"I'm willing, for the moment, to believe that this was a fluke." Demon said. "Maybe he was a part of it. Maybe he just turned a blind eye."

"Do you really believe that this was an isolated incident?" Bane asked incredulously.

"If there had been any other attacks, we would have heard something by now." Demon told him.

Maia's cell phone rang and she checked the caller I.D. "Excuse me." she murmured and stepped away to answer the phone.

"They could be doing it outside of Blackridge." I suggested.

"Then the stapans of the other cities would have been calling us." Demon said. "No stapan wants another kiss' members coming into their city and causing trouble."

"Vampires are pretty secretive." Kaz added. "Maybe the other stapans would just take care of it themselves."

"Hadrian would not do anything so foolish." Demon told him. "To allow his people to attack humans on another stapan's turf would start a war. That would definitely bring us into it and no one wants that."

We went into the library. Demon dropped into the desk chair. Bane sat in the edge of the desk, his favourite spot. I joined them, taking the chair in front of the desk. "Okay, so what is our next move?" I asked.

"We're going to have to start interviewing every supernatural in Blackridge." Demon said. "Someone must know something."

"But, will they be willing to tell *us*?" Riot asked. "Most supernaturals would rather face an angry sea monster than talk to us."

That reminded me. I took the opportunity to mention that monster in the lake to Demon. He grimaced. "This is the fourth one this month! Is there some kind of sea monster reunion going on in Blackridge that we don't know about?"

The library door opened and Maia came in. She snapped her cell phone closed and walked toward Demon. "I just had a phone call from an informant." she said and sank gracefully onto the sofa next to me while Bane poured her a glass of whiskey.

"Yes?" Demon prompted.

"I didn't quite catch everything he was saying. He was pretty upset." She sipped the whiskey and made a face. "Could I have something to water this down?"

I went to the small bar fridge and found her a bottle of water. "Thanks." she said adding some of the water to the glass. She took another sip and nodded. "That's better."

"Why was your informant upset?" Demon asked.

"He said he saw someone tonight that he thought you needed to know about." Maia said.

Demon raised an eyebrow. "Oh?"

"Apparently, he was in a bar on La Clare and a group of vampires came in. He said that it appeared that they were doing something they shouldn't."

We looked at each other. "That's the same bar where we found the others last night." I said.

Demon leaned forward intently. "Go on."

Maia took a deep breath. "He said that they were making friends with some humans and he doesn't think that the humans knew who and what they were. He heard that you were on the look-out for some rogue vampires so he called me."

"Are they still at the club?" Demon asked.

Maia shook her head. "No. They left some time ago."

"Damn. Did he recognize any of them?"

Maia frowned. "Well, this is where it puzzles me. He said that there was only one female vampire. She appeared to be the one in charge. He mentioned that she seemed familiar but he is not sure who she is."

"What did she look like?" Demon asked.

"He said that she was very beautiful. She had long black hair, curly, and she was a little shorter than I am with very pale skin."

We looked at each other. "It sounds like Darkmoon." Riot said.

Demon's mouth twisted into an ironic smile. "It sounds like ninety percent of the vampire population," he said. He turned back to Maia. "Did he get a good look at the others?"

"Not really. He wasn't paying attention to them, just her. He did say that there was probably five or six of them altogether."

Demon leaned back in his chair. "Okay, thank you for the information." he said. "Tell your informant thanks, too."

"I will." Maia sipped her whiskey. I watched in fascination as her tongue touched the rim of the glass to capture a stray drop. She set the glass on the table beside her and rose from the sofa. "Are you going hunting then?"

"We could." Demon told her. "However, I doubt that we will find them tonight. The vampires won't be heading back to their nest with their victims. That is the first place we would look. I am hoping that they will refrain from killing the humans since they probably know that the Enforcers and the Satana are looking for them."

Maia smiled. "Kick vampire ass, Deadlies."

Demon's eyes hardened. "We intend to."

CHAPTER TEN

W E COULD NOT SIMPLY march into Hadrian's house and execute Darkmoon because we *think* she might be doing something wrong. Even the Enforcers require proof. The informant's description was too vague. Black hair and a pale face weren't going to be good enough.

"We have no proof that these vampires were doing anything wrong." Bane pointed out. "The informant said he *thought* that the humans didn't know that their friends were vampires, but he didn't know that for certain. Other than the vampires who approached Kaz and Dev, we have no proof that there are any other rogues. There haven't been any news reports about the streets littered with humans found dead and their bodies completely drained of blood."

"So it is possible that we have killed all of the rogues." Riot said.

"Or the vampires are better at disposing of their victims' bodies than we thought." Demon said.

We discussed the possibilities of the bodies being sunk in the river (you can probably guess who suggested that) or being left in the woods somewhere. "I don't think so." Demon said frowning. "We would be getting calls from water and woodland creatures for miles around letting us know about the bodies just in case we mistake *them* as the perpetrators."

"What do you think the vampires are doing with the bodies then?" Bane asked.

Demon shrugged. "Someone or something is disposing of them," he said.

Bane's nose wrinkled. "You mean eating them?"

"It is a possibility."

"So, what are we going to do?" I demanded. "Wait until we catch them killing someone? How many humans will die first?"

"I know it is frustrating, Dev," Kaz said. "But, we have no choice. We can't just go around killing every vampire we come across."

"We should have asked Douglas."

"Douglas was not powerful enough to shake the stapan's control. He could not even defend himself. He could tell us nothing." Demon said tiredly, raking his hands through his hair. "I'll call Serkan again. He will know if there is anyone else of that description within the kiss."

Bane shook his head. "Other than Darkmoon there aren't any other sovereign females in Blackridge."

"We have to start somewhere. At the very least, Serkan can help us determine if we need to focus our attention on Darkmoon or someone else. We also need to know if there have been any strange deaths recently and link them to the vampires. Once we have something to go on, then we'll worry about hunting them."

"You can't do all of that tonight, Demon." Morgana said softly. She placed her hands on his shoulders and leaned forward to kiss the top of his head. Whatever arguments they had, however frustrated she was with him, it was clear that Morgana really loved him. "Try to get some rest. I know that you haven't been sleeping well in the last week. I hear you pacing at night."

"I don't need to sleep," he told her.

"Yes, you do. You've expended a lot of energy in the past few days." She gently stroked his hair back from his face. He looked up at her wearily and she smiled at him. "Even you can't keep up this pace. Come to bed."

He shook his head. "I have to call Serkan."

"You can do it tomorrow, Demon. Serkan will still be there." Morgana said firmly.

He stared at her for a moment and then rose slowly. "Very well, then. We will start first thing tomorrow morning."

We watched in silence as he walked slowly out of the library. A few minutes passed without anyone speaking. Finally, Bane broke the ice as he headed for the phone.

"What are you doing?" I demanded as he picked up the receiver.

"Calling Serkan." he informed me. "Maybe my brother needs to rest, but I sure as hell don't." He paused, staring at the phone in his hand. He wasn't certain how to make a phone call. He had never had to do it before. Up to this point, it had always been Demon or me.

That wasn't what was bothering him. "Demon is going to be really upset," he said softly without looking at us.

"Why?" Kaz asked frowning. "He was going to call Serkan too."

Bane just shook his head. Maia took the phone from his hand gently. "Let me make the phone call, Bane." she said. She dialled the number and turned to him. "What do you want me to say?"

He hesitated. Demon had always taken care of this part, too. "Uh...Put it on speaker phone."

"Hello?" Serkan's voice answered.

"Serkan, it's me." Bane said.

"Fechín, I have been trying to contact you."

"Um, this isn't Fechín. This is... Brandon." Bane told him. "Listen, we have to ask you something."

Bane explained to Serkan what had been happening and mentioned the female Maia's informant had seen. He asked about the females in the Blackridge kiss.

"Are you kidding me? Darkmoon would never tolerate other sovereign female in Blackridge." Serkan snorted.

"Fechín says we have to take everything into account. Is it possible that there could be another sovereign that she doesn't know about?"

"Anything is possible of course." Serkan said. He was quiet for a minute. "Let me check on a few things and I'll get back to you."

"By the way," Bane said. "Why did you want to talk to us?"

"Let me check into this first." Serkan paused. "The informant didn't happen to mention what colour the woman's eyes were, did he?"

"No, he didn't say."

"I see. Well, I will call back as soon as I have something." Serkan hung up.

"Now what do we do?" I asked.

"We wait." Bane said. "I hope when Demon wakes up, we will have more news for him."

I sure as hell hoped so too.

Demon staggered into the kitchen about an hour later with stubble on his chin and bleary eyes. I wasn't very surprised to see him. Demon doesn't sleep very well under normal circumstances. He went right for the coffee that we keep continuously brewing. As daemons, we don't require as much sleep as humans do, and when we are in the middle of a hunt, we sometimes go days without sleep. We keep the coffee on the go because even we have trouble running on only two hours' sleep.

"What are you doing up this early?" he asked me.

I didn't tell him that I hadn't gone to bed yet. When Maia turned in soon after Demon did, there had been no come-hither smile when she wished me good night so I assumed that she was tired and was going to bed to sleep. I would have hesitated even if she had asked me to join her. The shadow of Mike Scarletti was still hovering in the background no matter what Maia said. But, I was too wound to sleep, so I'd just spent the last few hours sitting in the kitchen at the huge wooden table, sipping coffee and eating whatever treat I could wheedle out of Hex. Fortunately, for me, she likes me because I'm always hungry and she always wants to feed someone. It's the perfect relationship.

"We called Serkan." I told Demon as he slid onto a stool across from me. "He said he didn't think that there were any other female sovereigns in Blackridge. He doesn't seem to think that Darkmoon would like sharing that honour."

"He is probably right." Demon said and took a tentative sip of coffee, sighing contentedly as the caffeine made its way into his system. He still required blood regularly but it had been a couple of months at least since he had last fed from another person. Since Maia was the first female visitor we'd had in the house in the last six months, I assumed that he had been using the bottles of blood kept in the refrigerator. Usually Demon got his blood from the supernaturals' blood bank but every so often, he would meet some young woman who was happy to donate her blood, not to mention her body, to him. It is rare since most humans don't know that vampires exist, but it does happen.

I watched him take another sip of coffee. "He said that he would look into it and get back to us." I went on. "He wanted to know if the informant had mentioned her eye colour. We said no and he seemed relieved."

Demon froze with the cup halfway to his lips. He set it down on the table slowly and looked at me. "Did he say anything else?"

His reaction puzzled me. "Just that he would tell us why he called us after he checked into this. What is all this about, Demon?" I asked.

Demon picked up his cup again. "You said he seemed relieved?"

"Yeah," I said. "It was almost as if…almost as if he had someone definite in mind." I finished slowly. I looked at Demon. He was staring into the cup with a haunted look.

"Do you have some idea of who she could be?" I asked him.

Demon grimaced. "Maybe." he sighed heavily. "Shit."

"Come on, Demon. You can talk to me. What's going on?" I asked. "Who are you so worried about?"

Demon got to his feet without appearing to hear me. "I have to talk to Serkan before he goes to bed for the night." he muttered as he left the kitchen.

Before I could determine whether I should follow him or not, Maia came in. She was wearing white panties and a short white halter-top. It was see-through. I made my decision and sat back down. I wondered if she was wearing it for my benefit, but since I still wasn't completely certain about where I stood or rather where Mike stood, I kept my hands to myself. However, that didn't stop me from admiring the view. After all, I *am* male.

Maia poured herself a cup of coffee as Demon had, but she added milk and sugar to it. Then she joined me at the table and took a sip before she spoke. "Good morning." she said softly.

"Good morning." I replied. Aware that I was still staring at her body, I made myself raise my eyes to hers. She was watching me with a small smile on her face. "You look nice." I told her.

She raised an eyebrow at me. "That's it? Just nice?"

I shrugged. "Okay, you look hot."

Her smile was eloquent. "Why don't you show me how hot?"

I shook my head. "No, Maia."

"Why not?" she demanded.

I opened my mouth to tell her why not but the kitchen door opened and Riot stomped in scowling. Even annoyed Riot still looked like Lust. "What the hell is eating you?" I snapped at Riot rather than answer Maia.

He stopped short and scowled at me. "What's it to you?"

Maia looked from me to Riot and rolled her eyes. "If I didn't know you two were friends, I'd think you disliked each other intensely."

"*We do!*" we snapped at the same time and Maia laughed.

The tension in my body eased and I shot a grin at Riot. "Come on, Riot, tell Uncle Dev all about it."

A smile tugged at the corner of Riot's mouth and he glanced at Maia who got to her feet with a smile. "Why don't I just leave you two to have your man-talk in private?" The doorbell rang. "Ah, saved by the bell." She left the kitchen.

I turned back to Riot. "Well?" I demanded. "Why are you stomping around the house and doing a poor impression of Wrath on a bad day?"

He had taken the seat that Maia had just vacated and fiddled with her empty cup. "It wasn't a *poor* impression," he protested. "I thought it was rather well done, actually." When I just stared at him, he sighed. "It's nothing, Dev. Just personal stuff and—did I imagine it or did the doorbell just ring?"

I frowned. "No, you're right. It rang."

"People don't pay visits at this hour."

Riot and I stared at each other. Humans wouldn't but vampires might, especially rogue ones that knew we were looking for them. We jumped up and drawing the weapons we still had strapped to us, Riot and I burst out of the kitchen and into the hallway. We arrived at the front door; blades at the ready as Maia reached for the doorknob. Kaz, Onyx, and Bane barrelled down the stairs in a pack. Apparently, the same thought had occurred to them.

"Maia!" I shouted. "Wait!"

Maia opened the door. We all halted in our tracks. It was Serkan. Maia turned to look at us and recoiled, her hand to her chest and her eyes wide. "Holy overkill, you guys!" she gasped when she saw all the weapons.

Kaz began cursing and sheathed his blade. "Don't you know any better than to open the door at this hour of the morning without checking to see who it is first?" he snapped at her.

"It's Serkan," she told him surprised.

"Did you know that before you opened the door?" he asked.

Maia looked sheepish. "No, I guess not. I'm sorry, Kaz." she said quietly.

He sighed and raked his hand through his hair. "No. I'm the one who should apologize. I overreacted. This whole thing with the rogues has got us all on edge."

She accepted his apology with a smile.

"May I come in now?" Serkan asked politely.

We had forgotten that he was still standing on the front porch. Embarrassed, Kaz nodded. "Sorry about that, Serkan."

Serkan stepped into the house and Maia closed the door behind him. He was tall and lean with long black hair and dark blue eyes. He would have looked like the stereotypical vampire if his skin had been paler. Instead, it was brown, as if he had spent his whole life out in the sun. He usually avoided wearing the cliché vampire black. He was wearing dark blue jeans and a white t-shirt with a brown leather jacket thrown over top. He had been in his thirties when he was turned into a vampire and that had been centuries ago. Serkan had been a nobleman of some kind and that is probably why he was a sovereign. He retained his regal bearing, even in modern clothing.

"There you are." We all turned toward Demon. He was standing in the doorway of the library. "No wonder you aren't answering your phone."

"I thought I should come in person." Serkan explained. "We must talk about this sovereign and get a better description of her from Maia's informant."

"The informant isn't here." Demon told him.

Serkan frowned and something about his expression poked at my subconscious. There was something important about it. It was something that I already knew, but couldn't quite grasp. "I have only a few short hours before I will have to return home to rest for the day." Serkan said. He turned to Maia. "Would you be willing to call your informant and try to get a better description of this woman?"

Maia's eyes widened. "Is it that important?"

"It is essential." Serkan said grimly.

Maia nodded. "Okay, I'll see what I can do."

"Thank you." Serkan said firmly. "Perhaps we should retire to the library while Maia makes her phone call."

Demon scowled. "What is going on, Serkan? Who do you think this woman is?"

"You know the answer to that as well as I do." Serkan asked pointedly.

"She is nowhere near Blackridge!"

"That is what I wished to speak with you about, but I need Maia's informant to give a better description before I can be certain."

Demon and Serkan stared at each other for another minute in silence. Finally, Demon sighed. "Come into the library."

As Demon moved past him, Serkan placed a hand on his shoulder, stopping him. "I would not ask this if it was not very important, Demon."

"I know." Demon replied flatly. He moved away from Serkan and went into the library. For a minute no one spoke. We were all watching Serkan as he gazed after him. There was a kind of longing in his face. I can recognize lust when I see it, but this was not it. Serkan's demeanour toward Demon puzzled me.

Suddenly, Bane cleared his throat and touched Serkan's arm. Serkan started and turned to look at him. The dazed expression on his face cleared as Bane gestured toward the open library door. Wordlessly, Serkan glided into the library. Bane stepped in behind him and the rest of us followed.

"Have a seat." Demon waved Serkan toward a chair and then sat down behind the desk. He leaned back in his chair and didn't speak again.

The following half hour was uncomfortably silent. It was a relief when Maia finally joined us. Serkan looked up at her and gestured toward the chair across from him. Demon joined them, taking a chair next to Maia. His expression was perfectly blank. The only sign that he was upset was the way that his hands grasped the arms of the chair, his hands and knuckles were perfectly white.

"Well?" Serkan said urgently.

Maia shook her head. "He claimed that he didn't get a good look at her and that he had nothing more to tell."

"What he did see of her was good enough to know that he did not recognize her." Serkan pointed out.

"That is what I told him and I was able to get a little more information out of him."

Serkan leaned forward. "Tell us exactly what he told you about the woman. Anything that he noted about her could help us identify her."

Maia looked from Serkan to Demon. They were both tense, looking at her as if their whole lives depended on her answer. "Okay, let me think." She closed her eyes for a moment. "He said that she wasn't very tall. She was probably an inch or two shorter than I am. She was not thin, but not fat either. She had a very feminine figure."

"She was attractive?" Serkan suggested.

Maia shrugged. "He seemed to think so."

"Was that all?"

"Well," Maia continued. "She was wearing a black dress."

Demon made a noise of disgust. "They all wear black. Vampires are so unoriginal."

Serkan laughed. "If you want originality, go to a daemon."

Demon smiled slightly.

Serkan turned back to Maia. "He observed nothing else unusual about the woman? Nothing that would set her apart from the others and help us recognize her?"

Maia nodded. "I asked about her eye colour since you asked about it."

"What did he say?"

"He seemed anxious when I brought it up. He said she looked at him and something about her scared the hell out of him. Her eyes were glowing in the dark and they were *purple*. It seems to me that would be something he would have mentioned the first time. I think, however, that he had been drinking."

Demon did not look as if he thought it was just drink. The colour drained from his face and his breathing became harsh, as though he had received a shock.

"Oh shit." Bane said. He had been standing beside his brother and now he took a step closer, placing his hand on Demon's shoulder. His face was white and tense.

Serkan sucked in his breath. "I knew it," he said in a harsh whisper. He was pale, too. "Oh god, Demon, it is Tanith."

Bane shook his head. "It *couldn't* be Tanith!"

Demon flinched. I wondered if anyone else saw it. He bolted to his feet and walked to the window, keeping his back to us. Who was the woman that she could make Wrath flinch?

"Did you know about this?" Bane asked Serkan. "Is this why you were trying to contact us?"

Serkan nodded. "A friend of mine mentioned that she had seen some strange vampires in Blackridge."

"So, there is more than one new vampire in town." Bane said. "Is it a whole kiss?"

"It may be. She mentioned a group, though she did not know how many there were exactly. She described a woman who resembled Tanith. That is why I wanted Maia's informant to come down with a more accurate description. I wanted to verify her identity."

"Who *is* Tanith?" Kaz asked.

Serkan was watching Demon. "Do you want to tell them, Demon, or shall I?" His tone was gentle.

Slowly he turned back from the window, his eyes despondent. "Tanith is the vampire that turned me," he said flatly.

We were speechless. "I thought you executed the vampire who did that!" I exclaimed.

"No. I killed the other vampires in her kiss, but I didn't kill her."

"If she's the one that actually turned you why didn't you kill *her*?" Riot frowned.

Bane moved to stand beside his brother, protectively. Serkan answered, "He couldn't kill her because he loves her."

CHAPTER ELEVEN

WE WERE ALL SPEECHLESS. Demon glared at Serkan, fists clenched at his sides. "I am not in love with her." he ground out.

"You did love her once, very much."

"Not anymore." Demon said.

Serkan rose. "Then why didn't you execute Tanith? How did she manage to escape you?"

"You know what happens after the turn!" Demon snapped. "I lost consciousness and when I came to, she was gone."

"But, you found her people."

Demon struggled to compose his expression and shrugged. "They were easy. They were afraid but not afraid enough to stop feeding from humans. I tracked them through their prey, but she was more careful. I have had no opportunity to kill her."

Serkan raised an eyebrow. "Why have you not hunted her down? It is not like you to sit by and do nothing."

"I *have* been hunting Tanith ever since she turned me!" Demon snapped, angry again. "I have never forgiven her or forgotten how she betrayed me!"

"Well, it seems that she has found you instead." Serkan said.

"Do you really think she has come here to seek out Demon?" Bane asked worriedly.

Serkan inclined his head slightly. "And perhaps she is murdering humans along the way."

"Are you blaming me for the rogue vampires?" Demon's voice was cold, but the flames in his eyes leapt.

Holy shit. Talk about pulling the tiger's tail. We all sucked in a breath and took a step back, staying well out of the range of his weapon. However, Demon didn't react the way we expected. His shoulders sagged and he sat down heavily in a chair near the window. "You're right," he said softly. "This is my fault." He leaned forward and put his head in his hands.

Serkan got up slowly and crossed the room. He laid a hand on Demon's shoulder. "I am not blaming you, Demon," he said gently. "Do not misunderstand me."

"I should have killed her when I had the chance." Demon said with his head still in his hands.

"Then why did you not do so?" Serkan asked.

"I did love her once." Demon said and looked up. "You were right about that. Things changed over time and I knew that she was dangerous. She will stop at nothing to get what she wants and she does not care who she hurts." He had a faraway look in his eyes. His expression said that he was remembering something unpleasant.

We were never exactly sure how Demon became a vampire. We knew that he had not been a willing partner in the turning, but that was all. I thought it strange because he should have just healed from the wounds. Instead, he had become a vampire. Besides, how do you turn an Enforcer against his will?

"So Tanith is a sovereign." Riot said.

"Oh, yes." Demon said.

"Is she very powerful?"

Demon nodded. "She is probably one of the more powerful sovereigns."

"More powerful than you are?"

Demon paused. "I...don't believe so."

Bane darted an anxious look at Demon. "Hex said a woman called asking for you last night. Could it have been her?"

"It could all be a mistake." Demon said.

"But, you don't really believe that either." Serkan said. "Now, I want to know what it is that you intend to do, *Wrath*."

Demon scowled. "You don't have to remind me of what I am, Serkan, or what it is that I do. If it is Tanith and if she is attacking humans, it is reason enough for me to execute her."

"Will you be able to do it, though?"

Demon gritted his teeth. "If she is the person behind the rogues we will find her and we will execute her." He repeated the words he had said to Hadrian. "There are no exceptions."

"This won't be easy." Kaz said. "If she has a brain in her head, she'll be well hidden."

"She is very intelligent." Demon assured us. "However, no one eludes us for long."

"I think we can agree that Tanith is not going to stand in the front yard and yell "yoo hoo" at us." I said. "So what's the plan?"

"It may not be as hard to find her as we think. She is a sovereign and some of Hadrian's people are following a sovereign vampire. He swears it isn't him or Darkmoon." Demon smiled thinly. "If there is another sovereign in Blackridge trying to take over his vampires then he'll want to help us."

"So we give him the heads up?" I asked.

"He may know about her already. I find it hard to believe that a sovereign could enter his territory without him knowing."

"But, if she is the rogue sovereign then why did he let Douglas take the blame?" Riot asked.

"Possibly because he knows that Tanith and I—" Demon broke off.

I shook my head. "Even so, Hadrian knows how you feel about rogue vampires. He would never believe that you would look the other way, even for someone you love."

"I am *not* in love with her. But, it is one possibility." Demon frowned. "And I haven't come up with another theory yet."

"What the hell is she doing attacking humans in Blackridge anyway?" Kaz said. "She must know that the Deadlies live here. If I were her, I'd want to steer clear of Blackridge."

"So what's her reason for coming here?" Riot asked. "She must want something other than Hadrian's vampires. There are thousands of other kisses. What is so special this one?"

"Maybe she's crazy." I suggested.

We all looked at Demon. He smiled a little and shook his head. "She is not crazy."

"She turned you so obviously she is not playing with a full deck." I pointed out. "So what's her game?"

Suddenly, the colour drained from Serkan's face and he sank back onto a chair next to Demon. Bane stood between them. Something flickered at the edges of my brain...something that should have clicked but it didn't. Even as I tried to grasp it, it slipped away again.

"She wants you to know that she is here." Bane said to his brother. His eyes were wide and worried.

"I was afraid of this." Serkan said hoarsely. "She *is* after Demon."

"Do you think she might try to hurt him?" I asked.

"I don't know."

"That is a pretty deadly game to play." Kaz said.

"I think he should be safe enough." Riot pointed out. "He is immortal and besides, it is quite hard to find us."

"But, not impossible." Kaz said. "The easiest way to find Demon would be to follow one of us or someone else associated with us—" He broke off and we all stared at each other.

"Like Serkan, for instance?" Demon suggested. He shot to his feet and ran out of the library. We all ran after him as he flung open the front door. As we burst out of the house onto the front porch, an engine roared to life. A car swung around in a circle, tires spewing gravel as they spun madly in an attempt to escape.

Demon's face twisted into a snarl, baring his sharp fangs. His blue eyes burned with fury. His black wings unfurled and stretched out. He flung himself into the air with a roar of wrath and soared over the car dropping in front of it at the end of the drive. The car screeched to a halt, the motor still running. Demon snarled at whoever was inside. He threw back his head and roared.

The people inside the car scattered like terrified chickens. Demon picked up the car and heaved it against a tree. The tree buckled and fell onto the car flattening it like a pancake. I hoped that there was no one left inside. It was a hell of a way to die.

"Get the sonofabitches!" Demon yelled.

We soared after the escaping intruders. Riot and I dove into the woods after a couple of them, flying through the branches and snapping them with our bodies and wings as if they were twigs. I caught one while Riot continued to chase down the other. I wrapped my arms around the struggling body of my captive, pinioning his arms to his sides.

"Be still!" I hissed in the captive's ear. "Or I'll execute you myself right here and now!"

Obediently, the person stopped struggling and I flew him back to the others. I landed on the front lawn where Kaz and Onyx had rounded up two others. Two men with long blond hair were huddled together on the grass, gazing up at Demon with trepidation. I tossed my own prisoner to the ground a little more forcefully than was necessary. He gasped, the breath knocked out of him. Riot returned with the woman he had captured. He dropped her onto the grass next to the others.

"Maia, turn on the outside lights!" Demon called out. His voice lowered dangerously. "Let's see who we have here."

Light flooded the front lawn revealing our intruders. "You have got to be kidding me!" I exclaimed.

The man I had captured fleeing through the woods was Mike Scarletti.

CHAPTER TWELVE

MAIA QUICKLY TURNED OFF the outside floodlights at Demon's command and we marched our guests into the house. Maia gasped and stepped back when Mike shuffled in. He couldn't even meet her eyes. He stared at the floor as Demon shoved him into the library along with his cohorts.

Maia came to stand in the doorway. I touched her shoulder. "Maia, you don't have to be here right now." I whispered.

Maia looked at me with eyes that glittered with unshed tears. "Oh my god, Dev," she began. "I'm so sorry. I—" she broke off, and her lower lip trembled.

That familiar feeling of panic was building in my chest again. I looked at her helplessly, not knowing what to do. I was just starting to speak when Morgana came to my rescue. I guess the commotion finally disturbed her enough that she decided to find out what was going on. She glided down the stairs to join Maia and me in the doorway.

"I'll stay with her." Morgana said quietly. "Demon needs you."

Gratefully, I slunk away leaving Maia to Morgana's tender care, feeling like a first-class heel. I should be able to comfort the woman I lo—No, I wasn't going to go there. Forcing my mind back to the business at hand, I wandered into the library and found myself staring down at not one familiar face but two.

"*Ophelia?*" I blurted. I looked around at the other Deadlies. "This has got to be a mistake, right?"

"I caught her in the woods." Riot said grimly.

I turned back to look at Mike Scarletti. "You do know that she's a witch, don't you? I mean, aren't you the one who thinks that anything supernatural has to be evil?"

Scarletti glared and suddenly he spat at me. The spittle landed on my boot. I glared at it and then coldly raised my eyes to him. "That's disgusting!" I snapped. "Do that again and I'll use your face to wipe it off!"

Riot and Kaz snorted. I think they were trying not to laugh, but that was not going to alleviate the seriousness of the moment. Demon was seriously pissed. He was all but breathing fire as he stood over the four captives.

"What the hell are you doing here?" he snarled at Scarletti, flashing his fangs. Usually he was better at hiding them than this. That he wasn't even trying was a bad sign. Scarletti opened his mouth and closed it again, too terrified to answer. Of course, he had always known what Demon was, but I don't think he had ever seen it up close, personal and pissed off.

"Someone had better answer me." Demon growled.

"We were sent by our sovereign," one of the others answered. I looked at him. I didn't recognize him, but I knew what he was.

Vampire.

And he had waltzed right into the Enforcers' turf. This guy must have been suicidal to come out here.

"How did you find us?" Demon demanded.

The vampire shrugged. "It was not hard to discover who is a liaison to the Deadlies. Scarletti told us about his girlfriend, but you took her away before we could find her." He nodded at Serkan. "He was the next choice. We were not expecting him to lead us to you so quickly."

My knees almost gave way under me. "Are you crazy?" I gasped. "You told the vampires where to find Maia?"

"They promised not to hurt her." Mike said coldly.

"*And you believed them?*" I yelled. "You really are stupid, Scarletti."

"Who is your sovereign?" Demon demanded.

The vampire looked at Demon. "I think you know her very well." He smirked. "Intimately, you might say."

Demon stiffened. "If you're trying to be clever, you're failing miserably," he hissed.

"This is no joke," the other vampire said hastily. "Sovereign Tanith has chosen you to be her eternal mate. You must be sensible of the honour." He and the other male vampire smiled at Demon as if they really believed it. We were all speechless. These two were either stupid or they were on something.

Demon stared at them. "Do I *look* pleased?"

The vampire considered that as he studied Demon's expression. His face turned pale. "Well, no."

"Where the hell do you fit into all of this?" I demanded of Scarletti.

Scarletti lifted his chin. "I approached her about helping me rid Blackridge of Hadrian and his nest of vipers," he said.

"And what do you get from this?" Demon demanded.

"There would be no further need for the Deadlies to be here." Scarletti said glaring at me.

For pity sake, the jealous twit had signed a deal with the devil to get rid of a romantic rival. "But, *she* was still going to be here! Did you think that she was going to just toddle happily off into the sunset as soon as Hadrian was gone?" I snapped. Scarletti stared at me, stupefied. Apparently, he had not thought that far ahead.

I made a sound of disgust. "She's a vampire, Scarletti! She may be trying to overthrow Hadrian so that *she* can control the vampires of Blackridge!" I yelled at him. "And she may be the one giving these little bloodsuckers the permission to go rogue!"

Scarletti frowned. "I don't know what that means."

The door banged open and we all started as Maia stalked into the room. Morgana hurried after her. "Maia! Maia!" Morgana said, frantically trying to distract her. It was no good. Maia was a woman on a mission.

Maia stopped in front of Scarletti, glaring down at him, eyes burning with fury. I have never seen her so angry. "What that means, Michael, is that your new best friend is allowing vampires to feed from unwilling humans!" she said coldly.

Scarletti smirked when he saw her. "I should have guessed that I'd find you here," he said tightly and he glanced at me. "Have you slept with him yet?"

"That is none of your business!" she snapped.

"You say that now, but just wait until you try to come crawling back," he said smugly. "And you are going to crawl. I guarantee it."

"I have never crawled for you, Mike, and I never will." Maia said.

He opened his mouth to speak.

"Shut up, Scarletti." Demon interrupted. He stared down at Ophelia. "And what do you get out of this?"

Ophelia smiled silkily. "Him." She pointed at Riot.

Riot looked startled. "*Me?*"

"If I help her, then she will let me have you."

Riot planted his hands on his hips and glared at her. "And exactly how did you think she was going to manage that?"

"I don't know." Ophelia said gazing up at him, dreamily. Moreover, she didn't care. She was only interested in the result. Of course, if Tanith had lied to Scarletti then she had probably lied to Ophelia too. There was no possible way she could deliver on such a promise.

"Are you getting this, Mikey?" I snarled. "Tanith promised you that once Hadrian was—what, dead—that the Deadlies would leave Blackridge? She came here to claim Demon as her eternal mate and she promised Ophelia that she could have Riot. Besides, do you really think that if Demon stays his brother is going anywhere? That makes *three* Deadlies that were still going to be here!"

"But, not *you!*" Scarletti snapped back.

I was beyond fury. I can honestly say that I saw red. I wanted to kill Mike Scarletti. I must have made a lunge toward him because I suddenly felt Bane's hand grip my arm. "Dev, cool it." he said quietly and sent a pointed look toward Demon.

I glanced over and saw that Demon's eyes were glazing over and his fangs were easing out of his mouth. I took a deep breath and tried to calm down. "Sorry." I muttered.

Demon pulled himself together and turned back to the vampires. "What happened to the humans you left the bar with?"

The first male seemed to understand now their danger. He shrank away from Demon, his eyes wary and frightened. The second male still wasn't getting it. He shrugged.

Shrugged.

"We fed and left them in the hospital parking lot," he said carelessly.

"You sonofabitch!" Kaz snarled and started toward the vampire.

"You admit, then, that you fed from unwilling humans." Demon said as he caught hold of Kaz' arm. His eyes filled with flames until there was no colour left except for that burning blue.

The second vampire seemed to understand then that perhaps this had been a bad idea all around. It was about time that he clued in. He exchanged worried looks with his partner.

"Scarletti," Demon said coldly, without looking at him. "Get the hell out of here. If I see you anywhere near this house or anyone connected with it again, it won't matter that you aren't a vampire."

"But—" Scarletti began.

Demon turned on him, eyes and fangs flashing. "You have ten seconds to get out of my sight because I am seriously reconsidering letting you go."

Scarletti realized that Demon was dead serious and fled the room. I went to the window and looked out. Scarletti was running like hell down the driveway. I had forgotten that Demon had wrapped his car around a tree. Oh, well. He probably had a cell phone. He could call someone to come and get him.

"This was my fault." Serkan said softly. We looked at him. He seemed shaken. His face was pale. His eyes were large and he was trembling. "I led them here."

We looked at him. Bane frowned. "Of course it wasn't your fault. How could you know that they were following you?"

Serkan didn't answer. He buried his face in his hands. Concerned, Morgana moved up beside him and patted his shoulder. "No one is blaming you for this, Serkan."

"Of course not," Demon said gruffly. "They could have just as easily followed Maia to us."

Serkan lifted his head. "I suppose so." He didn't seem convinced, however.

Demon glanced at the window. The sun was starting to come up. "Serkan, you had better take one of the rooms in the basement. There aren't any windows. You'll be safe there."

Serkan looked surprised. "Thank you, but you don't have to do that."

"You'll never make it home now." Demon told him.

"Come on, Serkan." Morgana said taking Serkan's hand. "I'll show you the way."

Serkan hesitated and studied Demon carefully. "Are you sure?"

"Yes." Demon walked over to him and touched his arm. "Don't force us to carry you down the stairs ourselves."

Serkan laughed. "Very well. Thank you." He allowed Morgana to lead him out of the room.

"Dev," Demon said turning to me. "You and Maia are going to take Ophelia into Blackridge. Drop her at Satana Headquarters. Daedalus will know what to do with her."

"I haven't done anything!" Ophelia cried out.

"It is possible that Daedalus won't have anything for which he can arrest you," he agreed calmly. "You may have to hang around the station for a bit while he does a thorough check, but if you're clear then he'll free you. If he does, you can take a message to Tanith."

"Which is?" Ophelia said petulantly.

"4218 East Brooks Street." he replied.

"What is 4218 East Brooks Street?" she asked.

"That's where she'll find the bodies."

About an hour later, we untied the vampires' bodies from the room in the basement. This one had windows and the two vampires were in there while the sun came up. You get the picture.

We ensured that they were dead before we put out the fire. We didn't want them to flare up again so Demon asked us to move them to a room without windows. They were still sizzling when Kaz and I dragged the bodies out of the execution room.

We paused at the first door and Kaz opened it. We started inside before we realized that the room was in use. Serkan lay on the bed, stretched out and looking, quite literally, dead to the world.

Kaz and I jumped back from the door. Kaz quickly closed it. We stared at each other in horror. "I've never seen Serkan...dead." He sounded rattled.

"Me neither." I said, my own voice shaking slightly.

"Let's try the next hallway." Kaz suggested.

"Good idea." I said hastily. We had never moved so fast in our lives. We ran down the hallway and quickly dumped the two bodies into a room. Kaz slammed the door shut and we made a fast exit out the back way, not daring to pass by Serkan's room again. I don't know about Kaz, but I never wanted to see Serkan like that again. It was too creepy.

Gasping for air, Kaz and I burst into the library. Bane and Demon were both there. Bane was sitting in front of the desk with his feet propped up on it. Demon was sitting in his usual spot behind it. They shot to their feet in alarm. "What's wrong?" Bane demanded.

Kaz and I looked at each other and decided it was better not to answer that. They would probably just laugh at us. "We were..." Kaz looked at me for help.

"We went for a run around the house." I said.

"*Voluntarily?*" Bane gasped.

I scowled at him. "I'm not that lazy!"

Two hours before sunset, three of us went out to deliver the two vampires' bodies to the address. We had searched the same warehouse earlier. One of Hadrian's boltholes was located there. If Hadrian found them first, then it would remind him that the Deadlies knew where it was. If Tanith found them first, then she would get the message that her chosen mate disapproved of vampires attacking humans.

Kaz, Riot, and I returned home after making our drop off and went to the library where we knew the others would be waiting. Demon and Bane turned to us, expectantly, as we came in.

"Two crispy critters, signed, sealed and delivered." I announced.

Bane rubbed his hands together. "Let the games begin," he said softly.

CHAPTER THIRTEEN

THE WAIT FOR TANITH or Hadrian to respond to our message seemed interminable. We sat together in the library as soon as the sun went down and stared at the phone. After about half an hour of this, Demon got up. "I'm going to the gym," he said quietly and left before anyone could speak.

The gym was in the catacombs. It had the usual work out stuff, like weights and punching bags but there were also dummies hanging from the ceiling to practice our skills on. I figured Demon was going downstairs to take some of his frustrations out on a dummy or two.

Now was probably a good time to warn him. "Don't go into the first room." I told him.

He turned back. "Why?" he asked curiously.

I hesitated. I really didn't want him to laugh at me, but he looked like he could use it. Finally, I swallowed my pride and told him. "Serkan is dead in there."

He stared at me while he tried to puzzle it out. Finally, he understood, but he didn't laugh. He gave me a slight smile. "Thanks for the heads up."

No one spoke for the first five minutes after he left the room. Finally, Kaz said, "I hate seeing him hurt like this."

"Demon is pretty much indestructible." I reassured him.

His eyes drifted toward me. "That's not what I meant. I meant, you know, emotionally."

"I don't like to see Demon vulnerable either." I agreed. Everyone looked at me surprised, I suppose, at my use of the word in describing Demon. I shrugged. "Well, what else would you call it? He looks like someone shot his dog. Twice."

"Dev is right." Bane said softly. "The last time he looked like that..." He trailed off and didn't finish the sentence.

The door opened and Maia drifted in, looking very tired. She went to bed shortly after we tied the vampires up. She couldn't bear to listen to them beg and did not want to witness their execution. To tell the truth, we didn't want her to see it either. Demon sent her to sleep in his room at the back of the house farther away from the execution room. I gave her earplugs, which she accepted gratefully. When she finally woke up, she spent most of the day in the kitchen with Hex, afraid to come out, in case we happened to be dragging our prisoners through the hallway at that time.

Maia dropped into a chair. "Is it all over?" she asked wearily.

"Yes." Bane assured her. He gave her a slight smile. "You look like you could use a drink."

"Wine would be nice if you have any."

"We do." Bane said cheerfully as he poured a glass and handed it to me to give to her. "Dev bought it. He insisted that we should have some here."

She looked up in surprise as she accepted the glass from me. "You bought a bottle just for me?" she asked, pleased.

"I know you prefer wine to whisky." I muttered.

Maia sipped the wine and smiled. "You even remembered that I prefer merlot. Mike could never remember that. Are you trying to seduce me, Dev Xander?"

I turned red and the others started to laugh. However, I was never one to take this kind of teasing lying down. I leaned over her, gazing deeply into her eyes. I brushed my lips over her cheek and down to her neck. "Absolutely," I murmured against her ear. "Is it working?"

Maia sucked in her breath and gaped at me. I laughed and straightened again. She scowled at me. "You have been hanging out with Riot too long."

"I taught him everything he knows. He's coming along nicely, isn't he?" Riot said, grinning wickedly.

Maia's cheeks flushed and she suddenly became intensely interested in her wine. "He's always been..." she trailed off, embarrassed.

"What?" I started to ask, but then the door opened and Demon came in.

He still seemed frustrated. Cement dust covered him from head to foot; even his wings were grey with it. I wondered if there were any cement blocks left in one piece downstairs.

"No one has called yet." Bane informed him.

Demon nodded. "I'm going for a shower," he said curtly. "If that phone rings call me. Do not answer it."

"Okay, but, Demon—" Riot began.

Demon was already heading upstairs.

An hour later, we were still in the library by the phone, waiting for it to ring. It was well past dusk now and no one had responded to our calling card yet. The tension in the room was so thick that it was practically suffocating. I paced to the window facing the side yard and flung it open. Everyone looked at me, but no one asked why I had done it. They understood.

"Maybe they haven't found the bodies." Kaz suggested.

"Daedalus released Ophelia." Bane said. "If she delivered her message, they found the bodies."

"What if she didn't?" Kaz persisted.

Bane raised an eyebrow. "If Wrath told you to deliver a message, would you deliver it?"

"Yeah, but I'm not a nut like Ophelia."

It was a good point. Bane did not have a response to that.

"What time is it?" Onyx asked for the hundredth time in the last hour.

"Six seconds since you last asked." I snapped at him.

Onyx glared. "You always were prone to exaggeration."

"Bite me!" I snarled.

"Would you two stop bickering?" Riot growled. He glanced at Demon, seated behind the desk. He had been there since he came back from his shower, staring at the phone as though it were a rabid dog ready to bite him. Onyx and I exchanged guilty looks.

"Sorry, Demon." I muttered.

"Yeah," Onyx said.

Demon did not respond.

Suddenly, the phone rang.

We all jumped and gasped, except for Demon. His face was calm, but his hand shook ever so slightly as he reached to pick up the handset. His voice showed no emotion as he answered. "This is Wrath."

Yikes. Usually he answered the phone as Fechín since phone lines are never one hundred percent secure from eavesdroppers, but he never *ever* answered as Wrath. He was going right for the throat.

He listened for a second. "Page, did you say? Dagmar Page, I see…Oh, yes, I am sure she does. I, too, wish to speak with her," he said in a quiet, angry tone. When he spoke again, his voice had become calm again. "We will meet at the Brooks Street address…That is non-negotiable…Oh, I think that she will. She does *not* want me to have to come and find her…What did you say your name was again…Right…Dagmar." He hung up without another word. He turned to us and stared at us in silence.

"Well?" Serkan demanded anxiously.

Demon shrugged. "We'll give Ms. Page a few minutes to relay the message and call us back." He was cool and calm. The nerves he had displayed earlier were nowhere in evidence even when the phone rang again ten minutes later.

"Answer that, Serkan." Demon said as he stood. "Tell Ms. Page that we are already waiting for them at Brooks Street. Tell them that they have fifteen minutes to get there."

"Or what?" Serkan asked, hand hovering over the phone while it rang.

Demon smiled coldly. "Just tell them that they have fifteen minutes to get there. They can fill in the "or what" themselves."

We flew to Blackridge. Serkan stayed behind with Maia, which pissed him off to no end. He wanted to come with us but Demon said no, he could handle it. Serkan had no choice but to remain behind, though it was obvious that he didn't like it. It wasn't that he didn't trust Demon. I think he didn't trust Tanith. I couldn't blame him for that. I was wondering if we were going to walk into an ambush myself.

The Brooks Street building was quiet. There were no lights on inside. Demon motioned for us to land on the roof. We came down carefully, making no sound. "Riot, there's a hatch over there. Go in that way and have a look around on the upper level. Dev, Bane, go with him. Onyx, Morgana, Kaz, you will follow me. We're going in through the window at the back."

I followed Riot and Bane to the trapdoor. Bane went in first and then motioned for us to come in. We scouted around the upstairs and checked the bolthole, but found nothing of interest.

"No one's home!" I announced, coming down the stairs.

Demon and the others had finished their search and were now waiting for the vampires' arrival downstairs. Bane and Riot stayed upstairs in case the vampires decided to try to sneak in that way. The rest of us kept our eyes open downstairs. Demon just nodded as I joined him, barely acknowledging me. He had his own thoughts to occupy him. I, too, had something to concern me.

Maia.

She had taken Mike's betrayal very hard. Just before we left, Maia and I had been alone in the library for a few minutes. She had tried to smile but it was a rather weak attempt. "Looks like I'll be here on a permanent basis. Hope you guys don't mind."

"You know that you're welcome here any time, Maia." I tried to offer the only comfort I could think of. "But, you know, Mike only did what he did because—"

She cut me off. "Don't tell me that he did it because he loves me because that is bullshit. He did it because he is jealous and possessive. He doesn't like my friendship with the Deadlies and more specifically he doesn't like my relationship with *you*."

I noticed that she changed the term when she referred to me. I didn't know what to do with that. I had had sexual affairs with women but I had never been in a relationship. Maia was the first one who had meant this much to me. She had the potential of becoming a relationship and that made me nervous. I've executed more supernaturals than I can count. I've faced down some terrifying things and laughed while they tried to kill me. However, the thing that actually terrifies me is having a relationship and falling in love. How weird is that?

What more Maia and I would have said to each other, I don't know because Kaz appeared in the doorway. "Demon's ready to go," he said giving me a pointed look. "You'd better get out here before he comes to look for you himself, which considering his mood could be very, very unpleasant."

I got it. Business first, pleasure later. I wasn't so sure that later was going to be pleasure or pleasant.

I left with the other Enforcers and I assume Maia went to bed. My imagination followed her from the library, up the stairs and to the bedroom door. I had to stop myself at the door of her bedroom. I didn't want to think about her snuggling down under the sheets, maybe naked. I groaned and put my hand over my eyes.

"They get under your skin, don't they?" Demon asked casually.

I looked up. His gaze wasn't on me. He was still watching the door so I scowled at him. "I don't know what you're talking about."

He did not respond. Instead, he suddenly stood straighter and cocked his head, listening. I strained my ears trying to pick up what it was that had caught his attention. Then I could hear it too. So did everyone else in the room. It was the distinctive sound of wings approaching.

"*The Graces!*" Demon added a few curse words. The rest of us moved in to stand shoulder to shoulder with Demon as the Graces flew in through the large bay door and landed a few feet from us.

There are seven Graces, but only three came in. The Graces look more human than we do. These three Graces had very pale skin and no horns. You would never have known that they were daemons or even supernatural had it not been for the white wings. Demon made no move as the tallest and blondest of them stepped forward. The man frowned when Demon did not acknowledge him.

"Hello, Wrath." The man's tone was cold, but he had used Demon's Deadly designation. It would have been a sign of respect had he not sneered when he said it. He should have known better.

"What the hell do you want, Ambrose?" Demon refrained from using the Grace's title. That didn't bother Ambrose as much as Demon's dismissive tone did. Ambrose believes that the Graces are superior to the Deadlies because we feed from sin and he and the other Graces feed from virtues. He never considers that perhaps draining away a human's virtue may not by the best idea.

Ambrose bristled, considering Demon's tone to be an insult. Ambrose has known the Deadlies long enough to know that if he was looking for admiration, he had come to the wrong people. Ambrose Grace may be Bravery but he is the biggest chicken-shit on the planet and we have no use for cowards.

Ambrose's face tightened in anger. "Must you be so insolent?" he demanded.

"What do you want?" Demon repeated, ignoring the question.

"What are you doing here?" Ambrose responded.

Demon's eyebrow rose. "What's it to you?"

"Are you waiting for someone?"

"How is that any of your business, Cowardice?" Demon growled.

Ambrose's handsome face twisted into an ugly snarl. Before he could answer, however, a small woman moved forward and stepped between Ambrose and Demon, her hand gliding along her older brother's arm. Carys' Grace is Love. She is petite and blonde and has what the humans would call the face of an angel.

"Ambrose," she said softly. "Don't start a fight with Fechín. We need their help."

I gaped at her. *"You need us?"*

She nodded solemnly. Demon frowned. "Why? What has happened, Carys?" he asked.

"We don't need the Deadlies' help." Ambrose sneered.

Demon glanced at him. "I wasn't asking you," he said coldly. He turned back to her. "Carys?"

She started to answer and then went still. "Bane?" she said softly.

Riot was coming down from the upper level with Bane behind him. When he saw the Graces, Bane froze. You know how they say Love is blind. Well, she really is. Bane hadn't said a word when he came down the stairs. No one had acknowledged his presence. So, how had Carys known that Bane was there? She was smiling and he was scowling at her.

"Bane?" she repeated puzzled by his non-response and took a step forward as if being pulled toward him by something we couldn't see. There was a wistful tone in her voice.

He abruptly turned to Demon, keeping his back to Carys, and suddenly changed shape, turning his skin to red and his blue eyes to red ones. He did this every time we ran into the Graces. Demon probably knew what was up with the red-skinned daemon thing, but if he did, he wasn't telling us. I had asked him once and he had told me to ask Bane. I did. Bane didn't tell me but he did teach me some swear words I had never heard before. I told him I was impressed and he laughed, but he never did answer my question.

"Why does he bother?" I muttered to Riot as he came over to join me. "It's not like she can *see* him."

"Still she obviously can sense his presence." Riot whispered back. He was smiling slyly. "That is very interesting, don't you think?"

"Well, yeah, but how does she do that?"

Riot shrugged, chuckling softly. "Whatever the reason, it makes Bane very uneasy."

Perhaps Riot was sensing Bane's lust for Carys but I didn't think so. It didn't look to me as though Bane desired Carys. It didn't seem that he even liked her.

"What are *they* doing here?" Bane demanded of his brother, jerking his thumb over his shoulder at the Graces.

"Apparently, they are asking for our assistance, just not very graciously." Demon replied dryly.

Bane's eyes widened. "*The Graces* are asking *the Deadlies* for help?" he asked, his voice oozing with sarcasm.

"We have asked for nothing." Ambrose pointed out.

Demon turned back to him. "If you want our help, then ask. If you're here out of nothing more than idle curiosity, then get lost. We're waiting for some vampires."

It was then that Zane stepped around Ambrose and moved to stand beside Carys. He didn't touch her, but there was possessiveness in his stance that was obvious. He was marking her as his territory.

Zane is almost as old as the twins are. He has long blond curly hair and blue eyes. His Grace is Intelligence. It is a misnomer, something like Ambrose being Bravery. He and Bane hate each other as evidenced by the looks of mutual disgust on their faces.

"Vampires?" Zane repeated. "Are you performing an execution here tonight, Fechín?"

"Possibly."

Zane and Ambrose exchanged looks. "Then we should be getting out of your way." Ambrose said, smoothly.

Demon grinned wickedly. "I thought you wanted our help."

"Yes, that is, no. We will talk another time." Ambrose said, hastily. He started to back away quickly. "We know where to find you."

Demon and Bane exchanged sly grins as Zane led Carys out of the warehouse. She turned her head as if wishing she could see us...or maybe, just one of us. Bane kept his back to them until he was sure that they were gone.

Our visitors departed, there was nothing to do now but wait. I was sure that the vampires had gone beyond the fifteen- minute mark, but as I have no concept of time (hey, I *am* Sloth after all) I couldn't really be certain. Demon didn't seem very worried about it.

Since there was nothing else to do, it seemed like the perfect time to razz Bane a bit. "So," I began. "Carys, huh?"

Bane's red eyes had turned back to blue as soon as the Graces had left. Now the flames flared in them and he growled at me. Stunned by the intensity of his reaction, I put up my hands. "Hey! Whoa. I was just saying. . ."

"Don't!" Bane spat.

"Sorry." I said. "I didn't know that it was an issue."

"There is no issue. Let us drop this subject," he said flatly.

Demon had been standing with his back to us, arms crossed over his chest waiting with his usual poise. Now he turned, looking less than dangerous in his concern for his brother. "Carys makes you uncomfortable."

"No. This *conversation* makes me uncomfortable. Graces and Deadlies have no business—" He broke off abruptly, as though he had said too much.

"What's wrong with a Grace being in love with you?" I asked.

"She is *not* in love with me. I'm a Deadly."

"You're also a very handsome man, even if I do say so myself." Demon said with a grin.

Bane returned the smile.

Suddenly, the warehouse door opened again and this time the vampires came in.

CHAPTER FOURTEEN

A QUICK GLANCE WAS enough to note that Tanith was not among the seven vampires who entered the building. They were all males. I was beginning to wonder if Tanith had any female followers at all.

A short, brown-haired vampire stood at the head of the group. Apparently, he was their chosen spokesperson. He studied us with haughty disdain. "Which one of you is Demon?" he demanded with a curl of his lip.

Immediately our hands went to our weapons and we waited for Demon to give us our cue. "*I* am." Demon said coolly. "Who the hell are you?"

The man hesitated for a moment as if he had just realized that we were armed but he pressed on. "I am Ferdinand. We have been sent by Sovereign Tanith herself to meet you," the man said as if we should be impressed.

Demon did not reply. So far, he was calm and controlled. The vampires had obviously mistaken his behaviour as a favourable reception but then they didn't know Demon as well as we did. After a moment of silence, Demon finally answered. "Is that it?"

The vampire's frown deepened. "Do you understand? We are Sovereign Tanith's delegation."

"I got that part." Demon's voice dropped to a growl.

Ferdinand nodded. "Excellent. Now then—"

"How many unwilling humans did you feed on before you came here tonight?" Demon asked, cutting him off.

Ferdinand stared at him, uneasily. Demon was clearly not behaving in the manner he had expected. "Un—unwilling humans?" he stammered.

"Definition of unwilling victims: people who do not want to be used for food or people who do not *want* to be killed." Demon clarified sarcastically.

Ferdinand paled. "We have killed no one," he said vehemently. "Her Majesty said…"

Demon stood staring at him, one eyebrow raised, his arms crossed over his chest, waiting for Ferdinand to stop stammering and choking.

"Yes? Just what did Her Majesty say?" Demon hissed in the same hypnotic tone he had used on the gang kid earlier. It didn't appear to have the same relaxing effect on the vampire. "Did she say that it was okay to feed on unwilling humans? Well, she was wrong. Around here, we call that going rogue. Do you know what happens to rogue vampires in Blackridge?"

The other vampires all took a step back except for Ferdinand. He was riveted to the spot, staring at Demon. "What?" he whispered.

"Well, *that* was a stupid question." I muttered to Riot.

Demon backhanded the spokes-vampire who flew across the room and straight through the concrete wall. Ferdinand lay on the ground, unmoving. Demon hadn't killed him, not yet, but the other bloodsuckers didn't realize that. They gaped at their unconscious friend and then, they were staring at Demon, right on the edge of panic.

"Are you going to kill us?" asked one of the vampires.

"It's what we do." Demon told them. He smiled, showing his fangs. "But, then we wouldn't find out what it is that Tanith wants."

Or where she is.

"I notice that she did not accompany you tonight." he went on.

"Oh," one of the vampires spoke up. "She's—" The vampire next to him nailed him in the gut with his elbow to shut him up. The blabbermouth vampire gasped and doubled over, but he didn't say anything more.

"Sovereign Tanith was uncertain of her welcome," the vampire with the killer elbow offered tentatively.

I snorted. "Gee, I wonder why? Perhaps she doesn't want to meet with the Enforcers after she's been slaughtering unwilling humans."

"Oh, no," the vampires all began to protest at once. "She would never do that! We have killed no one. All of our people live."

"You know, I do not think that I believe you." Demon told them contemptuously.

Demon's reaction seemed to puzzle the vampires. In the back of my mind, I thought how strange it was. It was something like the vampires we had toasted earlier. They seemed to feel that Demon was some kind of guardian spirit who had failed them in some way.

Demon made a sound of disgust. He glanced at us. "Let's finish this. They must be the ones that we're looking for." He drew his weapon and the rest of us followed suit.

The vampires gasped and took a step backward as if putting an extra foot of distance between us was going to save them. We moved up beside Demon forming a wall of wings, blades, and muscle. We began to advance toward the terrified vampires.

Suddenly, a rush of cool air that smelled of sandalwood swept through the open door of the warehouse. "Stop, Demon." the air sighed with a feminine voice. "Leave them alone. I am here."

Demon did not seem astonished. Instead, his scowl deepened. "Sending in the flunkies to take your lumps is just like you, Tanith."

The rush of cool air came again and with it, a woman appeared in the open doorway. My jaw dropped. I couldn't help it. Excepting Carys, I had never seen a woman so beautiful in my life. I glanced at Riot to see his reaction. He was watching her hungrily and not because he was thinking naughty thoughts about her but because most everyone else was, including me.

She glided into the room, every movement graceful. She was slender with just the right amount of curves. Long, dark curls cascaded down her back and long black eyelashes framed her eyes. They were purple, brilliant, and dark. She was movie star gorgeous and then some. It didn't take me long to remember the informant's description of the female vampire at the bar. It fit Tanith perfectly except she was definitely more than two inches shorter than Maia was. She was tiny.

"Demon," she said softly, her big eyes melting. "It's been so long. I've missed you." She said it as though he should reply in kind.

He didn't. He continued to glare at her, silently. I don't think he believed her.

She must have realized that too, because she stiffened. "You are still angry with me for turning you into a vampire."

"Well, aren't you the genius?"

"Is that why you killed my people?" Tanith asked.

"What, for revenge? No, Tanith. I executed them because they were killing humans."

"My people are not killing humans."

"The vampires who came to my house last night admitted to it."

"Impossible!" she said and sounded genuinely surprised.

"There is a sovereign vampire killing humans and giving the lesser bloodsuckers the okay to kill. They were seen leaving a bar with humans."

"That doesn't mean that they were unwilling." Tanith pointed out, amused.

"If you don't tell the humans what you are, then legally they are considered unwilling and that makes it murder."

Tanith frowned. "I cannot understand it. The vampires you killed should not have been in a bar and I certainly did not give them permission to hunt humans."

Demon smirked. "Well, isn't that a coincidence? There is a gang of rogue vampires running around the city killing unwilling humans and they show up right around the same time that you arrive in Blackridge."

"You know this for a fact?"

"A gang of them confronted two of the Deadlies the other night believing that they were humans and threatened to kill them." Demon gestured at us.

Tanith studied us. "It was very foolish of them to make that mistake."

"Wasn't it?"

"I do not recall missing any other people," she said.

"These vampires were the stapan's people." Demon told her.

"There you are then," she said triumphantly. "He must be your rogue."

"So, you think he gave permission to your vampires to murder humans?"

Tanith stared at him. "I see your point. No, I do not believe that my people have been in contact with the stapan."

"You know," Demon said casually. "It seems rather odd that no one appears to have control over these rogues. You don't. Hadrian doesn't."

Her lips thinned in anger. "I swear to you that I did not give anyone permission to do this, Demon." Tanith said.

"*Don't!*" Demon snarled suddenly. Tanith started and stepped backward hastily, her eyes wide and uncertain. "Don't you *dare* swear to me!"

"You don't believe me."

"No. Do you know why?" She shook her head. He leaned down until he was inches from her face. "You were seen in the bar with the rogues."

She gasped. "That is impossible!"

"I assure you that the person who saw you is very reliable," he told her coldly. "So, give me one damned good reason to trust you."

"I love you." She reached out to him. He snorted derisively and drew her hand back slowly. "I was nowhere near a bar tonight or any night." She frowned. "And I do not allow my people to go into bars. Drunken humans do not make good choices."

He raised an eyebrow and smirked in disbelief. "Your people haven't made any vampires since you came here?"

"Yes, of course, there has been one or two."

"Then they killed humans."

"They were the human mates of the vampires who turned them!" she said with a flare of temper. "They are still alive, Demon!"

"That is a matter of opinion."

"*Your* opinion?" she said sarcastically. "The humans were quite willing, I assure you. You can ask them yourself."

"Was the choice made freely, Tanith, or was some vampire persuasion involved?"

"Human mates often choose to become vampires!"

"I didn't."

The words fell between them like a stone. She hesitated.

"*I* didn't want to be *this*." He stabbed himself in the chest with his finger. "But, you didn't give me a choice, did you?"

"You were already immortal. You aren't any different than you were before."

"Oh, no, there's no difference at all." Demon replied sarcastically.

"You fed from humans before becoming a vampire." she insisted.

"I feed on *wrath*," he said. "I can do that without causing physical harm to the human. In fact, draining it away usually makes them feel better and there is no chance that I am going to kill them if I take a little too much. However, feeding on human blood is very different, isn't it? It's just a bit more dangerous.

Humans are fragile. If you become overexcited and forget yourself, you can kill your partner."

"Demon..."

"Then there is the issue of finding donors willing to share their blood with me," he went on bitterly. "That was never a concern before *you*."

There was never any shortage of willing women for Demon, but I didn't think he would appreciate it if I pointed that out right now.

Tanith's face softened. "Oh, Demon, I'm so sorry." She sounded like she meant it. "I didn't realize that you would take it so hard." That was an understatement. "I would never ever hurt you."

"It is too late for apologies." He took a step toward her but it was hesitant. There was regret in his eyes. He really didn't want to execute her. Maybe he did still love her in spite of his denials.

"Could you really kill me?" she asked softly.

"Yes."

"Even loving me as you do?"

"First of all," he said coldly. "I fell out of love with you the day I woke up with your fang marks in my neck."

"You were a willing participant in our intimacy that night!"

"Is that how you justify allowing your people to feed on unwilling humans? As long as the humans agree to the sex, they're agreeing to everything else too?" he asked coldly.

The weapon was still in his hand. Her eyes dropped to it. "You are making a mistake," she whispered. "Demon, please believe me. I have never lied to you and I love you so much."

Demon stared at her, hesitating.

"Wait!" someone called out. We turned and saw Serkan pushing his way past the vampires. "Wait, Fechín!"

Demon turned toward Serkan. "What are you doing here?"

"Don't do this, Fechín." Serkan gasped. "I just received a phone call from the chief. He said there was another rogue attack in the park about fifteen minutes ago."

"How did you get here from our place so fast?" Demon asked.

Serkan looked sheepish. "All right, so I followed you. I could not let you face this alone. My point is that witnesses in the bar said that the victim left with the female vampire about twenty minutes ago when Tanith *was already here*."

"It could have been one of her people."

Serkan shook his head. "The witnesses say the victim was talking to a woman with long, black curly hair and purple eyes."

Demon stared at him. "You think that someone disguised herself to look like Tanith?"

"Or we have made a mistake and it was never Tanith to begin with." Serkan said. "There could be any number of women who would match her description."

"What about the purple eyes? Those are not a common colour."

"Coloured contact lenses?" Serkan suggested. He put his hand on Demon's shoulder. "Listen, no one wants to see her pay for what she did to you more than I do." he said in a low voice. "But she is not guilty of this rogue attack."

"I nearly executed her." Demon said with dismay. "I nearly executed an innocent woman."

"She is hardly innocent, Fechín." Serkan pointed out. He snarled at Tanith baring his fangs. "She did turn *you* against your will."

Demon wasn't listening. "Those vampires this morning admitted that they attacked humans. So, some of her people *are* rogues." he said.

"They never said that she was with them when they did it." Bane added.

Demon was staring down at the weapon in his hands. "But, *someone* obviously was." Suddenly, he lifted his head and sniffed the air. "Do you smell something?"

I frowned and sniffed the air too. "Gasoline."

Demon stared at me for a half second and we both understood at the same time. "Run!" Demon screamed. He shoved Serkan toward the door and scooped Tanith into his arms.

We raced out of the warehouse, herding the vampires out ahead of us. Suddenly, there was a sound like thunder, a loud bang, and then a rush of intense heat at our backs. We plunged into the river as the warehouse rapidly went up in flames behind us. When I surfaced, I saw a figure running away from the site.

CHAPTER FIFTEEN

I STRUGGLED TO GET out of the water to chase after the person, but my wet wings kept dragging me down and by the time I managed to get out of the water and flop onto the dock, the person had disappeared.

Demon dragged himself out and flopped beside me, cursing. I agreed, giving vent to my own feelings in slightly less colourful language. Bane and the others crawled up beside us. Kaz and Riot scrambled to their feet and started to run in the direction the figure had gone.

"Forget it." Demon called after them. "You'll never catch him now."

They abandoned the chase reluctantly and we began hauling the vampires clinging to the dock out of the water. There were only six vampires. Demon groaned and turned to look at the warehouse in flames. "Damn it! We forgot someone."

"Oh crap!" I exclaimed. "The vamp you knocked out."

"He went through the wall." Riot suggested, hopefully. "Maybe he was far enough away from the building to avoid getting...you know..."

"Singed?" I suggested.

"I'll go and look." Kaz offered and jogged off.

We stood staring at the warehouse. Suddenly, Demon looked around. "Where is Tanith?" he asked.

The vampires we had hauled out of the river lay on the dock spitting out water and gasping for air. They looked at each other, blankly, and then out at the river. There was no sign of Tanith. The weight of her clothes had pulled her under. Demon cursed again and plunged back into the icy water. Seconds later, he surfaced carrying her in his arms. She was sputtering and coughing up water, but otherwise seemed okay.

Riot and I rushed to his assistance. Riot grasped Tanith's hand and hauled her out of the water while I did the same for Demon. Tanith gulped in air, trying to catch her breath again. She coughed and looked at Demon, sitting beside her. "You saved my life." she said softly and reached her hand out to touch him.

"You cannot drown, Tanith," he reminded her. Then he rolled away from her and got to his feet. He walked away to check on Serkan.

One of the vampires knelt next to Tanith. "Are you all right, mistress?" he asked. She looked at him coldly and did not reply.

Kaz was running back to us. We turned to him. He shook his head. "He's charbroiled."

"Damn." Demon said. "We better get rid of the body before the police and firefighters show up." He pulled his cell phone out of one of his armbands. He had insisted on making them of a waterproof material to protect some of our more delicate equipment. He made a quick call to the Boogeys. He closed the phone when he was done and tucked back into the safety of the armband.

"We need to get that body to the warehouse next door and shove it in the closet in the office," Demon said.

This time, Riot and I went. We found the body lying about ten feet from what was left of the warehouse. Kaz was right. There wasn't much left of our mouthy friend. "He stinks." Riot muttered.

"You wouldn't smell very pretty if you were burnt to a crisp either." I pointed out.

We each grabbed an arm and dragged him toward the other warehouse. Riot opened the door and gave a yelp. I dropped the vampire's arm and drew my weapon. Then I grimaced and re-sheathed it. "Geez, Beetlespaz! Could you try not to scare the shit out of Riot?"

"Sorry." Beetlespaz was standing just inside the door. "There is no one here, so I thought I would save you the trip through the warehouse."

"I thought Boogeys didn't like coming out into lit areas." Riot said once he had regained his composure.

Beetlespaz shrugged. "Some of the old ones, like my father, still fear that but

I haven't melted yet." He grinned. "Besides, if I didn't show up in the woods once in a while, what would the Sasquatch chasers do for entertainment?"

"You're too generous." I told him and handed him the vampire's arm. "Enjoy your barbequed bloodsucker."

"Aw. You didn't have to go to all the trouble of cooking him for us, but thanks." We watched him haul the body over his shoulders and walk back the way he had come. Flakes of burnt skin trailed behind him as he went.

I looked at Riot. He shuddered. "Let's get the hell out of here."

"Good idea."

We returned to the others. "Company's coming." Demon jerked his head in the direction of the sirens wailing in the distance. "Let's get the hell out of here."

"Our car is on the other block," one of Tanith's minions told us.

"We will escort you to your car to make sure you get there safely." Demon said much to our astonishment.

"Like hell we will!" Bane and Serkan announced.

"Okay," Demon said a few minutes later as we retreated toward the vampires' car. "Let's try to pull together an accurate description of this guy."

"We probably all saw something different." I pointed out.

"Between us we should be able to get some features that are the same."

"He was a big guy, tall, with broad shoulders." Kaz told him.

"I couldn't see his hair colour." Riot said. "It was too dark and he was too far away for us to see eye colour or any distinguishing features."

"No wings." Bane added. "So it wasn't one of the Graces."

I snorted. "They may not like us but they wouldn't try to fry us."

"That wasn't just someone setting fire to a warehouse. That was an explosion. Someone meant to kill not just to hurt." Demon suggested.

"Then maybe it wasn't aimed at us." Kaz said softly.

We glanced over at Tanith who was stalking behind us and pointedly ignoring her underlings. She stuck her firm little chin in the air, an obvious snub. Serkan was bringing up the rear. He was glaring at Tanith's back. The tension was thicker than the black smoke pouring into the sky behind us.

Demon shook his head. "It could have been a tall woman."

I shrugged. "Yeah, it could have been a Boogey too. It was hard to tell for sure."

"Or maybe it was a vampire." Demon said in a low voice.

We all thought about that. "I suppose so." Riot answered slowly. "Again, there was no way to tell for certain. It was too dark and he was too far away."

"Are you thinking of Hadrian?" Bane asked.

"The man was too tall to be Hadrian and he wouldn't soil his hands by burning down the place himself. He would have someone else do it." Demon said. "He knows that an explosion won't kill us but it might put one or two of us out of commission for a few days. That would seriously hamper our investigation."

"He also has reason to want Tanith dead. She is a strange sovereign on his turf." Bane said.

Demon looked at me. "Dev, you are very quiet. What are you thinking?"

"Mike Scarletti." I said. "Both of those motives could apply to him. He wants to get rid of us and Tanith used him."

Riot grinned. "Scarletti has a motive for wanting to get rid of *you*, not us."

I scowled at him.

"Dev is right." Demon interjected before I could tell Riot exactly what I thought of his theory. "We can't rule out Scarletti."

"Actually," Tanith's voice spoke behind us, making us jump. "You can."

Demon turned to her with an inscrutable expression. "He was at our house last night."

"So he told me when he came back this morning," she replied, to our surprise.

"He came back?" Demon asked raising his eyebrows. "He has a definite motive for wanting you dead. You made him promises. I would be careful with him if I were you."

Tanith frowned. "I promised him nothing." Then she hesitated. "No, that is not true. However, I did carry out my promise tonight which is why I know he could not be here."

I was puzzled. "But, I'm still here."

Tanith cocked her head. "Who are you?"

"Dev Xander."

She shook her head. "He mentioned no one named Dev. He did mention a woman named Maia. He wanted to be with her but apparently she prefers only other supernaturals."

Okay, so Riot's theory really did suck. I frowned. "So?"

She smiled. "I promised to bring her back to him."

I went cold. What had she done? Had she hypnotized Maia or threatened her? Had she tried to turn Maia into a vampire? The last seemed unlikely since she had to know that trying to turn Maia would kill her. I took a step forward, drawing my blade. "You crazy bitch! If you hurt Maia—" Kaz caught my arm. It was probably a good thing because I think I would have executed her on the spot.

Demon had stopped walking and turned to face her. "Where is Scarletti?" he asked worriedly. "What have you done to Maia, Tanith?"

"I have done nothing to Maia." There was a hint of jealousy in her voice. "And don't worry about Scarletti. He is recovering nicely." She beamed as if she had done something particularly intelligent. "I made him a vampire."

Holy shit. Mike Scarletti, Super Cop and self-righteous ass—a vampire.

Demon groaned and covered his face with his hand. "You *didn't*."

Tanith frowned again. "Well, Demon, why not? If you are worried that he was unwilling," she added hastily. "Let me reassure you that *he* approached *me* with the idea."

"The worst part is that I believe it. How long ago did you turn him?" Demon asked.

"At sunset tonight as soon as I woke up. He decided that if this woman preferred supernatural men then he would become one. The simplest method was to become a vampire. I could have sent him to Madame Zola, the voodoo priestess but," she waved her hand. "Zombies are *so* unappealing."

"That was not very long ago." Kaz said.

"He would not be fully recovered yet." Demon said. "However, it is not impossible that he should be able to get up and walk around. Inadvisable, but not impossible."

"I don't believe this." I muttered.

She looked from me to Demon. "What have I done wrong?" Tanith asked, apprehensively.

"If this was really his idea, then you have done nothing wrong," Demon assured her. "Since you have nothing to hide, then you will not mind if we accompany you to wherever you are staying so we can interview your people."

It was a challenge and she took it as such. She lifted her chin and looked him squarely in the eyes. "I have no objection."

"Good." He turned to Serkan. "I suppose you came in your car?"

Serkan nodded. "I will head home now."

"No," Demon said. "Come back to our house."

Serkan seemed uncomfortable. "Thank you, Fechín, but you see I haven't fed yet."

Demon frowned for a moment and then, slowly, he smiled. "I see. You were going to visit a lady friend."

"Yes."

Demon moved closer to Serkan and lowered his voice. "All right, but I don't want you to go home. Come to our house after."

"Why?"

"Tanith and her people know where you live. I don't like it."

Serkan was surprised. "You are worried about me."

"Yes." Demon admitted.

Serkan gave Demon a small, but pleased smile. "Perhaps I will go right to your house. You have enough bottles of blood?"

"There is enough to feed a small army of vampires. Don't worry about that. You will not be eating me out of house and home."

Serkan nodded and then, casting a looking over his shoulder at Tanith, he drew Demon aside out of her hearing. "Are you certain that you wish to let her live, Fechín?" he asked in a low voice.

Demon lowered his voice too. "Something about this just isn't sitting right. Some of Tanith's people are rogues and yet Hadrian claimed the ten vampires that stopped Dev and Kaz were *his* people. Somewhere in the middle of this damned puppet show, there is a sovereign pulling the strings and if Tanith isn't the puppet master, I think she knows who is."

"And she is protecting him or her."

Demon nodded.

"I see your point." Serkan said. "However, she could be in danger if she returns to her current residence."

"I'm sure that she will be fine. She will be accompanied by the Enforcers after all." Demon said dryly.

Serkan scowled at Tanith. "At least let me help escort Tanith back to her hideout."

"*No*, Serkan." Demon growled a warning. "I'll be fine."

"Go on, Serkan," Bane said. "I'll watch out for him."

"Watch out for yourself, too." Serkan urged quietly. Demon was fuming, ready to snap at both of them. "I would not want anything to happen to either of you."

With a final meaningful glare at Tanith, Serkan left. The vampires had come in two cars. Demon, Riot, and I followed Tanith into first one, a dark red luxury car. While Demon and Riot got into the back seat with Tanith, I rode in the front with the other vampire. I kept my back to the door so that I could see what he was doing at all times and, more importantly, I could see what Tanith was doing.

The vampire who was driving the car was a bundle of nerves. He seemed unconcerned that I was sitting next to him, but he kept glancing in the rear view mirror at Demon as if he expected him to turn into a rabid killer any second. Riding in a car with Wrath will do that. Still, he was worried about the wrong Deadly. Demon and his weapon may have been in proximity, but *I* had better access to him than Fechín did.

Tanith seemed blithely unaware of the tension in the car. She sat in the back between Demon and Riot, smiling dreamily. She was silent for a few minutes and then, she could no longer contain herself. She turned to smile up at him. Demon did not return her smile. He stared at her coldly, but didn't speak.

"So, Demon, do you have a girlfriend or a wife?" she asked lightly.

"Not for the last couple of months."

Tanith looked surprised. She had clearly expected a denial of both. "You had a girlfriend then?"

"Yes." he smirked sarcastically.

"Oh." Tanith turned away again.

"Well, what did you expect, Tanith?" he demanded. "Did you think I pined away for you over the last few centuries?" He paused. "By the way, did you happen to call me last night?"

Tanith looked surprised. "No. Why?"

He shook his head. "It's not important."

Tanith was quiet for a minute and then she asked, "Who was she?"

"Who?"

"Your girlfriend." she sneered.

"That is really none of your business." His eyes narrowed and he frowned. "Are you trying to pick a fight with me?"

"Don't change the subject. So, what was her name or didn't know you know it?" she asked sarcastically.

"Yes, I know what my girlfriend's name was."

"*Girlfriend*," Tanith sneered again. "Why don't you just come right and say that she was your lover?"

"Okay. She was my lover."

Tanith drew back as if he had slapped her. Her voice caught and she turned her head abruptly, but I could see that her eyes glittered with tears. *"Demon."*

A look of guilt passed over his face, but he quickly suppressed it. "You asked." he pointed out.

Riot leaned across Tanith to whisper to Demon. "If she's going to cry, I'm bailing out of this car. When it comes to crying, hysterical women you're on your own, Demon."

"I am *not* going to cry!" Tanith snapped.

She didn't say any more about Demon's girlfriends. She didn't look at him again and Demon turned back to watch where we were going just in case we ever needed to find the place again. I wondered if the vampires knew what they were doing. You know, showing the wolf where the sheep hid out.

About ten minutes later, it appeared to be getting light out. I glanced at my watch. 11:45 PM. I frowned at the bright sky. That couldn't be right. I looked at Tanith to see if she was melting. Nope. In fact, I don't think she had realized that the sky was getting brighter. "Demon," I said softly.

"I see it." he responded, sitting forward.

We all looked out the windows. There was something odd about the glow. It was probably all the black smoke that accompanied it. "Fire!" I gasped.

"How much do you want to bet that it's Tanith's place?" Demon added grimly.

Tanith gasped. "My people!" She leaned forward and placed a hand on the driver's shoulder. "Drive faster, Osmond!"

"Yeah, step on it, Jeeves." I added.

The driver sped up in response to Tanith's order, but didn't answer me. He gave me one dark look and then turned back to watch the road.

"Do not get pulled over unless you would like to explain our wings to the human cops?" Demon growled at him.

We reached the fire before the police or the firefighters. They were probably still busy with the fire at the warehouse but I was sure that someone would dispatch another engine and crew soon. It wouldn't leave us much time to see if there were any survivors. Demon must have thought of this too because he sent us on a hunt around the grounds.

We returned quickly to the sound of sirens. "Did you find anyone?" Demon asked. We all shook our heads.

"Either no one was here or they didn't make it out." Riot said.

"They could have gotten out and high-tailed it." I suggested.

"Let's get the hell out of here." Demon said.

"But, I have new people in there!" Tanith wailed. "They will be trapped inside their coffins!"

We looked at each other. "Scarletti," Bane said.

We stared at each other, gritting our teeth. Finally, Demon sighed. "Okay. Here is what we're going to do. I am going in to look around and see if there is anyone else."

"Won't you burn?" one of the vampires asked.

Demon gave him a long look. "No." He turned to Tanith. "Where is the coffin room?"

She stared at him blankly as if she had never heard of such a thing. She was clearly in shock. He grasped her shoulders and gave her a little shake. "Tanith, we need to get your people out fast! Where the hell is the coffin room?"

She clutched his arms and stared up at him with frantic eyes. "It is in the basement. The door is in the kitchen at the back of the house. It is a single room, so you can't miss it."

"All right I'm going in." Demon told us. "Kaz, you, Dev and Riot, you come with me. Onyx, take Tanith and her people back to our house."

Holy shit.

Even Onyx gaped at him. "Don't stand there!" Demon snapped. "Get going! Morgana, go with him!"

Onyx hurried the vampires back into their cars. Tanith paused as Onyx held the door of her car open. "Demon," she called out. He glanced back at her. "Be careful. I would not have anything happen to you." Then, she got into the car and they took off.

Demon stared after the car for a second and then shook his head. "Let's haul ass," he said.

We ran around to the back of the house. Demon didn't bother checking to see if the door was locked. He and Bane linked their arms around each other's shoulders and kicked it in. Black smoke poured out and flames were already starting to inch their way into the kitchen. Suddenly, we heard screaming from somewhere inside the house. My blood ran cold when I heard it. Someone had awakened to find himself in hell.

"Let's go!" Demon yelled and we plunged into the burning house.

The screams were coming from the basement. It occurred to me as we headed through the flame and smoke into the basement that it might be Scarletti. We were trying to follow Demon, but we couldn't see him through all of the black smoke. We only managed to keep up to him because Demon couldn't see either. Ahead of me, I could hear him running into things and cursing as he tossed items aside. When I heard him mutter, "Oops, that one was full" I guessed that we had found the coffin room.

"Kaz, we have one. Get him out of here." Demon called out. A second later, Kaz raced past me.

"Who are you?" a female voice snapped in a voice edged with suspicion. "How did you get in here?"

"We are here to get you out. Now, how many of these coffins are in use at the moment?"

"How do I know you're really here to help?" the woman demanded.

"Look," he snapped. "You can stay here and fry or you can take your chances with us."

"I don't even know who you are!"

"Enforcers," Demon said bluntly.

She went silent.

The sirens were getting closer. "Demon," Bane shouted in a panicked tone. "Cops are coming!"

"There were only two coffins in use," she said at last. "One you found. I am standing next to the other."

"If she has use of her legs, why the hell is she still here?" I muttered.

"She's probably a beschermer." Demon told me bluntly.

A beschermer is a vampire who guards the other vampires in the kiss, especially the stapan. She had apparently been set to watch over the newest vampires while they recuperated from being turned.

"I can't see so you're going to have to direct me to you." Demon told the woman. "Now, I am standing at the base of the stairs. Where are you?"

The woman gave them directions to where she stood. The twins groped their way through the darkness until they found the woman and the casket that she was guarding. I heard the squeak of the lid and a grunt as someone hefted what was inside over his shoulder.

"I've got this one. Move it, Dev." Bane said. Riot and I ran up the steps. I heard Demon and Bane coming up behind me. We rushed out into the cool night.

Kaz was already gone. I got a look at the person slung over Bane's shoulder. It was a woman.

We looked at each other. "I sure hope Kaz has Scarletti." I said.

The sirens were pulling up at the front of the house and we heard shouting and the sound of wood cracking as the firefighters broke through the front door. We soared off into the night.

CHAPTER SIXTEEN

WE ARRIVED AT OUR house a few minutes after Kaz. He was just walking in the door with his burden when we hustled in behind him. Demon had carried the beschermer and he set her on her feet as he walked through the door. Tanith was standing at the library door with Serkan and Morgana, but I didn't see Maia. I felt a surge of relief. I didn't want Tanith to meet Maia until someone explained to her that she was not Demon's girlfriend. I had a feeling that bad things could happen to Maia otherwise.

"Take them both to the catacombs." Demon said walking away from the woman.

"Demon—"Morgana gasped.

"Later."

"Demon, I really think that you should—"

He was already heading down the stairs and we all followed. There was one long hallway with three doors on either side of it. At the end of this hallway, was another hallway with another four rooms. The basement of our house is all cement, painted white. There are no frills about this area.

"Very nice," Tanith commented, her voice oozing with sarcasm. "But, excuse me, since you do not need to sleep during the day, why so many coffin rooms?"

"Not all vampires like to sleep in coffins. These six rooms are guest rooms and they have beds in them for when we have company like Serkan." Demon told her. He glanced back over his shoulder, eyes hard. "However, not all of the rooms are impenetrable by daylight. Three of the rooms have windows. Those are our execution rooms."

Tanith sucked in her breath sharply. "Is that where..."

Demon turned to his brother who was still carrying the female vampire over his shoulder. "We'll give her room four." Demon said. He unlocked door and held it open for Bane who stepped inside and gently laid the woman on the soft bed inside. Tanith peeked inside nervously and then relaxed when she had assured herself that there were no windows.

Demon had his back to her. "Since they haven't done anything wrong that I know of," he said without turning around. "They won't go into a room with a view."

"Room with a view." one of the vampires repeated. "Cute."

"You wouldn't think so if we locked you in one." Demon said flatly, as he unlocked the door of room five and waved Kaz in.

Kaz laid the man on the bed. I heard him gasp. "Shit!"

Demon stepped in, frowning. "What is it, Kaz?"

Kaz hesitated. "Bane," he called out. "Do you happen to have Scarletti?"

Bane followed his brother into the room. He shook his head. "No, I had a female. Don't you have him?"

"Apparently not," Kaz said dryly. He looked up at Demon. "Uh oh."

Demon spun around with a snarl and stormed through the crowd of people to the beschermer who was still standing at the bottom of the stairs. "I thought you said—" He stopped short.

She smiled at him. "Hi."

Demon stared at her as if he had seen a ghost. He shook his head. "No way," Demon's voice was a hoarse croak. "No *way.*"

Tanith looked from one to the other curiously. "Do you two know each other?"

It took me a minute, I'll admit, but I did recognize her. Her blond brown curls used to be shoulder length but now almost reached to her slim waist. Her big golden brown eyes were smiling. Her face was pretty, not beautiful, but it was a unique face and not one that you soon forgot. "*Kit?*" I gasped.

Kit smiled at me and then darted an apprehensive look at Demon who was still staring at her, thunderstruck.

Tanith was frowning as her eyes moved between the two. "Kit, what happened to the young man who was with me tonight?"

"Was he the tall, handsome one with the dark curly hair?" Kit asked.

"Yes. Michael Scarletti."

Kit's nose wrinkled and I had the impression that she didn't think much of him either. "The newest male went out shortly after you did." she said.

"Scarletti left?" Demon said at last. He looked dazed, like someone awakening from a dream.

Tanith frowned. "But, where would he go?"

Suddenly, my heart dropped out of my chest. "Oh, shit!" I exclaimed and thundered back up the stairs.

I burst into Maia's room having run all the way up the stairs and down the hall. Maia sat up in bed with a start and gaped at me. Then when the sleep had cleared from her brain and she recognized me, she smiled slowly. "Why, Dev, fancy meeting you here." she purred. The others burst in behind me and she sighed. "And company."

"Maia," I gasped, relieved to see that she was okay. "We need you to step out into the hall so we can check the room."

"I'll take the grounds." I heard Demon say behind me. "Bane, come with me." I heard them running back down the stairs.

Kaz and Riot moved into the room behind me. "Check every damn square inch." I told them.

We checked the closet, under the bed, under the dresser, *in* the dresser. Vampires can fold themselves into the damnedest places, though in hindsight, Scarletti probably would not have fit inside a dresser drawer, but I was not taking any chances. As I leaned out of the window to see if Scarletti was hiding in the tree or clinging to the sill, I felt someone come up behind me and gently touch my back. I jumped and spun around.

"Dev, what's going on?" Maia said surprised by my reaction.

"Maia, please go back into the hallway." I ordered.

She stared at me. Her face was full of concern as she reached up to touch my cheek. "Dev, you're shaking!"

I caught her hand and pressed it to my lips before releasing her. "Maia," I begged. *"Please!"*

She nodded slowly and took my hand again gently. "Okay. But, only if you come with me."

125

"I can't." I told her.

"Take Maia down to the kitchen, Dev." Serkan came into the room. He patted my shoulder trying to reassure me. "I will help search the room."

I did not try to resist as Maia led me from the room. It occurred to me that she might just refuse to leave the room unless I did too. It seemed a better plan to go and take her with me. As we passed Tanith, I kept Maia on the other side of me and urged her down the stairs ahead of me. I glanced back at Tanith. She was snarling, baring her teeth. She took a step forward.

"Don't do anything stupid." I warned her quietly. "She's not Demon's."

Tanith was still glaring as I hustled Maia down the stairs. Maia was frowning at Tanith. "Dev," she whispered as I herded her down the stairs. "Who is that woman?"

I shook my head. I was huddled so close to her, I was half pushing her down the stairs, away from that bedroom with its easily accessed window. I was not looking forward to telling her what Scarletti had done.

Maia pushed open the door to the kitchen. Hex was there, bustling about. She stopped and her eyes widened in concern as we came in. "Dev, what on earth—"

"I'm not sure what's going on." Maia told her. "But, it must be something pretty bad. The upper hallway is filled with vampires and Dev looks as though he's seen a ghost."

"I'm a Deadly. Ghosts don't scare me." I told her.

"Well, you look terrified." Maia said firmly. "And your hand is freezing!"

I looked down at my hand. My skin was blue, a sign that I really was terrified. My skin would stay blue until I was no longer terrified. I could be blue for a long time. Sometimes it sucks being half shapeshifter.

Hex shoved a mug of something hot into my hand. I glared at it suspiciously. "Is this tea?"

"Just drink it." Hex ordered.

I took a tentative sip. It was coffee. I took a big gulp this time and let its warmth seep through the mug into my hands. It wasn't going to make a difference to me, but it might prevent Maia from getting hypothermia while she held my hand.

The back door opened. I jumped to my feet and automatically drew my weapon. Bane came in. I didn't bother to replace my weapon in the sheath. Instead,

126

I laid it on the table. I felt better having it easily within reach. As I sat back down, I sensed both women staring at me.

"Did the room check out?" Bane asked, as if my aggressive reaction was normal.

"I don't know." I told him bitterly.

He studied me for a minute. "They kicked you out?" he asked finally.

I nodded.

"Drink your coffee, Dev, and try to relax." He paused and lowered his voice so Hex, standing by the sink, wouldn't hear. "It *is* coffee, right?"

"Would I be drinking it if it wasn't?"

Bane grinned as Hex turned to glare at us. "I'm going back outside to see if Demon found anything," he said, starting for the back door.

"I didn't hear any blood curdling screams." I called after him. "I bet he didn't."

Bane flashed me a grin. "I believe that I will take that bet. If my brother so chooses he can hit his prey so fast that they would not have time to scream."

That was true, but we probably shouldn't be saying so in front of Maia. Of course, she didn't know that Demon was out there hunting her boyfriend.

Bane left again and I could feel Maia's eyes on me, curious and waiting for an explanation of our strange behaviour. I didn't speak. I sat drinking my coffee.

Finally Maia burst. "Dev, if you don't tell me what is going on, I'm going to scream! You busted into my room at midnight and wake me out of a sound sleep. You didn't even come in alone! Then, you throw me out and turn the room upside down looking for... *something*. There is some female vampire upstairs glaring at me as if she wants to rip my throat out. I think I deserve an explanation!"

"I was looking for someone, not something." I corrected. She made an impatient "keep talking" gesture with her hands when I did not say any more. I sighed. "We were looking for—" I stopped.

I had to explain this the right way, if there was one. I couldn't just jump in with both feet and blurt out that her boyfriend had had himself turned into a vampire and that I was afraid that he might come looking for her, but that is exactly what I did.

The words just burst out of me like a dam breaking. Maia stared at me as if I had lost my mind. I told her everything, starting from the meeting with Tanith and winding up with the discovery that Mike had left Tanith's house, probably in search of Maia. She sat quietly on her stool, her lips parted in astonishment.

Tears sprang into her eyes. Strange to say, I didn't feel that familiar surge of panic. Instead, I reached out to hold her hand. "Maia," I said softly. "Don't cry. We'll find Scarletti. I'm sure that Demon can help him."

"Why?" Maia choked back tears. "Why would Mike *do* this?"

"He did it for you. He loves you." I admitted, even though I hated to do it.

"That makes no sense! He hates everything supernatural!"

"He doesn't hate you."

"But, I'm a *shapeshifter*, Dev!" Maia snapped. "Mike is a vampire! God, I can't believe I just said that! We're not even the same supernatural species!"

I withdrew my hand from hers and sat back. My mother may have been a succubus but I was as far away from being a shapeshifter as Mike was. "I guess you're right. My parents were different species and look how their marriage ended up." I said with a touch of bitterness.

I got to my feet, angrily, and stalked to the sink, dumping the rest of my coffee. I stood there for a minute, finally grasping the reality that Maia and I had no future. I was attracted to her and she was attracted to me, but in her eyes, two different supernatural species couldn't be together.

"Dev?" she said quietly.

I took a deep breath, steadying myself, before I turned back. "Yes?"

"Were you looking for Mike in my room?"

I nodded. "We have reason to believe that he'll come looking for you eventually. If not tonight, then some time."

Maia shivered. "God, Mike." she said softly.

I had never believed Maia's claim that her relationship with Scarletti was over but hearing the regret in her voice, I couldn't take it. "I guess it doesn't matter that he's not the same species after all." I snapped and punched the swinging door on my way out of the kitchen.

"Where are you going?" Demon appeared beside me, seemingly out of thin air.

I yelped and spun around to glare at him. "What the hell are you doing sneaking up on me like that?"

He ignored that. "Why are you leaving Maia alone in the kitchen with Scarletti on the loose?"

"Why not?" I demanded sarcastically. "After all, did any of us bother to ask Maia if she *wanted* him to come and get her?"

Demon stared at me, head cocked. "Where did that come from?" he asked thoughtfully.

I shook my head as I pushed past him, too hurt and angry to talk to anyone, even to my best friend.

CHAPTER SEVENTEEN

THE LIBRARY IS USUALLY Demon's retreat when he is feeling stressed. He seems to find it relaxing and I was definitely feeling stressed, so I thought it was worth a try. Flinging open the library door, I stopped short when I realized that I busted in on something I shouldn't have. When the Satana had arrived earlier, we had been busy so Serkan had asked Daedalus, Jordis, and Medea to wait in the library. Riot was there now as well, leaning against the desk staring coolly at the three officers.

I muttered an apology as I backed out of the room. Riot stopped me. "You might as well stay here. As soon as I find Demon we'll be having a meeting."

"I can get him." I told him. "He was just in the hallway. I think he's gone upstairs."

"I'll get him. I need some air." Riot said and strode from the room. There were sparks in his eyes.

Shit. I backed up against the wall and let Riot out of the room. I knew Morgana could do that when she was angry, but I had never seen Riot do it before. "What the hell is wrong with him?" I asked Daedalus as the door slammed behind Riot.

Daedalus shrugged. "He hasn't confided in me since he was a very young boy. I assume it has something to do with a woman. It usually does with him." He darted a quick look at Jordis.

Jordis was blushing and I realized that I had been so involved in my own problems that I had forgotten all about Riot's weird behaviour the other night when he had to ride in the van with Jordis. "Is there a problem between you and Riot?" I asked her.

"Of course not!" she protested. Her blush deepened and Daedalus gave her a look that screamed "liar."

Riot returned a few minutes later with Demon and Maia. I stiffened and tried to suppress my unreasonable anger, reminding myself that, no matter what was going on between us, she was still a part of this team. I couldn't escape her and I resented her for that.

Maia came to stand next to me and I tried to inch away without it being obvious, but she moved closer, linking her arm through mine and snuggling in against my side. I could have fooled myself into believing that she actually cared about me. I knew better. It was clear that I was fun to flirt with but Mike was the man she loved. I couldn't move away from her without causing a scene, so I gritted my teeth and coped with it the best I could.

"Daedalus," Demon said as Riot retired to a corner of the room far away from our guests. "What brings you here?"

"There was a fire in an abandoned warehouse on Brooks Street." Daedalus said grimly. "They haven't made it official yet, but it looks like arson. The investigator is looking at the owner to see if there is anything in his background to suggest that he might have set it himself for the insurance."

"What makes them suspect arson already?" Demon asked casually. "I thought these investigations took days."

"A gasoline can was found at the scene." Daedalus gave us a hard stare. "But, they think that there must have been some kind of detonation because they had reports of a loud bang before the whole thing went up."

"Interesting."

"I also spoke to a source who tells me that three of the Graces entered and left the building several minutes before the explosion occurred. The same source also mentioned seeing several people running out only seconds before the explosion. At least seven of the people had big black wings."

"Did your source happen to see who set the fire?" Demon asked.

Daedalus shook his head. "There was too much smoke."

"He says."

"She."

"Whatever." Demon eyed him for a minute. "Daedalus, if you already know that we were there, then why did you come all the way out here to ask the question?"

A smile flickered over Daedalus' face. "The informant tells me she saw a Boogey removing a body from the scene so I want to know if this was an execution and who the other people were. Secondly, I thought you might want to speak to my source because, despite her assurances that she didn't see who set the fire, I don't believe her either."

Demon inclined his head slightly in acknowledgement of this professional courtesy. "I would like to question her. Who is the informant?"

"Viola Nerida."

I rolled my eyes, but Demon managed to restrain himself. Viola is a siren who lived under the docks by the warehouses. "Viola is a nut! Why didn't she just tell you what she saw?" I exclaimed.

"She doesn't want to talk to me because despite knowing me for hundreds of years, I'm still a cop. She has asked to talk to Kane." Daedalus explained to me.

"Why me?" Riot frowned.

"She says you're hot."

Riot rolled his eyes and Demon and I began to laugh.

"You're the least threatening of the Deadlies as far as Viola is concerned. If I sent one of my officers to question her, I would be worried about her seducing him. Her siren song doesn't work on you." Daedalus pointed out.

"It's the other way around." I added.

Riot glared at me but Daedalus nodded. "If she has anything to tell, she'll tell it to you," he said.

"Fine," Riot groaned. "I'll head back to the warehouse and see if I can find her, but someone has to come and protect me. Viola has wandering hands."

"Kaz can go with you." Demon said. "If she sees me, Viola may clam up."

"What about the vampires?" Daedalus asked.

Demon gave a quick rundown of this evening's excitement, mentioning Mike Scarletti's recent transformation, but skimming over his own previous relationship with Tanith.

"Huh." Daedalus grunted when Demon had finished. "Are you sure that you can trust this woman, Fechín?"

"Not in the least." Demon replied promptly. "That is why I'm keeping an eye on her."

"All right. As long as you know what you're doing."

"I do. Keep your friends close, but your enemies closer. That isn't a suggestion, Daedalus. We Deadlies live by it."

Daedalus and his officers left. I turned to Demon. "You consider Tanith an enemy?"

"Of course," Demon replied with surprise. "I would be a fool to trust her."

I agreed with that. "Does that include Kit?"

He frowned. "Yes, it includes her. Why shouldn't it?"

"You consider *Kit* an enemy?" Riot said in disbelief. "Demon, seriously—"

"Yes, seriously!" Demon snapped. "She is not the same woman that we knew. She is not our friend. It is a mistake to think of her that way."

"But—"

"It has been more than a hundred years." Demon pointed out. "What do we know about her life during that time?"

"But, she's *Kit*." I reminded him softly. "She is who she has always been, Demon. You were the one who nicknamed her Kit, remember?"

"Dev. . ." I heard Maia say behind me and she touched my arm.

"Damn it, Dev!" Demon burst out. He pointed his finger at me. "She is Tanith's *beschermer*! Do you know what that means? It means *you don't trust her*! She is on Tanith's side and as far as we know Tanith is allowing vampires to feed from and murder humans!" He looked and sounded desperate. I had never seen him this upset except when he went Wrath.

"Do you really believe that Kit would be a part of that?" I demanded. "After all, you were the one who taught her the rules of being a vampire."

Demon hesitated as the door of the library opened and Kit drifted in. She moved with the grace of a dancer. There had always been something elegant about her. Even wearing the shabby dress we had found her in, she had sophistication.

All expression disappeared from Demon's face as she closed the door behind her. She turned and stared back at him with the same lack of expression. When neither of them spoke after a minute, I decided to break the ice. Besides, it gave me a good excuse to move away from Maia now without drawing attention. "Hey." I said.

She glanced at me and a smile spread over her face. "Hey, Dev."

I smiled back. "You remember me."

Her smile widened. "Of course, I do. How could I forget the men who burst into my bedroom to rescue me from a bad dream?"

"You screamed." Riot reminded her. "We thought—" He broke off, not wanting to bring up bad memories for her.

"Yes," she said softly. "I know. I remember how shocked I was that you would come to my rescue with such ferocity."

"We may have overreacted a bit." I admitted.

Kit laughed. "Maybe a just bit." she agreed, jokingly. She looked at Maia. "Seven people burst into my room, blades drawn and ready for a fight. I have never seen anything quite so fearsome in my life."

Maia laughed. "I can just imagine."

Demon raised an eyebrow at Kit. "Speaking of protecting, shouldn't you be down in the catacombs with Tanith?"

She ignored his sarcasm, still smiling. "She is in the house of the Enforcers. Who would be fool enough to come after her here? She is well-protected."

"Apparently, you don't know Mike Scarletti very well." Riot snorted.

"Do you think she is well-protected here?" Demon asked. "Have you forgotten what we do?"

"Not at all." she said. "I have good reason to remember."

We fell into an awkward silence. We met Kit when we were hunting the rogue vampire that attacked her. It had not been his intention that she should survive the encounter. Demon changed that.

Suddenly, Demon stared at her, suspiciously. "Did you happen to call here the other night?" he asked.

She seemed embarrassed. "Yes, actually, I did."

"How did you get our phone number?"

"I still had it from when you first gave it to me," she replied softly.

"Why didn't you tell Hex who you were?"

"I wanted to talk to you, not Hex."

"Oh." Demon looked confused. "Well, what did you want?"

Kit's face softened into a smile. "Maybe, I just wanted to hear your voice again," she said over her shoulder as she left the room.

We all turned to look at Demon. He was gaping at the closed door, dumbfounded, and his cheeks were ~~pink~~...

I struck out the word "pink" because Demon objects to the word as applying to his manly face.

Demon was ~~blushing~~.

I have now kicked Demon out of the room. I hate it when people read over my shoulder.

CHAPTER EIGHTEEN

RIOT AND KAZ TOOK off to visit Viola before daybreak. By sunrise, the siren would be soundly sleeping under her dock, safely tucked away from the prying eyes of humans. Demon stalked off upstairs after his confrontation with Kit. Bane went after his brother. Onyx took off somewhere too, but no one much cared where. It left me alone with Maia. I fled as soon as I could. I did not want to be alone with her.

I wandered into the kitchen to see if Hex was baking anything. She wasn't in there and I remembered that it was still very early. She was probably asleep. As I was raiding the cookie jar, I heard someone coming and thought it might be Maia, so I ducked out the back door with a handful of cookies.

I walked around outside, eating my cookies and admiring the night sky. The most beautiful painting in the world can't touch it. Soon the sun would start to come up and the stars would disappear, but in the meantime, they were magnificent, scattered across the night sky like thousands of diamonds. Guess that is where the song comes from.

I stood in the front yard feeling, if not content, at least relaxed. Suddenly the front door opened and I looked around. It was Bane. He spotted me and came down the steps to join me. He did not speak as we stood side by side gazing up at the stars.

Finally, I spoke. "Okay, give it up. What the hell is going on with Demon and Kit?" I demanded.

He did not pretend not to know what I meant. That is what I like about Bane. He will give you a straight answer if possible. "I can't say for certain what happened between them, Dev. I can only speculate."

"So," I said, gesturing for him to continue. "Speculate."

"After Kit's attack," he began. "When Demon insisted on bringing her home with us, didn't you find that odd?"

"Well, no." I said surprised. "I guess I didn't really think about it. I mean, he rescued her from the vampire. He is the one who fed her and finished the turning. I just assumed that he felt responsible for her."

"I did too." Bane admitted. "I always thought that he meant to turn her over to the stapan of the city before we left. However, when she lived with us, there were a few times when I saw her watching him. It worried me."

"Why?" I asked.

Bane shook his head. "I can't say for sure but I thought that there was something going on between them. I think that she fell in love with Demon and maybe he knew it."

"Uh oh," I said. "Do you think she told him how she felt and he responded badly?"

Bane frowned. "Oh, hell, Dev, I don't know. If she had made any such confession, he certainly would not tell me about it. But, when she disappeared that night, I did wonder."

"Perhaps she felt it was better to leave than to go on living in the same house with him, knowing that he didn't love her back." I suggested. I felt Bane's inquisitive gaze on me, but I didn't look at him. I understood exactly how Kit must have felt. I didn't want to be around Maia if she was still in love with Mike Scarletti. I would rather she left now and let me get over it in my own way if I could. Having her here was hell.

"Maybe you're right. Perhaps he felt guilty. He was rather touchy after she left." Bane went on.

"Touchy?" I echoed incredulously. "No one dared speak to him for weeks afterward because he would snap our heads off rather than look at us. I actually pitied the vampires he hunted in the first few weeks after." I shuddered. "I thought the other night was bad, but it can't compare to the weeks right after Kit left."

Bane shuddered too. "Yeah."

"Do you suppose that she is still in love with him?" I asked.

"It certainly looks like it to me." Bane said.

"Do you think he feels guilty and to make himself feel less guilty he is trying to convince himself that she is a rogue?"

Bane frowned. "I would never have believed that of him, but it certainly seems that way, doesn't it?"

We both fell silent as a black car pulled into the driveway and Riot and Kaz got out. They walked toward us. The sun was just starting to break the horizon now. I hoped they got their information before Viola went to sleep.

"How did it go?" Bane called out.

"Oh, we can't wait to give you all the gory details." Kaz said, dryly. He glanced around. "Where's Demon?"

Riot was less interested in Demon's whereabouts. He had noticed the seriousness of our mood. He looked from me to Bane and frowned. "Is everything all right?"

"Yes." Bane said. "We were just talking about Kit."

Riot smiled. "I've always liked her."

"So have I." Kaz said. He paused. "Do you think Demon is right? Is she one of the bad guys?"

"I don't know." Bane answered.

"Poor Demon," Riot said quietly. His golden eyes were full with a sadness I didn't understand.

"Do you think that she is a rogue?" Bane asked.

Riot looked thoughtful. "Since we are talking about Kit, my first instinct is to say no. However, Demon has a point. What do we know about her? She lived with us for a span of six weeks, maybe two months. While I would not agree that she is completely untrustworthy, I would advise caution."

"Usually, Demon would be the first one to give the same advice. It is not like him to overreact like this." Bane said.

"I agree that this behaviour is a little out of character. I assume that it has something to do with the, er, feelings that seeing Kit and Tanith has aroused." Riot said.

Bane frowned. "What feelings?"

Riot smiled slightly. "The lust is so heavy in the air that I could eat it with a spoon. I am surprised that no one else has noticed."

Bane frowned again. "Is it coming from Kit or Tanith?"

Riot gave him a funny look. "Do you think he is uncomfortable because he thinks they are lusting for him?"

Bane returned the look. "Isn't that what you meant?"

"No."

Bane's eyes widened. "Oh."

"If both women are going to be living here, this could make things very tricky." Kaz pointed out.

"Morgana isn't going to like this either." I added. "It's bad enough when Demon has one girlfriend in the house, but if she knows that Tanith and Kit are after him too...whew. The three of them will be at each other's throats."

"I'll put my money on Kit." Riot grinned.

I grinned back. "Why?"

He shrugged. "Demon did train her to fight, after all."

We started walking toward the house.

"Yeah, but Morgana is a Deadly and immortal." Kaz pointed out.

"Even winning a fight won't make Demon love her." I said. I was in complete sympathy with her. "This unrequited love stuff sucks."

I guess I was a bit too vehement. Everyone's faces turned to me, startled. I jammed my hands into my pockets, embarrassed by my outburst and feeling a bit defiant at the same time. I glared at Bane, Riot, and Kaz, daring them to make something of it.

They looked at each other and then Riot laid his hand on my arm. "Dev—"

I pulled away from him abruptly and stalked into the house. I didn't want their pity. I think Demon got off easy when Kit just left.

I stormed right through the house and into the backyard. I spent about an hour just pacing. It had rained a bit the night before and there were mud puddles scattered about. When Hex came out and saw me stomping around, splashing her clean laundry with mud and hacking off the tops of the flowers in her flowerbed with a stick I had found, she grabbed the garden hose and drenched me with water. Then she gave me a lecture that scorched my ears. I told her that I felt better for having my temper tantrum. I probably should have kept that information to myself. It certainly did not improve her mood.

"You're wanted back at the house for a meeting!" she snapped at me.

I slunk back into the house. I figured I had to be safer in there with Maia and an edgy Demon than facing Hex over her soiled laundry and destroyed garden.

I paused in the kitchen to grab a few more cookies since I had not gone in for breakfast. I figured, hey, if ice cream is supposed to console a broken heart, cookies could work too. Besides, Hex bakes the world's best cookies.

With one cookie in my mouth and six in my hand, I pushed open the swinging door and stopped. Morgana was standing in the middle of the hallway, glaring at the floor. I swallowed the cookie, hastily, and cleared my throat, making a bit of noise as I entered the hallway. I had once surprised her accidentally and ended up flat on my back with the wind knocked out of me. Rather humiliating, considering that I was a lot bigger and stronger than she was. Morgana looked up and I felt it was safe to approach. At least I did until I saw the expression on her face. She was seriously pissed off.

"What's wrong?" I asked warily as I moved toward her. I stayed just out of reach though in case she was looking for someone to take out her frustrations on.

"Why does that...*Tanith* have to stay here?" she demanded with a snarl.

I shrugged. "Demon wants her here, where he can keep an eye on her."

"What the hell do we care if some vampire gets exterminated?" she snapped.

I eyed her. It was a little odd that she only mentioned Tanith, but then Demon had once been in love with Tanith. Perhaps Morgana didn't consider Kit competition.

"If it's the rogue vampires who are trying to kill Tanith then wouldn't it make sense to keep her close so we can find out who they are? They won't try once and then back off you know." I explained.

Morgana frowned at me. "So, she's bait?" she suggested doubtfully.

I latched on to that. "Yeah, that's right. She's bait."

Morgana was quiet for a moment. "Dev," she said at last. "Do you think he still loves her?"

I started to say no, but then I remembered how he had looked with the blade in his hand, preparing to execute her and I wasn't sure. Morgana saw my hesitation and turned away. "Forget it." Her voice caught.

I reached out and caught her arm, gently. "Morgana, I'm sorry."

She flared up, yanking her arm out of my grasp and turning on me. "I don't need your pity, Dev."

"I wasn't offering pity."

"It sure sounded like it."

"Look, I know you love him, but—"

She was already walking away. I knew that she was hurting. Maybe I should have lied just to keep her from Tanith's throat. We had enough problems as it was. Morgana would not hesitate to stake her claim on Demon openly and considering how Tanith had reacted when she thought Maia was Demon's girlfriend; it seemed inevitable that two women were going to clash at some point. Personally, I did not want to be around when they did. I didn't think the house could stand up to that kind of abuse. Thank goodness, it was Demon's problem, not mine. Mine was somewhere in the house and it was starting to look a hell of a lot less volatile than his.

I decided that it was safer to avoid any further discussion of Tanith. I followed her down the hallway. "Where is everyone?"

"Demon is in the library." Morgana responded.

I rolled my eyes. "Thank you. Is everyone else there too or did you bother to take notice?"

She swore at me as I turned away and opened the library door. She followed me inside and closed the door with enough force to make one of the books fall off the shelf on the other side of the room.

Demon was leaning against the edge of the desk. He raised his eyebrow at her. "Problems, Morgana?"

She flushed. "Not at all." she responded coolly and settled onto the sofa next to Kaz.

Demon turned back to me. He smiled. "I see Hex found you." He nodded at the cookies.

I glanced down at them too. "I stole them." I admitted. "Considering that she found me in her garden, I doubt she would have given me cookies."

Demon gave me a look. "Is that why you are wet?"

"Yeah, she turned the hose on me."

"What the hell did you do?"

I shrugged, trying to look innocent. "I was just pacing."

He raised his eyebrow, waiting for me to continue. He knows me too well.

I sighed. "Okay, I may have destroyed a few flowers and ruined the laundry, but I had a good reason."

"It must have been something serious if you were willing to risk Hex catching you mistreating her garden." Riot added with a grin.

I glared at him. "It was just a couple of flowers." I protested. "It isn't as though I trashed the whole thing. Besides, I think she was more pissed off about the laundry."

I passed around the rest of the cookies and sat on the edge of the desk next to Demon. "So was Viola's information helpful?" I asked.

Riot waved his hand, dismissing the siren. "Viola was a bust. All she wanted to do was grope me, and Kaz was no damned help rolling on the ground laughing his ass off."

Kaz grinned. "But, poor Viola hadn't been with a man in so long, Riot. She was just overcome by your beauty and manliness."

"Asshole," Riot responded and bit into his cookie.

"I told you," Demon said to Riot. "Her information wasn't completely useless. She did see someone running away who might be easy to find. Her description was rather unusual."

Riot waved his hand again. "Demon, how many vampires are running around with black hair and wearing jeans?" he said scornfully.

"Riot," Demon said in the same tone. "How many vampires are running around who look like that and are male *and* drop crosses?"

"The bloodsucker had a cross?" I frowned. I mean, the whole thing about holy items repelling vampires was bullshit, but you didn't often see religious vampires.

Then it hit me. *"That black-hearted, pinheaded sonofabitch!"* I yelled.

"Don't hold back, Dev. Tell us how you really feel." Bane said dryly.

"It *was* Scarletti after all!" I snarled.

"It certainly looks that way." Demon said.

"Do you think he torched Tanith's house too?" Kaz asked.

"He might have." Demon said. "Once she turned him, she had outlived her usefulness to him. He must have decided to rid Blackridge of Tanith's vampires and eliminate the competition at the same time. Having all of us in the warehouse together must have been very convenient for him."

"Eliminate the competition." Riot grinned at me. "That would be *you.*"

"Scarletti overlooked one thing." I said dryly. "I am not his competition. I think he is taking Maia's flirting with me a bit too seriously."

Demon gave me an odd look. "Perhaps you don't take her flirting seriously *enough*." he told me.

I scowled at him. "What the hell do you know? You don't even see what's going on right in front of your face!"

Demon drew back, looking startled and hurt by my outburst. "Dev, I'm sorry. I didn't mean to upset you."

I took a deep breath. I admit that I was touchy and I didn't want to say something I would regret later. "No, Demon. I'm sorry. I overreacted. Look, I just don't want to talk about Maia."

"Okay, fair enough." he said. "But, if you do want to talk, you know that I am willing to listen."

"Thanks. The same goes for you."

Demon blinked and then looked away. "Right." he replied.

"Could we please get back on track here?" Bane demanded, glaring at his brother. "We know that Mike Scarletti started the fire or at least we have a good reason to suspect that it was him. He is a supernatural now and that puts him under Satana jurisdiction."

"And ours." Riot added. "Technically, he should go on the List."

"I think that would be a bad idea." I said reluctantly. "I mean, yeah, if Scarletti was trying to kill Tanith, then he needs to be stopped, but maybe it shouldn't be us hunting him down. You know, because of Maia."

"I see your point." Demon agreed. "But, Maia knows that murder, even a murder attempt that fails, is an executable offence. If someone breaks the law, he or she goes on our list."

"I know that she knows it here." I pointed to my head. "But, it's different when it's someone you love."

The others looked at me, incredulously. "Are you serious? Maia isn't in love with Scarletti, you ass!" Kaz said.

"Whatever her feelings are for him now," Demon interrupted. "Executing Mike may put a strain our friendship with her. Perhaps we should just leave it to the Satana to deal with him."

"Besides," I added. "Don't we have enough to do hunting down a rogue sovereign?"

The others agreed, reluctantly. Demon reached for the phone. "I'll call Daedalus."

CHAPTER NINETEEN

"ARE YOU SURE YOU want us to do this, Fechín?" Daedalus asked. His muffled voice came through the speaker. "This is usually your domain."

"It's better this way."

"It means a trial." Daedalus warned. "That may be harder on Maia than an outright execution."

Suddenly, the door opened and Maia came in. We all froze.

"Fechín, are you still there?" Daedalus' voice asked.

"What's going on?" Maia asked, puzzled by our consternation. "Did you find Mike?"

There was silence on Daedalus' end of the line at the sound of her voice.

"Not exactly," Demon told her.

"Gotta go!" Daedalus said, hastily, and we heard a click.

"Coward," Riot muttered.

Maia walked over to Demon. "Tell me what's happened."

Demon explained Viola's information and that we were turning the investigation over to the Satana. Maia's expression seemed to grow darker with each word.

"Are you sure that's wise?" she asked, at last. "I know that they are trained officers, but Mike is a vampire now. They're trained to arrest criminals, not to execute them."

"All Satana officers are trained in the proper procedure for executing a target."

"Theoretically," she said. "But, I'll bet there isn't one in a hundred of them who have even *seen* an execution, let alone participated in one."

Demon shot a look at me. "Dev seems to think that it would upset you if we were the ones who hunted Mike."

Maia stared at him and then wheeled around to face me. "This was your idea?" she snapped.

I nearly stepped backward, stunned by the vehemence in her voice. "I—I just thought that maybe it would make it hard for you to keep working with us if we executed your boyfriend." I stammered.

She gasped. "Mike is *not* my boyfriend! We broke up months ago."

"It was two days ago." I reminded her, irritably.

She planted her hands on her hips and glared at me. "I moved out of Mike's apartment eight months ago. You think I'm still in love with him!" she said in an accusatory tone.

This time I did take a step backward. There was anger and frustration in her tone that I didn't understand. "Maia, I just wanted to protect you."

"I know you did!" she shouted at me. "What are you protecting me *from*, Dev?"

I opened my mouth and closed it. I had done something to make her angry. I didn't know what it was and Maia was looking at me as though I should know. "You love him. I didn't want to be the one to execute the man you love." I shrugged helplessly.

"You are not listening to me!" she yelled. Suddenly, she balled up her fist and punched me in the shoulder.

"Ow!" I gasped. "What did you do that for?"

Instead of answering, she grabbed the waistband of my jeans and dragged me closer. Then, she kissed me hard. It took a second for it to sink in, and then I put my arms around her and kissed her back.

Finally, she sighed shakily and drew back. "I love you so much, Dev," she murmured. Maia's arms were still around my neck and she kissed me gently on the lips with each word. "I want you, not Mike." She touched her lips to my cheek. "I love you," she repeated quietly.

"Shit, Dev!" I heard Riot say. Someone grabbed my arm, catching me as my knees gave out, and sat me down into a chair. I looked around in a daze and saw a circle worried faces hovering over me.

"Are you okay?" Demon demanded. "Your skin is completely blue! I don't mean just pale blue, I mean *blue.*"

"Damn, half-assed shapeshifting—Hey!" I sputtered as Bane tried to force brandy down my throat. I glared at him. "Are you trying to drown me or help me?"

"I heard brandy was good for people who were in shock," he said defensively.

The room *was* tilting a bit. "I am not in shock!" I insisted and turned to Maia. "Look, don't tell me this if there is even the slightest chance that you might change your mind."

"Not a snowball's chance in hell." she said firmly. "Or a vampire's chance against the Enforcers if that makes it any clearer."

I have never been very good with expressing my emotions, especially this kind of emotion. I told her how I felt the only way I knew how. I stood up, pulled her into my arms again and kissed her with everything I felt, but couldn't say. The kiss softened as Maia's arms wound around my neck again.

I was vaguely aware of a noise in the background. "Bells," Maia said dreamily as I lifted my lips from hers. "I actually heard bells." She looked as dazed as I felt.

"That was the doorbell." Bane said dryly.

"I'll get it." Kaz left the room.

I glared at Bane and Demon who were both biting their bottom lips and staring at the floor. "It *could* have happened!" I said defensively.

Riot started to laugh. I glared at him too. Maia's lips brushed over my chest and she snuggled against me. If she was trying to distract me, it was working.

"I heard bells," she said decisively. "And it wasn't the doorbell."

I rested my cheek on top of her head and closed my eyes, smiling. "I've been in love with you for three years," I told her, finally. "And I'm jealous as hell of Scarletti."

There. It wasn't pretty but I said it.

She laughed softly. "You assumed that because you picked me up at his apartment, I was still living there."

"You were carrying a suitcase with clothes in it." I reminded her.

"I went there to get a few things that he kept promising to give back and didn't. He had one of my suitcases and some of my clothes. It made sense to put the clothes in the suitcase. Why put them in a bag and carry an empty suitcase?"

"You are so practical." I said, smiling down at her. "That is such a turn on."

"Oh brother," Bane said, rolling his eyes.

"No one asked you." I told him and kissed Maia again.

The library door opened and Kaz came in, jaw tight and eyes angry. We straightened; alerted by his manner that something was very wrong. "There's a police officer at the door—" he began.

"*Out of the way, demon!*" a male voice screamed and Kaz was shoved hard from behind. Kaz stumbled a few steps and a thin man with brown hair stepped into the room.

Mistake. BIG mistake. I pushed Maia behind me for safety and opened my mouth to yell at the jerk, but Kaz had it under control. He grabbed the man by the front of his shirt and slammed him against the wall with enough force to shake the whole house. "The name is Kaz," he snarled and yanked the man around by the shirt, pointing at Demon with one finger. "*That* is Demon and I suggest you use a bit more respect in your tone when you deal with him!"

Demon put on his cold, menacing Wrath face. "Who the hell are you and what are you doing here?" he asked in a tone that matched his expression.

Before the man could answer, Maia peeked around me and gasped, "Todd?"

"You know him?" Demon asked, pointing at the man.

She nodded. "This is Officer Todd Cooper. He is Mike's partner."

146

CHAPTER TWENTY

TODD COOPER WAS NOTHING like his partner in appearance. While Scarletti was a big, dark, fiery man with big heavy features, Cooper was a foot shorter with brown hair and pale skin. He had a slender build but he was in better shape than Scarletti who carried a bit of extra weight around his middle. Cooper had a narrow face with sharp features and keen brown eyes. The only attribute the two men seemed to share was their bad attitude.

Cooper lost some of his attitude after Kaz slammed him against the wall. Demon stood over him. "Sit down," he ordered.

Cooper dropped into a chair. He stared up at him, terrified, and Demon hadn't even flashed fang yet. He just knew instinctively that this was the man to fear.

Demon crossed his arms over his chest, his expression stony. "What do you want here? How did you find us?"

"That's my business." Cooper said.

Demon smiled thinly. "When did Scarletti contact you?" he demanded.

Cooper looked up in astonishment. "How did you know that he called me?" An explanation for it occurred to him and his mouth tightened. "You stay the hell out of my mind you—you—"

Demon's eyes narrowed. "Tread carefully, Cooper. I have no need to read your mind. Really, why else would you be here? You could not have known who we were or where to find us unless Scarletti told you."

When Cooper didn't respond, Demon went on. "Now, I am going to ask again and you are going to use a civil tone when you answer. When did you last speak to him?"

Cooper toyed with the idea of thumbing his nose at Demon, but when he weighed it against the probable result, he wisely decided against it. "Last night." he answered grudgingly.

"Before or after he became a vampire?"

Cooper's mouth opened and closed again. His lips tightened and he turned on Maia. "This all *your* fault!" he snarled at her. "He would never have done anything so crazy if he hadn't been so desperate to get you back!"

Maia glared at him. "Michael is a grown man, Todd. He makes his own decisions, stupid or otherwise."

Cooper rolled his eyes. "Oh, *please!* You made such a big deal out of the fact that he didn't understand you because he wasn't *supernatural.*" he sneered.

"I never asked him to do this." Maia told him. "I didn't care that he wasn't a werewolf. He was the one who made the big deal out of it."

Cooper snorted. "I told him that dating someone like you was a risky thing to do but he wouldn't listen to me!"

"He should have." Maia said coolly. "If he had listened to me when I broke up with him nearly a year ago, he wouldn't be in this mess and I refuse to take the blame for any stupid decisions he has made in the last eight months. If he wants to find someone to blame he should take a good long look in the mirror."

"*You bitch!*" Todd hissed.

Okay, up until that moment, Cooper was merely annoying. He had just crossed the line to insulting and since it was my woman that he was insulting, I picked him up by the shirt collar and slammed him against the wall again. I was pleased to see that he hit hard enough to leave a dent.

"Watch your mouth." I snarled. I lifted him off the floor by the throat. His feet dangled. "One more foul word out of you and Demon will be the least of your problems."

Cooper made a gurgling noise. Behind me, I heard Demon say, "Put the nice police officer down, Dev." His tone was mild, but when I glanced over my shoulder, his expression was not. "He will be very respectful and polite."

I slowly lowered Cooper to the floor again. He gasped and stumbled away from me.

"Next time," Demon told him, coldly. "You go *through* the wall. Understand?"

Cooper nodded.

"Good boy." Demon waved him to a chair. At least he didn't say, "Sit" and pat Cooper on the head. "Tell us exactly where you saw Scarletti last and exactly what he said to you word for word. I don't want to hear your own interpretation."

"Shouldn't the Satana be in on this?" Kaz interrupted. "After all, we gave them this case."

"Call them, Maia." Demon said.

Maia moved to the phone while the rest of us we kept our eyes on Sergeant Shithead. Maia hung up a few minutes later. "They're sending an officer to take Cooper's statement."

"You called Satan?" Cooper gasped. His face was white again and he looked like he was going to pass out.

"*The Satana*," Demon corrected. "That is the supernatural police force."

Cooper blinked at Demon and then turned to Maia. "Is there such a thing?"

"Yes, there is such a thing." Maia said sarcastically. "Who do think keeps the supernaturals in line?"

Cooper smirked. "Do you really want me to answer that?"

"No. Now shut up before you wear out your welcome."

Cooper shut up and remained rooted to his chair, gripping the arms, while the rest of us stood around him, eyeing him coldly.

Ten minutes later, the doorbell rang. No one moved. After another minute, the doorbell rang again.

"Someone has to go and let the officer in." Demon said at last.

"I am not leaving Maia." I said firmly.

"I'll get it." Morgana started for the door. "I sure hope it isn't another cop or Scarletti's mother or something. I think I've had enough of humans for the day." she called over her shoulder. She returned a few minutes later with Jordis.

Jordis glided across the room. "Good afternoon, Fechín." She stopped and stared Cooper, curiously. "Is this the witness?"

Her red skin and daemon horns were too much for Cooper. He leapt to his feet and pointed an accusing finger at her. Jordis had to step back or Cooper's finger would have been up her nose. "Tempt me not with this demon slut!" he screamed.

"Take that finger out of my face before I break it!" Jordis snapped at him.

Riot was already moving across the room. "Third time's the charm," he said. He grabbed Cooper by the collar with one hand and hurled him straight through the library wall.

Demon and I stepped over to join Riot. We peered through the Cooper shaped hole in the wall. He was sprawled face down in the hallway on the other side.

"You're fixing that." Demon told Riot.

Riot made a face. Kaz leaned through the opening, too, and studied Cooper carefully for a minute. "I think he's dead," he announced finally.

"He better not be. How are we going to explain that one to Daedalus?" Bane asked. He stepped through the hole and crouched down beside Cooper. He laid his fingers along the pulse in the man's neck. "He still has a heartbeat." He moved his hand along Cooper's back and leaned down close to his face. "He is still breathing."

"Is anything broken?" Demon asked stepping through the hole as well.

Bane ran his hands over Cooper's frame and then shook his head. "Not that I can tell but I'm not a doctor."

"Maia, call Claire. We'll have her take a look at him just to be sure." Demon said without turning around.

Dr. Claire Bridges is an old friend of ours. We have known her since she was eighteen years old. She is fifty-eight years old now. Many years ago, she had been Riot's lover. After a while, she decided that Riot was not the type of man she could bring home to Mom and Dad. Though she has been married three times and has four children, she remains a good friend to all of us.

Demon, Riot, and I were waiting in the front foyer when Dr. Claire arrived some fifteen minutes later. She is a small woman, more than a foot shorter than Riot. Claire has long black hair, which was slowly starting to turn gray. Her green eyes lit up when Riot stepped forward and greeted her with something more than friendly kiss.

Claire drew back from him with a shuddering sigh and a slightly dazed smile. "Wow." she told him.

Riot raised an eyebrow at her. "That's it? Wow?"

She grinned. "I can't say what I was really thinking out loud, darling. I might shock Demon and Dev's delicate sensibilities."

"Don't mind us." I told her. "Please go on just as if we weren't here."

Demon started to laugh. Claire shook her head. "Hello, Dev. Are you behaving yourself?"

"Not unless someone is pointing a weapon at me." I told her.

"And sometimes not even then," Riot added giving me a stern look.

Claire finally noticed the hole in the wall. She blinked. "Oh, my goodness! What did that?"

"Not what," I told her. "Who."

"He is in the library. His name is Todd Cooper. He had an accident with the wall." Demon explained and led her back into the library where we had moved Cooper.

Cooper was lying on the sofa and had regained consciousness. He hadn't spoken, however. There was fear in his eyes as he watched Demon's approach. I had to wonder at that since Riot was the one who hurled him through the wall.

Demon stopped beside the sofa. "This is Todd Cooper." He waved a hand at Cooper. Todd flinched away from the hand.

"Well." Claire said as she followed Demon into the library. "Hello, Mr. Cooper. Let's just have a look at you, shall we?"

"Officer Cooper." Demon told her.

Claire looked up sharply. "He's a police officer?"

"Yes." Demon said.

"Human?"

"Yes." Demon explained Cooper's presence.

Claire glanced toward the hole in the wall again. "May I assume that it was you who assisted Officer Cooper in making the hole in the wall?" she asked Demon.

Riot spoke up, sheepishly. "Actually, I was the, er, propellant."

Claire looked at him, startled. "It isn't like you to lose your temper like that." she frowned. "What on earth did he do?"

Riot's eyes darted to Jordis. "Well, uh—"

"It doesn't matter." Demon broke in much to Riot's relief. "We just want to make certain that his injuries are not life threatening."

Claire approached Cooper who shrunk back from her. "What are you?" he demanded in a hoarse whisper.

She stopped, frowning, and glanced back at us.

"He wants to know if you're an unholy fiend like the rest of us non-humans." I told her bitterly. I was getting sick of people treating us like monsters.

Claire rolled her eyes and then turned back to Cooper. "I am just as human as you are, Officer Cooper," she told him.

This did not seem to reassure him. Cooper's eyes darted from her to us. "Are these evil spirits controlling you against your will, too?" he whispered.

"Young man," Claire said coldly. "No one has been able to control me since I was fourteen. Now, sit up and let me have a look at you."

Cooper tried to sit up but the pain was too much for him. After a minute or two of struggling, he finally gave up, sinking back on the sofa, pale and sweating. I took pity on him. "Here," I said, reaching out. "I'll help you."

"No!" Cooper said, alarmed.

I hesitated, my hand still extended.

"Oh, don't be stupid, man!" Claire snapped when Cooper shrank back from me. "If the Enforcers wanted you dead they would hardly have called me to come here and make sure that you were okay, would they? Does that sound like the behaviour of evil monsters?"

Cooper shook his head.

"Then, let Dev help you. I haven't got all day." Claire said crisply.

Carefully, Kaz and I assisted Cooper into a sitting position. Demon set a pillow behind his back to help support him. Cooper stared at us, intently, while Claire made a quick examination of him, muttering to herself, and shaking her head.

"Well?" Demon asked when Claire rose to her feet with a sigh.

"He'll live," she said. "There is not as much damage as I would have expected from his having been thrown through a wall by someone of Riot's strength. I would say he's damned lucky his neck isn't broken, but he's got a dislocated shoulder and some bruising."

"Can you do something for him?" Demon asked.

"The best I can do is put him in a sling and give him some pain medication. He is going to hurt like hell tomorrow and he won't be able to drive himself back into town. Can one of you give him a ride?"

"We can take care of that in a minute." Demon said. "However, we cannot let him go just yet. He owes us some answers."

Jordis stepped forward but Demon held up one hand to stop her. He turned to Cooper and fixed him with an icy glare. "Remember your manners," he said. Cooper nodded, and then Demon stepped back and let Jordis do her thing.

"When did you last see Scarletti?" Jordis asked.

"Last night." Cooper said. "He was waiting outside my apartment when I came home after my shift."

Jordis noted it down. "Did he tell you that he had been turned?"

Cooper frowned. "Turned?"

"Into a vampire, I mean."

"Oh. No, he didn't say anything at first. He just kept talking about Maia and about how he was going to get her back. I noticed that he didn't look well. He was sweating and shivering at the same time. His face was so thin and pale. His eyes looked too big and there were dark circles under them. I thought he had the flu. I said something about him looking like death warmed over. He laughed." Cooper shuddered. "God, I'll never forget that laugh as long as I live. That's when he told me what he had done."

"What was his purpose in sending you out here?"

"He wanted me to talk to Maia and tell her that he still loved her and wanted her back. He said that he would forgive her for everything if she would come back to him now."

"Forgive *me*?" Maia sputtered.

I put my arm around her waist and drew her closer to me. "Maia," I whispered. "Let it go."

"Was that all?" Jordis prompted.

"No, I was supposed to convince her to come with me to meet him." Cooper looked up at Maia. "He just wants to talk to you. He loves you and in spite of every good reason I could think of for him to forget about you, he seems to want to give you another chance."

Maia didn't say anything but from the look on her face, I would say she had a few choice words for Officer Todd Cooper that he wasn't going to like. So far, she was restraining herself admirably.

"What if Maia chose not to come with you?" Jordis asked.

Cooper seemed uncomfortable now. "You must understand that I advised strongly against this."

"Cooper, just answer the question." Jordis said pointedly.

"*Officer* Cooper!" he snapped. She stared him down without replying. He answered with clenched teeth. "If Maia refused to come with me, he said that I was to set up some fireworks in the woods behind the house. Just small ones." he added hastily seeing our expressions. "Then Mike would come later tonight to set them off. When everyone ran outside to see what was going on, he would slip in and find a way to make her listen to him."

"What was he going to do if she refused to listen to him? Was he going to kidnap her?" Demon broke in.

Cooper looked uncomfortable. "He didn't seem to think that it would come to that if he could just talk to her without any interference from you."

"Where is Scarletti now?" Jordis asked.

"I don't know. He wouldn't tell me where he was hiding out. He said his apartment wasn't safe because they know where he lives." He jerked his chin at us.

"More likely, Scarletti was afraid that his partner would sneak in and stake him while he slept." I muttered to Kaz.

"I would." Kaz agreed.

Maia gritted her teeth in anger as she turned her back on Cooper. Demon reached out and touched her shoulder lightly. Her body relaxed instantly as Demon drew off some of the anger. His hand slid away and Maia smiled at him. "Thanks."

He smiled back. "Any time."

Cooper looked from one to the other, sneering. "Are you sleeping with this one too?"

"That is none of your business!" Maia snapped.

Cooper snorted. "I told Mike that you were nothing more than a—"

Before he could finish the sentence, Demon dragged Cooper up from the sofa by his shirt collar. He squawked in terror and clutched Demon's hands as if that would prevent Demon from beating the hell out of him. "You were doing so well." Demon sighed. "You really ought to learn to curb your tongue, Todd." He glanced at Jordis. "Are you done with this man?"

"I suppose I'll have to be," she said, bemused.

Demon nodded and turned back to Cooper. He gazed deeply into Cooper's eyes and in a few seconds, a glazed look came over Todd's face. "You were never here." Demon told him. "You have never heard of the Deadlies. You injured your shoulder when you were playing football with some friends. Mike Scarletti is not a vampire. He is on temporary leave from his job for mental health issues."

I grinned. I was pleased with Demon's explanation for Scarletti's odd behaviour when he came to find out if Cooper had managed to convince Maia to come and talk to him.

"Cooper, are you listening?" Demon asked.

"Yes." Cooper said in a faraway voice.

"Where are the fireworks?"

"In the woods."

Demon grimaced. "I need details, Cooper. I want to know how many and where you set them exactly."

Cooper admitted that he had set about ten large screaming fireworks and a bunch of smaller ones along the back of the bush. Bane, Kaz and Onyx went out to look for them while Demon sent Cooper into dreamland.

"Riot, take him home." Demon said, handing Cooper over to Riot.

"Is it okay if I hit every bump in the road along the way?"

"It won't matter. He won't feel it."

"Damn." Riot swung Cooper into his arms and left the room.

"Well, we've got a good lead." Jordis said as Claire bustled out of the room behind Riot. "We may not know exactly where Scarletti is, but we can stake out Cooper's apartment and catch Scarletti there."

Demon nodded.

"Are you sure that you don't want to be in on the capture?" Jordis asked.

"We're sure." Demon said. He paused. "Jordis, make sure that someone is close to Cooper in case Scarletti is disappointed."

Jordis was surprised. "Why? Do you think Scarletti is going to hurt him?"

"I have met many, many people like Mike Scarletti over the centuries. They are bullies as humans and it gets worse once they get a taste of vampire power. It goes to their heads." Demon told her. "Also, Scarletti is a new vampire. He doesn't know anything about how to feed the hunger, whether he uses humans or animals. I doubt that he has fed properly since he ran off. The hunger will make him more dangerous."

Jordis nodded. "Okay, I'll make sure that there is a guard on Cooper until we catch Scarletti."

She glanced out of the library window and froze. I looked over to see what had caught her attention. Claire and Riot were standing next to Claire's car. It seemed that they were saying good-bye. Okay, they were making out. Jordis turned away from the window, abruptly. "I have to give my report to the chief before night fall," she said flatly. "He'll need time to get a team over to stake out Cooper's apartment."

She spun around and stalked out of the library and we heard the front door open and the soft murmur of voices in the hallway. The door slammed and Riot came into the library looking as depressed as I had ever seen him. We all watched him for a minute as he went to the front window and stood staring out. Then he turned to us, his face expressionless. "What do we do next?"

"We turned Scarletti over to the Satana, but we've still got a rogue sovereign out there. So," Demon shrugged. "We go hunting, but first things first." He went behind the desk again and picked up the phone.

"Who are you calling now?" I asked.

He glanced up and grinned. "Pizza." he said. "I'm starving."

CHAPTER TWENTY-ONE

THE OTHERS DECIDED THAT I should meet the pizza guy at the door. The kid was about seventeen years old with a few pimples and wearing an orange baseball cap with the pizzeria's logo on the front. The orange and black uniform did nothing to enhance his complexion and it was at least two sizes too big for his thin, gangly body. He eyed me suspiciously when I answered the doorbell. I couldn't blame him. I was wearing jeans but I also had on a long black coat indoors and no shirt underneath. I must have looked crazy to him and our order didn't do anything to dispel the impression. "Did you order ten pizzas?" he demanded.

"Yeah," I told him.

"Are you having a party?" He glanced back over his shoulder. There were no vehicles in the driveway save Demon's van and the kid's brown, piece of crap hatchback.

"Something like that." I waved the money under his nose to get his attention.

The kid eyed me, ignoring the money. He struggled with his curiosity until it finally got the better of him. "Isn't it a bit hot out to be wearing a coat?" he asked.

"Heat doesn't bother me." I told him truthfully.

"Why don't you turn down your air conditioning?"

I eyed him back. "What air conditioning?"

"Why else would you be wearing a coat in the house?" the kid demanded, mystified.

I have always found that telling the truth is the surest way to make people think you are lying to them. I shrugged. "It's to hide the wings."

"Wings?" The kid started to edge away from me.

"Yeah, I have big black wings."

The kid snatched the money out of my hand and fled to his car, no doubt thinking that I was crazy like every other adult over twenty.

Ha. Little did he know.

Everyone else was already in the kitchen getting plates, drinks, and paper napkins out as I breezed into the kitchen, balancing ten pizzas in one hand.

"I think I traumatized the pizza delivery kid." I announced.

Bane was setting plates out on the large wooden table. He paused. "What did you do?" he sighed.

"I told him the truth." I paused pretending to think about it. "Just so you know we're probably going to have carloads of teenagers driving by and daring each other to sneak up and knock on the door."

The others frowned and looked at each other. I could tell that they were thinking, "We just don't want to know." I laughed.

As we sat devouring our pizzas, we plotted our stratagem for the evening. True to his word, Bane insisted on accompanying his brother in spite of Demon's assurances that he had fed.

"When? How?" Bane demanded.

"You forgot who." I said as I grabbed another piece of pizza and took a big bite.

We all paused and then looked at Demon. He scowled at us with a piece of pizza halfway to his mouth. "I drank one of the bottles in the fridge."

"Bummer," I said, scooping up second piece of pizza.

"All right, but I am still going with you." Bane told him.

"Whatever." Demon rolled his eyes. "Riot, Morgana and Kaz, you can cruise the bars on the east and west ends of the city since there is only one strip club. Riot, you are going to have to wait in the car there."

"The second bummer of the evening," Riot sighed.

We had learned our lesson the hard way. Many years ago, we had followed a target to a burlesque house. That should give you some indication of just how long ago this was. The dancers had followed Riot around offering him private dances, much to the annoyance of the management and the paying customers. A brawl ensued and our target escaped, for the moment. Afterward, we started calling Kane "Riot" whenever we wanted to tease him and it stuck. Demon had never allowed him on another hunt in a strip bar (or burlesque house) again.

Demon ignored Riot's pout. "Dev, you and Onyx to take the south end bars." I was not pleased, but I didn't say anything. I scowled at Demon though to let him know that I wasn't happy to be stuck with Onyx. He ignored me too.

"What about you and Bane?" Kaz asked.

"We'll check the north end bars and clubs as well as the park, though I doubt the vampires are going to hit that very often. It's too open."

"That's it?" Morgana said. "We're just cruising bars?"

"It seems to be the rogues' hunting ground of choice and since we have only a few hours tonight in which to hunt, I thought we would start with the obvious places. However, if you happen to have any better ideas, please feel free to share them with the rest of us." Demon said coolly.

Morgana flushed. "I wasn't second-guessing you."

"It seems to me that all you have been doing lately is complaining about my leadership."

Morgana started to say something, but changed her mind and turned away from him. She finished her pizza in cold silence.

"Okay," Kaz said to Demon. "What do you want us to do if we spot the rogues? Should we corner them or follow them?"

"If they are with a human, try to get the human aside so that the vampire doesn't become alarmed. Find out if the human knows that the person he or she is with is a vampire. If not, then try to detach the vampire from the human prey discreetly. Tell him that you are an Enforcer and then, politely suggest that he might want to rethink his dinner plans."

Kaz laughed. "We'll tell them we have Wrath on speed dial. That should be enough to send them screaming into the night!"

The rest of us laughed too. "Apparently, we need to have a discussion about the definition of *discreet*." Demon teased. "Try not to execute unless you absolutely have to. Take some time to question them if you can. If anyone offers information, call me. We need one of the vampires to give up the rogue sovereign."

"What about Tanith?" I asked. "Any luck there?"

He shook his head. "She swears that she does not know who it is."

"Do you believe her?"

"No."

I sighed. "This would be so much easier if the rogues would just wear t-shirts that say, "My name is such-and-such, and I feed on unwilling humans.""

"A nice thought, but since they are unlikely to be so accommodating, we'll just have to find them the old-fashioned way." He turned to check the time on the old pendulum clock hanging on the wall. "If everyone is finished eating, we have an hour to sundown so let's get ready."

We went to our rooms to put on our equipment and met in the front foyer about twenty minutes later. We were not loaded up with weapons. Demon had forbidden the long blades in case the bouncers at the bars wanted to pat us down. They might think the wings were just a bulky shirt, but there was no mistaking the shape and feel of a sword.

Serkan was coming down from upstairs. It seemed a trifle early for Serkan to be up and walking around, but then he was a sovereign. Maybe that made a difference. What did I know about vampires? I didn't know any others except for Demon and daytime or nighttime, it didn't make a difference to him.

Maia came up from the basement with Kit. Maia walked over to join me. She kissed me on the cheek. "Good evening." she intoned in the perfect imitation of a movie vampire.

I rolled my eyes. "Very funny."

She giggled.

"What were you doing in the basement?" I asked.

"Visiting with Kit."

"Having a little girl talk?"

"We were both bored. She's really nice."

"Don't get too comfortable with her, Maia." Demon warned. "She could be one of the rogues."

"I have a hard time believing that."

So did I, but I didn't say so. Kit stood by the basement door, her gaze steady on Demon. He focused on Serkan, pointedly ignoring her.

"Are you hunting tonight?" Serkan asked Demon.

Demon gave him a curt explanation while Serkan gave him a disapproving look that clearly said, "Is this any way to speak to me?" Demon glared back and Bane scowled at both of them. I frowned as I watched them. There was something...something...

"I will accompany you." Serkan announced calmly when Demon had finished. "I have always wanted to join a hunt."

"The hell you will!" Demon exploded. The rest of us took a step backward. "This isn't fun and games, Serkan! These people are dangerous! You being a sovereign will not protect you!"

"I am aware of that." Serkan said coldly. "Do not speak to me as if *I* were the child here, Demon."

To my utter astonishment, blue flames flared in Serkan's eyes.

I gasped and sputtered for a moment. Finally, my brain made the connection. "Holy shit!" I exclaimed.

Everyone turned to look at me. "What?" Kaz asked.

I gaped at him and pointed at Serkan. The flames were gone. His eyes were cool and composed once more. I darted a look at the twins and in that moment, I knew that I was right. Demon shook his head slightly and glanced toward Kit. He didn't want me to say anything in front of her.

"It was just a moth." I muttered. It was lame. I knew it was lame. The others knew it was lame. Bane raised his eyebrow at me. I shrugged.

"Your, er, guests will be rising soon." Serkan pointed out, hastily turning the subject. "What are you going to do about them?"

"There are plenty of bottles of blood in the refrigerator." Demon turned stiffly to Kit. "Help yourselves. There is more where that came from."

"Thank you," she replied quietly.

"You are going to leave them here alone?" Serkan asked.

Demon studied Kit for a moment and then shook his head. "I had not thought of that. One of us will have to stay behind. You will have to come with us. You're not immortal and I'm not taking any chances." Demon told him. "Kaz, would you stay? We're expecting some more of Tanith's people to show up tonight."

"I knew it was too good to be true." Kaz sighed. "Yeah, I'll stay."

"Thanks. Sorry, Kaz, but it cannot be Riot because some of the vampires *are* females after all. I don't want to come back to them trashing our house over him and I'm not crazy enough to send Greed and Gluttony out together without a chaperone."

"I was so looking forward to going hunting with Lust." Kaz said mournfully.

"You'd be hunting for women instead of the rogue vampires." I accused.

"And anyway," Kaz went on. "What's wrong with wanting a little female attention?"

"Ask Rowan." I retorted.

"Ouch." Kaz made a face. "I'd rather not. I like my balls right where they are."

"I suppose it doesn't matter if the humans trash the bars over Riot." Bane added dryly.

"It isn't *my* bar." Demon pointed out.

Riot laughed.

Demon turned to Serkan. "You can come with Bane and me. Maia, you can go with Dev and Onyx."

"Wait a minute." I protested. "Why is Maia going?"

"Do you really want to leave her in the house with Tanith?"

"Kaz will be here." I pointed out. "Besides, I could stay with her. I just don't want her out in Blackridge with Scarletti still on the loose."

"She will never be safer than she will be with you." Demon said. "I don't think Scarletti will try to grab her in a public place. He's not that desperate."

He and I stared at each other. The word "yet" hung between us. I hoped the Satana would find Scarletti soon.

"I'll be fine, Dev." Maia reassured me. "You and Onyx will be there to protect me. I'm certain that Onyx likes me enough to stop Mike from kidnapping me, though he might turn a blind eye if Mike comes after you."

To my surprise, Onyx began to laugh. "Now that's not true! I would rescue Dev...after five or ten minutes of watching him get his ass kicked."

As I stood with my mouth hanging open, I heard the others start to laugh. Then, I started to smile too. Perhaps they were as surprised as I was. It wasn't often that we heard Onyx crack a joke or laugh.

"It's not as bad today, is it?" Demon asked softly.

Onyx' smile disappeared. He shook his head and looked embarrassed.

"Tell me if you need anything." Demon urged.

Onyx nodded. "I will."

"What about me?" Kit asked softly.

Demon looked startled and then, he wiped the expression from his face. "Shouldn't you be protecting your sovereign?" he suggested coldly.

"I consider hunting the rogues to be protecting her." Kit replied in the same tone. "If I can prove that Tanith has nothing to do with the rogues, then you won't execute her and I won't need to find a new job."

"Your generosity is truly awe-inspiring." Demon said, wryly.

"I am alone in the world," she reminded him. "I cannot afford to have generous feelings toward every master. They tend to take advantage."

Demon didn't speak for a minute. Finally, he said, "I'm sorry, Kit."

"I don't want your pity, Demon. I want——" She broke off and turned away, but I saw tears welling up in her eyes. She went back down to the basement.

Serkan cleared his throat. "Is there something you would like to tell me, Demon?" he asked when Kit was gone.

"No." Demon said flatly. He wrenched the front door open and then slammed it, making us all jump. We stared at him as he stalked past us to the stairs.

"It's still daylight," Demon said. "If Serkan is coming with us we will have to wait until full night."

"That gives us almost another hour to wait." Bane told him.

"I know it." Demon said as he stormed up the stairs. "Take a break everyone. This is going to be a long night."

An hour later, we met in the front hallway where Demon was waiting impatiently for the rest of us to join him. He held the keys to the jeep (black of course) in his hand. "Grab a set of keys and let's go."

Riot took two sets of keys from the hall table. "You can have the luxury car," he said to Maia, handing her the other set of keys. "You drive. The idea of Dev driving a car is more frightening than facing the whole pack of rogues by myself. I'll drive the Vette."

"The hell you will!" Morgana scowled.

I scowled at him too and started to say something but he was already turning away. I began to plot my revenge as I watched him toss the keys to the Vette into the air. Demon quickly caught them before they landed in Riot's hand.

"What are you doing?" he asked in amazement.

"*You* are taking the van." Demon held up another set of keys. "And Morgana is driving."

"Ha!" I stuck my tongue out at Riot drawing a glare from him.

Demon turned and dropped the keys into Morgana's outstretched hand. "Sorry about the van, Morgana, but it is the safest way to travel with Riot."

"I can deal," she said. "Thanks for the keys." She held them up right under Riot's nose.

"And why does *she* get to drive?" Riot demanded.

"I'm driving because I'd like to come back in one piece." Morgana replied coolly.

I snickered and Riot glared at me. He pointed a long finger at me. "Shut up, Dev!"

"Try to keep Riot out of trouble, will you?" Demon told her.

"If you have some way for me to knock him out cold for the night, he'll be no trouble at all."

"Bring an army." Riot scowled at her.

She pointed at Demon and raised her eyebrow pointedly. Riot groaned. Demon laughed and tossed the jeep keys into the air and catching them again. He opened the front door. "Good luck, Morgana." he called over his shoulder as he went down the front steps. Bane and Serkan followed him.

Morgana gave Riot a shove toward the open door. "Let's go, hot stuff. Time is a-wasting." She hustled him into the van's passenger seat and then climbed into the driver's side, still laughing. He looked completely dumbfounded. I doubt Riot had ever been treated this way by a woman in his entire life. We watched them drive away.

"That was interesting." Onyx remarked.

I had been expecting to see his usual unpleasant smirk on his face and was surprised to find that his expression was one of mild amusement. I grinned back but I was puzzled. I was used to a jealous, green-eyed Onyx. Right now, his eyes were blue. I couldn't conceal my surprise. Onyx gave me a rueful smile. "You didn't know that my eyes were blue, did you?"

"I did." I told him. "But, I had forgotten until now."

"Demon keeps telling me that I owe all of you an apology and an explanation. Perhaps he's right, but not now," he said. "Let's go hunting."

I grinned at him. "You got it."

Onyx and I followed Maia to the car. Onyx got into the back seat without a word of complaint, leaving the front seat to me. I stared across the roof of the car at Maia and shook my head in disbelief.

By the time we reached the fourth bar, it was close to two o'clock. It was a Goth bar owned by a vampire. Everyone inside was under the age of thirty and proving their individuality by wearing the same clothes (black) and having their hair dyed the same colour (black) and wearing the same makeup (white and black), even the guys.

We hadn't seen very many vampires and the ones we did see did not appear to be doing anything wrong. Onyx and I warned them about the rogues and told them to call Serkan or us if they saw anyone misbehaving with the humans. They all agreed that they would, but as the last one walked away with an air of relief, Onyx said, "They won't call."

"One might have a pang of conscience." I suggested.

"Why should they?" Onyx asked. "We don't know who the rogue sovereign is and they know we're not going kill them without a damned good reason."

"You could threaten them with Wrath." Maia suggested. "That usually works." Maia waited for Onyx to answer and was surprised when he didn't. "Doesn't it?"

"It hardly seems fair to Fechín," he said, slowly. "We're making him out to be a kind of Boogey man."

"He is the Nightmares' Nightmare." I said. "The vampires named him that, not us."

"Aren't we just perpetuating the impression? Isn't there more to him than that?" Onyx insisted.

Earlier, I noticed a young woman eyeing Onyx with a tremendous amount of interest. Having worked up enough courage, she finally approached him and asked him to dance. Before he could refuse, I leaned in and whispered, "She's cute. Go on."

He looked back at me, startled. "We're working," he whispered back.

"No one here is supposed to know that except the vampires. She isn't a vampire."

"What about Fechín?"

"What he doesn't know won't hurt us."

Onyx grinned and wandered off with the pretty, young woman to the dance floor, a large square of wood in a sunken area in the middle of the room. There were steps leading down to it from all four sides. The non-dancers could stand at the railings or sit at one of the tables scattered around it to watch. Maia and I moved closer to the railing and stood watching them for a minute.

"I don't understand it." I muttered, watching the girl's eyes light up as Onyx leaned in to say something to her.

"What, that Onyx can dance?" Maia asked.

I made a face. "I knew *that*. It's just that he's not acting like himself."

She smiled. "He's being friendly and flirting with a girl."

"Well, yeah."

Maia's smile faded and she looked thoughtful. "It must be so hard being Riot's little brother. Riot constantly outshines him."

"That is hardly Riot's fault. It's who he is."

"I know, but it must make Onyx' Deadly so much worse."

I frowned. "Explain."

"You sound like Demon." she teased.

"Just tell me what the hell you're talking about." I growled.

She kissed me and we forgot what we were discussing for a minute or two. Finally, she drew back, a little breathless. "Getting back to Onyx..."

"Onyx who?"

She laughed. "As I was saying, I think that Onyx' jealousy is like Fechín's wrath. When there is too much, he can't control himself."

"You mean the jealousy can overwhelm him?" I thought about that. "Fechín rips rooms and vampires apart when he goes Wrath. Onyx gets obnoxious when he goes Green-Eyed Monster. It makes sense."

Maia and I looked back at Onyx. He and the girl were standing by the bar now, chatting and having a drink. "Fechín said it wasn't as bad today and Onyx said no." I went on. "So Fechín must know or suspect that Onyx is struggling. I wonder why he didn't tell us."

"Perhaps he feels that it isn't his place." Maia suggested.

Okay, so now I was regretting every nasty thought I had ever had about Onyx. We had been friends once. When he started behaving like a jerk, I had just become so irritated with him that I never tried to figure out why he had changed. The others dealt with him the same way, except for Demon. He understood what it was like when your Deadly overwhelmed you to the point that you couldn't control yourself.

"I feel so ashamed." I said. "He said he was going to apologize to us but I think we're the ones who owe him an apology."

"Maybe all he wants is for everyone to be as understanding with him as you are with Fechín." Maia suggested.

I smiled down at her and felt the need to kiss her again. When I drew back, she seemed pleasantly dazed. "You are so smart." I told her.

"I can do some algebra if you want." she said breathlessly.

166

I laughed. "Any excuse to kiss you is a good excuse."

"If 2X minus Y equals..."

I didn't let her finish. I leaned down to kiss her again and stopped. "Dev?"

"Just a minute, Maia, hold that thought."

Darkmoon, Hadrian's mate, was standing at the top of the stairs watching the dancers. She was not a tall woman or particularly beautiful but she had an impressive air and her lovely brown eyes angled up slightly at the tips giving her an exotic appearance that many men found compelling. That is why Darkmoon was so successful at persuading humans to let her feed from them and if she was a rogue that made her dangerous.

I watched her for a minute, waiting to see what she was up to before I moved in. I tried to attract Onyx' attention discreetly. Suddenly, Darkmoon turned her head and saw us across the room. She smiled at me, flashing her fangs. I bristled at the arrogance of the challenge. So, she wasn't afraid of me, eh? Well, I could change that. I darted across the room, moving so fast that it would seem to the human eye or the vampire eye that I had disappeared. I reappeared right behind her. She was frowning at the spot where I had been standing.

"You wouldn't be so damned cocky if Wrath were here." I hissed in her ear.

Darkmoon gave a little start, but she quickly recovered her poise and didn't turn around. "I have done nothing wrong." she informed me in a low voice.

"For your sake, you'd better be telling me the truth, Darkmoon."

"Are you threatening me, Sloth?"

"Take it as you will. You have heard that there are rogue vampires in Blackridge?"

"I have."

"If you know anything about the rogue vampires, you had better tell me now. You wouldn't want me to mistake *you* for one of them, would you?"

"I was under the impression that you had already executed the rogue sovereign." She was maintaining her bored expression and though her eyes were roving around the room as though I was of no consequence, her body was tense.

"Were you?" I laughed softly.

Her jaw tightened in anger. "Hadrian said that the Enforcers executed Douglas."

"Did Hadrian say that he had witnessed the execution?" I demanded.

She finally turned to look at me and slowly it dawned on her that perhaps Hadrian's trick hadn't worked after all. There was a flash of fear in her eyes.

I smiled, satisfied with her reaction. "I see that I have your attention. Let me give you some advice. Don't believe everything you are told. Gullible doesn't suit you."

Darkmoon's mouth tightened. "You arrogant—"

Darkmoon didn't finish her sentence as Onyx and Maia joined us. I doubt it was a compliment, anyway. Onyx stood on the other side of Darkmoon, eyeing her with distaste. "Is everything all right here, Dev?" he asked. "Should I be making a phone call?" His cell phone was open in his hand and his thumb hovered over the buttons. I knew it was all for show. Onyx was technologically illiterate. He would probably end up calling Australia instead of Demon.

However, the message came through loud and clear. Darkmoon turned away haughtily and then paused when she saw Maia. Darkmoon smirked. "Ms. Severn, fancy meeting you here. I hear that you are living with the Enforcers now."

"Where would *you* hear something like that?" Maia asked coolly.

"I, too, have my informants. Have you also taken to hunting with them?" The tips of her fangs flashed. "You should be careful. Hunting supernaturals could be a very dangerous pastime for a tasty-looking little human like you."

Maia's eyes flashed. "It could also be very dangerous for anyone who forgets that I am a werewolf."

"Of course, *some* vampires actually prefer werewolf blood and the battle to get it would be half the fun." Darkmoon told her. She gave Maia a smirk and started to walk away.

I grabbed Darkmoon's arm. She looked up at me and hissed, "How dare you! Let go of me!"

"Lower your voice unless you want to take this somewhere more private!" I snapped.

"I'm not afraid of you!"

"That's your first mistake. Let me just remind you, that I have authority to kill a rogue vampire, too."

"You have no proof that I *am* a rogue," she pointed out with an evil grin.

"You threatened Maia." Onyx said.

"Oh no," Darkmoon shook her head. "I simply gave her some friendly advice. Ask Fechín. He will tell you that himself."

"I could just kill you anyway." I told her.

She lifted her chin and glared at me, haughtily. "Fechín would be furious!"

I shrugged and smirked at her. "He would forgive me eventually and you would still be dead."

Darkmoon tried to yank her arm away but I didn't let her, not right away. Onyx moved in closer. Something gleamed in his hand. He turned it slightly so that we could see that he was holding a short blade. Darkmoon looked up at his cold expression. Too many of the supernaturals forgot that Demon was not the only Enforcer that they should fear. When she realized she could not just pull away from me, her eyes widened in alarm.

"Now, let me give you some advice. Threatening someone under the Deadlies' protection is also a very dangerous pastime and very, very foolish." I warned her quietly.

She gave me a speculative look and nodded slowly. "I am beginning to realize that."

"See that you remember it." I released her arm.

She inclined her head slightly. "Good evening, Dev Xander." She disappeared into the crowd. A few minutes later, she gathered up her little entourage of vampires and left the bar.

Maia shivered. I put my arm around her. "She's one of them, Dev." Maia whispered. "She has to be the ringleader."

"She is right though. We don't have proof of that and she knows we won't just kill her without reason." I said. "My only consolation is that they left without taking any humans with them."

"They can always find others." Onyx pointed out.

"But, they won't try tonight. They know we are out looking for them. Darkmoon won't risk it."

Suddenly, my cell phone vibrated. I nearly jumped out of my skin. Maia found it in the pocket of my jeans and answered it. She held it up to me. "You have a text message from Fechín."

I took the phone and quickly read Demon's message. "Let's go." I said to Maia and Onyx, closing the cell phone. "Fechín is calling us in."

CHAPTER TWENTY-TWO

DEMON, BANE AND SERKAN were just getting out of their SUV as we drove up. Morgana and Riot were behind us in the van. I got out of the car and glanced over my shoulder as Riot got out of the passenger side. He was grinning. There was lipstick on his cheek. Maybe he didn't get to drive but someone made it up to him. I rolled my eyes at Maia. She smiled.

"Any luck?" Riot called out to Demon.

He shook his head. "All the vampires we saw were behaving themselves. What about you two?"

Riot smiled, widely. "You could say that I had some luck, but no vampires."

"Just a bunch of horny humans," Morgana added and she wrinkled her nose at Riot.

"They were just happy to see me." Riot said good-humouredly.

"Ugh."

Riot laughed.

"So why did you call us in so soon?" Onyx asked Demon as we walked toward the house.

"I got a phone call from someone telling me to come home." Demon said, worriedly. "It was not from Kaz, but it was a male."

"You called Kaz to check on him?" I asked.

"Yes, he wasn't answering the phone."

Bane opened the front door and I heard him gasp. I whirled around and bounded up the front steps to peer in over his shoulder. The house looked like a tornado had ripped through and upturned everything.

Demon pushed past his brother into the hall. They looked at each other and alarm spread over their faces. "Kaz!" Demon shouted and raced down the hallway to the kitchen. "Kit! Tanith!"

Bane darted into the library while Riot headed into the basement. "Kaz, answer us!"

"I'll check the parlour!" Morgana said and raced down the hallway.

I looked over at Onyx. We turned and ran up the stairs together. "Hex!" I hollered.

"Kaz, where are you?" Onyx threw open the door to Kaz' bedroom and ran inside.

I stopped suddenly, hearing a soft sob coming from the bathroom between Kaz and Riot's bedrooms. I looked at Onyx. He nodded.

"You wait on this side." I whispered.

Onyx drew his sword and stood beside the bathroom door while I slipped silently into Riot's room. Cautiously, I drew my sword as I approached the bathroom. I flung the door open. I heard someone gasp and scramble toward the other door. I stepped inside and flipped on the light as Onyx flung open the other door.

Hex barrelled into Onyx and screamed when he grabbed her shoulders. "Hex, it's us! You're okay." he assured her.

Hex stared up at him for a second and then burst into tears.

"*Demon, they're in the basement!*" I heard Riot yell.

"Stay with Hex." I told Onyx and raced back down the stairs. I reached the basement door right behind Demon. He ripped the door off its hinges and tossed it against a wall. Bane was right behind me as we plunged down the stairs. At the foot of the stairs, I saw Kaz. He and Riot were kneeling beside someone lying in a heap at the bottom of the stairs. We drew nearer and I saw that it was a female. Her blond curls were soaked with blood. There was a stake protruding from her chest.

"Kit!" I gasped.

"No. Oh no, Kit." Demon whispered and he dropped to his knees beside her. He stroked her hair gently.

"It was Scarletti." Kaz said in a dazed voice. There was dried blood smeared over his chest. He looked at Demon, miserably. "I couldn't stop him, Demon. I'm so sorry."

Demon didn't appear to hear him. "Kit. *Damn it!*" he screamed and then wrenched the stake out of her chest. Blood poured out of the wound and Kit's eyes opened. She screamed and blood seeped from her mouth. Her eyes rolled back in her head. She was dying right in front of us.

Demon picked her up and held her in his arms. "Come on, Kitten. Stay with me." Demon urged. Her eyes opened again and tried to focus on Demon. "That's right, open them up and look at me." He pulled the dagger strapped to his arm and slashed his chest, wincing as the blade cut just a little too deep. Blood welled from the wound and picked her up, cradling her against his body. "Come on, drink up."

She shook her head weakly. "I c-can't..."

He forced her mouth to open slightly, allowing the blood from his chest to drip onto her lips. "*Please!* You must drink before I heal! Morgana, get her a bottle of blood from the fridge! Hurry!"

Morgana ran back up the stairs.

He helped Kit lift her head and pressed her mouth to the wound on his chest. He buried his face in her hair as she began to suck, drawing strength from his blood. Even as we watched, Demon's wound began to heal. I would have panicked except that the hole in Kit's chest was healing at the same rate. By the time Demon's wound was gone, so was hers. He still held her tightly against him, his face buried in her hair and her face burrowed against his chest. I heard her sniff. She was crying.

Finally, Demon lifted his head. "Tell me what happened," he said to Kaz, hoarsely.

"I was in the kitchen checking the back door to make that it was locked." He froze. "Hex!"

"She's upstairs with Onyx." I assured him. "She's okay, just a little shaken."

Kaz sighed in relief. "I can't believe that I forgot about her."

"You were in the kitchen." Demon prompted.

Kaz nodded. "I heard a loud crash and I tried to push open the kitchen door, but there was something against it. I pulled it open and found that someone had pushed the big china cabinet in front of it." He looked rueful. "I'm afraid I shoved it aside a bit hard when I came out. I may have broken a few things."

"Don't worry about that. Go on."

"Well, I heard screaming in the basement and I ran downstairs straight into a stake."

Demon studied Kaz' face intently. "Scarletti hurt you?" he asked.

Kaz grimaced. "Yeah, the bastard got me in the chest." His hand passed over the blood smears. "Before I had healed enough to go after him, he was long gone. I was about to call you when you came in."

Kaz paused and shook his head slightly. "Demon, I really think that Scarletti has lost his mind. He didn't look sane."

"How long ago did he leave?" I asked.

"It must have been about half an hour ago."

"Do you think he was the one who called you?" I asked Demon.

"Someone called you?" Kaz asked surprised.

"Why would Scarletti call me?" Demon asked.

"Well," Kaz said thoughtfully. "He was quite upset when he discovered that Maia wasn't here."

"And what better way to find her than to call us and get us to bring her to him." Demon said.

We all stared at each other. I swore, and then Bane, Riot, and I raced back up the stairs and out into the yard. Serkan and Maia had still been outside when we found Kaz and Kit. They had been too far away from the house to hear the commotion. They were coming toward the house as we rushed out. We hustled them inside while Bane explained what was going on.

The colour drained from Maia's face. "Oh, my god." she whispered. "Did he... is Kit..."

"No, she's okay." I assured her. "But, you need to stay in the basement with the others. Scarletti might still be around."

"I will help you look for him." Serkan said.

Bane shook his head. "No, Serkan. You go to the basement too. We don't want you getting hurt either."

Serkan looked as though he was going to argue but he stopped, seeing the worried look on Bane's face. "Very well." he murmured.

Serkan took Maia into the basement while the rest of us searched for Scarletti. He was gone. Perhaps he reconsidered kidnapping Maia when he saw that she was not alone. Perhaps he had not had time before we came back out of the house. Perhaps he had not made the phone call after all. Whatever the reason, I was grateful.

We returned to the house. Everyone was in the basement. Onyx and Hex were there too and, thankfully, she was unharmed. Hex explained that she had been cleaning the bathroom when the commotion started and she locked herself in.

Kit was sitting on the bed in one of the rooms drinking the bottle of blood that Morgana had brought for her from the refrigerator. Maia sat on one side of the bed next to Kit and Tanith sat on the other. Demon leaned against the wall by the door, the indifferent expression firmly in place. I felt better knowing that while we had been outside, Demon was watching over the women. They could not have been safer.

"He's gone." I said flatly. Maia came over and nestled against me. I wrapped an arm around her, pulling her close. I could feel her fear and mentally cursed Mike Scarletti. I was suddenly glad that Demon had insisted on her going with me tonight. "How the hell did he get in?"

"Dev's bedroom window is broken." Onyx said quietly. "He must have climbed in through there."

"He was upstairs while Hex was there." I shuddered. "At least he didn't find her."

"No, but a few of Tanith's people had arrived." Kaz said. "Apparently, they spent last night with various friends. Some had not fed yet tonight so when I went to the kitchen, I decided to load up a laundry basket with some bottles of blood for them. The next thing I hear is screaming and crashing. I came downstairs and saw Kit lying at the bottom of the stairs."

Demon glanced at Kit. "I had just been outside," she explained. "I came in and heard someone in the basement. I went downstairs and found Scarletti standing over one of the other vampires. He was staking her." Kit stopped speaking and took a deep breath. Her voice shook. "I went after him to stop him and he yanked the stake out of the other vampire and attacked me with it."

She stopped and buried her face in her hands. Demon made a slight movement toward her, then stopped and leaned back against the wall again.

"It was not your fault, Kit." Tanith said quietly. "You did what you could."

"Where were you during all this?" Demon asked her.

She looked up at him. "One of my people locked me in one of the rooms and went to help Kit." Her voice faltered and she looked away. "He is one of the dead."

"How many of the vampires are dead?" Demon asked.

"Six." Kaz told him. "Two were staked and four were just slaughtered. He must have had some other weapon. I don't know what it was."

"One of the machetes is missing from the wall upstairs." Onyx said quietly.

Kaz shuddered. Demon touched his shoulder. "Where are they?" he asked gently. He stopped Kaz as he started toward the door. "No, don't come out and show me. Just tell me."

"Down the hall toward the rooms with a view," Kaz told him.

Demon stepped out into the hallway beside me. In the darkened hallway, I hadn't noticed the bodies. Two were in the hallway. The legs of a third were sticking out of one of the rooms. I didn't see the other three. "The new vampires are two of the victims." Kaz added.

"Shit." Demon whispered. For a moment, we all stood in silence, our heads lowered in respect for the dead.

"We'll get them cleaned up." Bane said finally, laying a hand on his brother's shoulder.

Demon was still staring at the floor, his hand flexed into a fist. Kit came out of the room now and took his hand in hers. He glanced at her, questioning. She smiled. "Thank you for saving my life...again." She looked down at her blood soaked chest and grimaced. "It isn't as much fun as raising the moon, but—"

"*What?*" Serkan snapped. He glared at Kit and then at Demon.

Demon shook his head hastily and then looked back as Tanith joined them. "You are unhurt?" he asked.

Tanith took his other hand with a smile. "I am fine."

Demon looked down at the two women's hands in his. "Scarletti is a dead man," he said roughly. "I'm going to kill him."

"I thought that we were going to let the Satana handle this." Bane said.

"Oh no," Demon hissed. "He came into our house, killed people under our protection. He belongs to the Enforcers now."

He let go of Tanith and Kit's hands. "You should have another bottle of blood," he said to Kit.

"I'll get it." Maia offered.

Kit turned to her. "You don't have to do that. I will come upstairs. I feel much better now." She looked a bit puzzled. "Better than I've ever felt in my life actually."

"I'm so glad, but you can't make it up the stairs without support. You can hardly stand up by yourself." Maia held out her hand to Kit.

"Ms. Severn is right, Kit." Tanith said quietly. "Go along." Kit could not ignore Tanith's orders. Finally, she took Maia's hand and obediently followed her upstairs.

Demon watched her go with an odd expression on his face. Tanith touched his arm. He looked down at her. "Thank you," she said.

He frowned. "For what?"

"For caring about my people, even if they are Nightwalkers." She stood on tiptoe and lightly kissed him on the mouth. Then she followed Kit and Maia up the stairs.

Riot and Kaz went out to find the remainder of Tanith's people and bring them back to the house before dawn. They freaked out a little when they discovered that many of their friends were dead. Once they realized that they had not been executed Enforcer-style they calmed down and helped us clean. At least, those who didn't get sick did.

The clean up took a lot longer than the vampires had to be awake. Just before daybreak, Demon sent them off to bed while the rest of us continued to scrub blood off the walls and fix broken furniture. Demon tried to convince Kit and Kaz to get some rest, but they refused.

"I don't think I could close my eyes right now without seeing—" Kaz broke off shaking his head. Demon didn't say anything more about going to bed, but he and Bane insisted on cleaning up in the basement by themselves. Kit and Kaz didn't argue.

By noon, we were finished. I helped the twins stow the bodies in one of the few windowless rooms that had a closet. After we carried the last body in, Bane closed the door. Demon pulled out his cell phone but instead of flipping it open, he stood staring at it. There was a look of horror on his face. He was probably seeing the same thing that we were, bodies hacked to pieces and covered in blood. Kit and Kaz, covered in blood.

Bane waited for him to pull himself together, but when Demon didn't move after a minute or two, he touched his brother's arm. "Demon, are you okay?"

Demon gave himself a little shake and his expression went blank. "Yes, of course. I'm fine."

"Did you forget Nightscare's number?" I asked.

Demon scowled at me, looking more like his usual self. "No." He dialled the number.

Bane and I went upstairs leaving him to deal with the Boogeys. When we reached the top, Serkan was standing there. "Where is Fechín?" he demanded.

Bane and I exchanged looks. "He's in the basement calling Nightscare to come and get the bodies." Bane told him.

Serkan started to push past us and Bane caught his arm. "Don't. Serkan, don't."

"Did you happen to notice that Kit was up after daybreak?" Serkan demanded of Bane.

"Yes." Bane admitted.

"She said that she raised the moon. You know what that means. Did you know about this?"

"No."

Serkan made a noise that sounded suspiciously like "humph." "Okay, I admit that I didn't even think about it." I said. "How the hell did Kit manage that?"

"There is a legend that when two vampires feed from each other at the same time they can, temporarily, become Daywalkers. This is called raising the moon."

"They feed at the same time as what?" I asked with a slight smile.

Serkan nodded slightly. "Yes, they usually do it during sex."

"Does it work?" I asked curiously.

Serkan shook his head. "Any vampires that I know of who have tried it have all died attempting it."

I frowned. "Wait a minute. You think that Demon and Kit—"

"You're overreacting." Bane told him. "They may not have raised the moon at all." Serkan gave him an incredulous look and Bane shook his head. "No, even I don't believe that."

"You are not taking this seriously enough, Bane." Serkan said.

"You can walk in the daylight too." I said. "So what happened? Did you raise the moon?"

Serkan hesitated and shook his head. "No. My ability is from a different cause."

"Does it have something to do with the fact that you're Demon and Bane's father?" I asked quietly.

Bane bit his lip and darted a look of panic at Serkan. Serkan stared at me. "How did you know?" he asked.

"I guessed." I admitted. "Something has been bothering me for a few days and last night when I saw your eyes flame up like that, the thought crossed my mind that the twins really look like you." I shrugged. "I put two and two together and came up with a father. So does that have something to do with you being a Daywalker?"

"No. Demon once fed me in order to save my life. Just drinking some of his blood is what gave me this ability. Demon did not feed from me."

"Kit also fed from Demon when he rescued her." Bane pointed out. "Maybe—" His eyes widened. "Oh, crap. What if, to achieve this ability one just has to feed from the true Daywalker?"

"You mean that any vampire could become a Daywalker just by feeding from Demon?" I gasped.

The three of us stared at each other, appalled by the implications.

"We thought that it worked for me because I am Demon's father." Serkan said. "We thought my blood might have something to do with it. We could not be sure. But, if he was able to turn Kit into a Daywalker too, then it is entirely possible that this could work with anyone."

Bane looked worried. "That is not something we would want to get around. If other vampires find out, we will have major problems."

"Yes." Serkan said quietly. "Vampires would be hunting Demon in order to steal some of his blood."

"They won't be gentle about it either." I said. Of course, it would probably get them executed, but they might risk it anyway just on the off chance that they could escape and become Daywalkers too. Some vampires wouldn't be more dangerous that way, but the ones who would risk all to get that blood are the ones who would be.

"Can I ask you a question?" I said to Bane. "Why didn't you tell us that Serkan is your father?"

"It was safer for Serkan to have no association with us. If the people we hunt knew who he was, they might try to use him against us." Bane said.

"That makes sense." I said. "I don't like the idea of Serkan being a criminal's hostage either. Don't worry. I won't tell anyone."

Bane smiled. "I did not think that you would, Dev."

"I do think the other Deadlies ought to be told though." I said. "It isn't fair for us to be working in the dark like this. They should know the risks of a vampire getting his hands on Serkan or Demon or even Kit."

"I don't think that Kit's or my blood could be used that way." Serkan pointed out.

"The vampires just might try it anyway." I said.

"Okay, fair enough." Bane agreed. "I'll talk to Demon."

"Ah, yes. I almost forgot." Serkan said. His eyes glittered with anger as he started for the basement steps and I had a feeling that Demon was in for a fatherly lecture.

Bane must have thought the same because he grabbed his arm to stop him. "Serkan," he said in a low voice. "It would not be wise to confront him right now."

"Confront whom?" Demon's voice asked coldly. We turned. He was standing in the basement doorway, glaring at us.

"Did you raise the moon with Kit?" Serkan demanded.

Bane winced. "Way to be tactful there, Serkan."

"I do not feel tactful." Serkan snapped. "Do you know what you have done?"

"This is none of your business, Serkan." Demon said. "I am a grown man."

"But—"

"Drop it, please."

"Very well," Serkan said stiffly. "But, you are making a mistake. You are my son and I love you."

A look of guilt crossed Demon's face. "Serkan, I'm sorry. I didn't mean to be rude."

Serkan looked guilty too. "I am sorry too," he said in a gentle tone. "I shouldn't have jumped on you. You are right. You are grown up now. Sometimes, I forget." He sounded wistful.

"Get some rest," Demon said gruffly. "It has been a long day."

Serkan shook his head. "Indeed it has, and you have had less sleep than anyone."

"I don't need to sleep."

Serkan flared up instantly. "Like hell, you don't! You look like crap!"

Demon scowled at him. "*Thanks.* You look ready to fall over yourself. Go to bed."

Serkan crossed his arms over his chest. "I will go to sleep when you do."

"That is so childish!"

"That is the deal."

"Boy, now I know where you get it." I murmured to Demon.

Demon gave me a cold look and then sighed. All of his energy seemed to drain out of him and he looked exhausted. "All right, Serkan, you win. Let's finish cleaning up and go to bed."

"The clean-up is done." I told him.

"Go to bed, Demon." Serkan said gently.

Demon nodded tiredly. "Okay, maybe for a few hours."

Serkan, Bane, and I followed Demon up the stairs. He turned at his doorway, frowning. "Where is everyone else?" he asked.

"They went to bed an hour ago." I told him.

"Quit stalling." Bane growled at him. "We're not leaving this hallway until you go to bed."

Demon rolled his eyes and disappeared into his room. Bane's room and mine were on either side of Demon's room. I started back to my room. Bane went to his. He started to open his bedroom door then, realized that Serkan was still standing outside Demon's room.

"Serkan," Bane said. "I thought you were going to bed."

Serkan nodded at the door. "I will once I am sure that he will stay put."

Bane and I exchanged looks. "Good luck." I told him. Bane went into his room and I opened the door to mine. I stepped inside and closed the door. I turned and stopped dead in my tracks.

"Maia?"

CHAPTER TWENTY-THREE

"WHAT ARE YOU DOING in here?" I admit that I was somewhat dumbfounded to find her in my bed and apparently unclothed. Her eyes opened sleepily and she sat up.

I made a strangled noise as the blankets slid down her body, exposing her breasts. I turned my head, trying to slow my breathing as she groped for modesty. "I'm sorry," she said. I risked a peek and was intensely disappointed that she had pulled the blankets over her shoulders. "I gave my room to Kit and I didn't know where else to go."

"Why isn't Kit in the catacombs with Tanith?" I asked.

Maia made a face. "She doesn't want to be down there right now. Can you blame her?"

Hell, no. *I* didn't want to be down there after seeing the walls splattered with her and Kaz' blood. I couldn't imagine what it would be like for them, but Kaz didn't have to go down there to sleep.

"It was nice of you to offer Kit your room." I said.

She smiled. "You could be nice too and let me sleep in your bed."

"Yeah, that's fine. No problem." I started to back up toward the door. "I'll just go and see if Demon or Bane wouldn't mind if I slept on their floor."

She sighed in exasperation. "I could be even nicer and let you stay here with me," she said quietly.

181

Oh, shit. "I don't think that's a good idea." I said.

"Here I was thinking that it was the best idea anyone had had all day." Maia said playfully.

"You are killing me." I told her agonized. "I don't think I can sleep with you in my bed, Maia."

Her eyes met mine. "I wasn't intending to sleep."

I started toward the bed and then stopped. I was determined that I was not going to take advantage of an exhausted woman, even one who was as hot as Maia was. She smiled as if she understood what I was thinking. "Dev." she said softly.

"Yes?"

She threw back the covers. "Come to bed."

That was all the encouragement I needed. I caught sight of one long, tanned leg and the struggle was over. I walked to the bed and Maia rose to meet me. Her arms slid around my neck. She kissed me gently and drew me down to the bed with her.

"I love kissing you. You taste so good, Dev." she sighed.

I lifted my head to look at her and smiled. "Let's see if you taste as good."

I began to kiss my way down her body. "Mmm," I traced my mouth over her breasts. "Delicious."

"Dev." Her breath caught.

"I love you, Maia." I laughed softly and continued to move downward.

"I love you too." she sighed.

I felt a hand caress my shoulder and I cracked open one eye. It was dark outside now. Moonlight streamed into the room, casting everything with a silver glow. I rolled over and sat up abruptly. "Oh, shit! How long have I been asleep?"

"Not long actually." Maia told me. "It has only been about an hour."

I looked down at her, surprised. "It couldn't be. It was daylight when I fell asleep."

She laughed. "It was almost nightfall then! We've been making love most of the afternoon." She gave me a sultry though tired smile.

I felt as though I had run twelve marathons but that smile made me consider running the thirteenth. I reached for her and someone knocked on the door.

"Damn it!" I exclaimed as my mouth moved over her belly.

Maia moaned. "I agree. Don't answer." Her breath caught as my lips skimmed her inner thigh.

182

"If I don't, they'll break in thinking that Scarletti got us." I told her ruefully as I sat up. "You'd better cover up and I'll get rid of whoever is at the door. And it had better not be Riot."

Maia laughed as I yanked on some pants. I stalked to the door and flung it open glaring at Kaz who leaned against the wall. "What do you want?" I snapped.

"Daedalus is in the library." Kaz said. "He has news about Scarletti. Where is Maia?"

She appeared behind me wrapped in a sheet from the bed. Kaz stared at her blankly. "Oh." Then a smile slid over his face. "*Oh.*"

I pointed a finger at him. "One word about this to Riot and I'll beat you senseless. Tell Demon I'll be there in five minutes."

Behind me, I heard a muffled giggle and Maia's soft mouth kissed my shoulder. I stifled a gasp. "Make that a half hour."

Maia's giggle turned into a soft moan and she traced my shoulder blade with her tongue. I felt my eyes glazing over. "An hour. Just give me one hour." I slammed the door in Kaz' astonished face. I turned to scoop Maia up and carried her back to bed.

"Demon's going to *kill* me." I muttered as I hastily shoved my legs into my pants.

"I doubt it." Maia said languidly. She was sprawled in the bed with a dreamy grin on her face.

I stopped for a moment with my pants at my thighs and debated getting back into the bed. No, that is what got me into this in the first place. Demon was going to kill me despite Maia's assurances. I yanked my pants the rest of the way up.

"I told him an hour." I reminded her, groaning. "It's been," I checked the clock and stifled another groan. "Two hours and forty minutes. You've been making love to a dead man."

Maia laughed and sat up. "You felt pretty lively to me," she teased. I made a move toward her. "No." She shook her head, smiling. "I know what you're thinking."

"Oh yeah," I challenged. "You think so?"

She smiled. "I know so because it's the same thing that *I* am thinking. But you'd better get downstairs."

"If I don't come back alive I just want you to know that this was the most amazing afternoon of my life." I sighed.

Maia burst into laughter and I left the room before I invited myself back into the bed. I almost made it into the library before Demon came out of the room and into the hallway. He closed the door behind him and started for the stairs. He stopped when he saw me on my way down.

"I know! I'm late. I'm sorry." I said as I reached the bottom.

"*Really* late." He smiled. "You don't look like you're not sorry at all."

"So you're a mind reader now?" I asked.

Demon laughed. "If that big grin on your face is any indication, you have good reason not to be sorry."

I grinned back sheepishly. "Yeah."

Demon looked at the floor and then, glanced up at me, his smile gone. "Dev?"

"Yeah?"

"I am very happy for you and Maia."

I smiled, a little embarrassed. "Thanks, Demon."

I followed him into the library. Daedalus and Medea were waiting for us. Daedalus flicked an impatient look at me. I got the impression that he had wanted to start the meeting without me, and Demon wouldn't let him.

"Are we all ready now?" he asked sarcastically.

Demon didn't answer immediately. He stared at Daedalus steadily for a moment and then walked around behind the desk to sit down. With a careless gesture toward a chair, inviting them to sit, he took control of the meeting, disregarding Daedalus' annoyance.

"All right, Daedalus," Demon said. "Tell us what happened with Scarletti."

Undaunted by Demon's cool tone, Daedalus sat back in his chair. I wondered if he would forget and lean back too far. I admit I was half hoping that he would fall on his ass. If he did, I knew I would never be able to stop myself from laughing. It wasn't because I was resentful. Daedalus' sarcasm hadn't upset me. I was too much the daemon myself to be offended. This was just my immature side peeking out.

Embarrassed, I darted a look around to make sure that no one was watching me watch Daedalus. Apparently, I wasn't the only childish idiot in the room. Bane was leaning forward in his chair also watching Daedalus intently. His expression practically screamed, "Fall! Lean back and fall on your ass! Oh, *please!*" Bane looked over and caught me watching him. We exchanged sheepish grins. We glanced back at Daedalus as he finally tried to lean back and almost fell. He managed to right himself before he hit the floor, much to our disappointment. I heard Bane stifle a groan. I had to look away before I burst into laughter.

"We had two of our officers staking out Cooper's place. I sent two of our daemon officers that look human so Scarletti wouldn't become suspicious if he saw them." Daedalus explained. "They didn't see Scarletti but about 9:00 PM or so, Cooper left the apartment building. One of the officers followed him in case he was going to meet Scarletti."

"He didn't?" Demon asked.

Daedalus shook his head. "Cooper went to a restaurant and ordered take-out. Then he stopped at a liquor store for some wine. He picked up a lady friend after that and they went to a movie rental place."

"Who covered the apartment while Cooper was out?" Demon asked.

Daedalus sighed. "Jordis was the one who stayed behind. She called about fifteen minutes after Cooper left and said that she had seen someone go into the building that looked like our boy. I told her not to approach him without backup, but unfortunately the guy she had seen was already gone before back-up arrived."

"Does she know where he went?" I asked. "Did he go to Cooper's apartment?"

"She thinks that he did because she saw the light from the outside hallway when the door opened. He didn't turn the lights on in the apartment but she thought she saw a shadow moving around inside." Daedalus said. "Unfortunately, she didn't see him leave again. She is still staking out Cooper's place or she would have come out to give you her report herself." He shot a look at Riot and for some reason I didn't believe Daedalus' explanation.

"I was one of the back-up officers." Medea added. "We searched the building, but found no sign of Scarletti. If we had been able to make contact with Cooper we could have asked to search his apartment for clues, but Jordis tells us that he would probably go into hysterics if we approached him."

"She's right, he would. Damn." Demon said softly. He looked up at Daedalus. "Well, Scarletti is ours now. We'll get him."

"I don't think that is a good idea." Daedalus frowned. "I am sorry that he got away, Fechín. However, I think it would be a mistake to give him to the Enforcers."

"Why is that?"

"I know what he did to your friend and I understand you wanting revenge, but that is not the way to deal with Scarletti."

"My friend?" Demon asked.

"The girl. What's her name? The beschermer."

Demon stiffened. "Her name is Kit and she is not my friend."

Daedalus looked confused. "I thought Kaz said—"

Demon glared at Kaz who seemed uneasy and wouldn't meet Demon's eyes. "Kaz is mistaken." Demon said coldly.

Kaz slunk behind me. "Hey, don't hide behind me!" I protested softly.

"I'm hoping that he won't throw something because he might hit you." Kaz hissed back.

"That's not going to help." I whispered. "You're taller than I am and he has really good aim."

"Who is this Kit anyway?" Daedalus was asking.

Demon shrugged. "She is Tanith's beschermer."

"No, I mean who is she to you?"

Demon hesitated. Finally, he said, "I rescued her from a vampire many years ago."

Daedalus waited for more information, but seeing none was forthcoming, he shrugged. "That's it?"

"That is it."

"So, you are ready to hunt Scarletti down yourself and execute him because he almost killed a woman who is not your friend?"

Demon hesitated. Daedalus smiled and shook his head. "You are fooling yourself, Fechín."

"Scarletti is a vampire and an attempted murderer." Demon pointed out. "That makes him ours."

"Yeah, and you once knew and cared about the woman he tried to kill," Daedalus said as he got to his feet. "And that makes it personal."

"I never said that I cared about her." Demon said stiffly.

"You didn't have to."

Demon rose as well. "He goes on the execution list just like anyone else would." he insisted.

"Fechín, I have known you a long time. I have to admit, I have never seen you execute out of revenge."

"This is not about revenge." Demon crossed his arms over his chest. "He should have been on our list from the beginning. The only reason we hesitated was for Maia's sake. I think that even she would agree that Scarletti has crossed the line and should be executed."

"We can do that."

Demon shook his head. "Your officers don't have enough training to deal with someone in Scarletti's state of mind. One of them will get hurt. I do not wish to see anyone else harmed."

"Me either. How about this," Daedalus was in negotiation mode now. "Give us a week to keep investigating the case. If we cannot find him, then we will turn him over to you."

Demon shook his head. "That is not good enough. He is after Maia and determined to have her. He has proven that he is a danger to her and anyone else that gets in his way. Six vampires died here, Daedalus. They were innocent."

"Do you think Scarletti might hurt Maia?"

"We don't know what he has been doing for the last twenty-four hours since the attack here. Kaz said he looked insane. Cooper described a vampire that has not fed in a while. If Scarletti isn't feeding then the danger has increased tenfold. That is why he needs to go on the list."

Daedalus struggled to come up with another reason, but he had run out. Finally, he nodded. "All right, Fechín. He goes on the list. He belongs to the Enforcers now."

He took a last look at Demon's dark expression and glowing eyes and shook his head. "Poor sonofabitch."

CHAPTER TWENTY-FOUR

DAEDALUS WAS STILL RELUCTANT as he handed over everything that they had on Scarletti. There was more than one file and I expressed surprise to find that they had so much information on a human police officer. "We have been watching him for years." Daedalus admitted. "We started taking notes when we started working with Maia actually. While we trust her, we did not trust him."

"I know he's a jerk, but why didn't you trust him?" I asked.

Daedalus shrugged. "The Enforcers didn't trust him and, more importantly, Fechín didn't trust him. He is suspicious of everyone at first, but he never warmed up to Scarletti. There had to be a damned good reason. The rest of you didn't like him either. It looks as though you guys were right on the money."

"I didn't realize that we were your bad guy barometers."

"That is why you are the Enforcers." Daedalus shrugged again. "You must have been picking up something from him that put you off."

I had never sensed any Sloth coming from Mike. My dislike of him had to do with a different type of Deadly entirely. However, I had never asked the others if they sensed any of their particular Deadlies from him.

After Daedalus and Medea left, we sat down to plan our strategy for hunting down and executing Mike Scarletti. Demon teamed up with Onyx and Riot since Scarletti's strongest emotions were most likely to be wrath, jealousy, and lust.

They would be able to follow those emotions. It would not be easy, however, since those three "sins" are quite common throughout the human and supernatural races. Sifting through the morass of emotions would take some time and that was something we did not have.

"We have another problem now." Demon went on. "We have been compromised. Scarletti still knows where we are. Unlike Cooper, I had no opportunity to erase that piece of information from his mind." He shook his head. "I should have done it before I let him go the first time, but I didn't think he would ever come back."

"What are we going to do then?" Bane asked. "Scarletti isn't exactly close to the other vampires in town so I doubt that he is going to pass the information on to any other bloodsuckers."

Demon smiled slightly. "I was more concerned about him using the information himself."

"Are we going to have to move?" Onyx sighed.

"I'm sure Rowan would be happy to put up some invisibility wards for us." Kaz offered. "He wouldn't be able to find us then."

"Oh no," Demon said. "I want him to be able to find *us*. I just don't want him to find anyone else living here."

Demon got to his feet and moved around the desk to join us. "It is clear that Tanith and her vampires cannot stay here. Even if he isn't after them in particular, they are in danger as long as they are here. They can move to a new place and Scarletti will probably leave them alone."

"Are you thinking about putting them up in one of our safe houses in Blackridge?" Riot asked.

"No. I don't want Tanith or any of her people knowing where those houses are and Scarletti could still find her there."

That is a bad thing?" Bane sneered.

"We don't have to like her." Demon told him. "But, we do have to protect her. Tanith probably has a hideout aside from the one that burned. Most vampires do. The people who did not come here are most likely there now waiting for her. Some of them may be in with the rogue sovereign so I am going to suggest that she make contact with them, but not join them until we clear up this business. She will have to find somewhere else to stay."

"Then, might I make a suggestion?" Serkan said. "I will take them to my house."

We all turned to stare at him. "That is out of the question." Demon said firmly.

"She will be safe there with me, Demon."

"Yes, but will you be safe with her?"

"I can take care of myself. Besides, you have nowhere else for her to go. Scarletti is not likely to find her at my house."

"It's a good idea." Bane added. "Serkan can keep an eye on her."

Demon looked as though he was going to fight it but then he shrugged. "Okay. Serkan, you are in charge of Tanith and her vampires." He looked at me.

"Maia can't stay here either because she *is* Scarletti's target." I said grimly. I had known that without Demon having to tell me.

"Are we going to hide Maia at the safe house then?" Riot asked.

Demon shook his head. "No, I want her as far away from Blackridge as possible, but not so far that we can't get to her if we need to. We want some place that Scarletti will never think to look for her."

"I know a place." I said suddenly.

Demon had talked Tanith into staying away from her people for a short time. She made the phone call to tell them that she was fine and to ensure that no one else was hurt. She reported that everyone was well and would stay hidden until she came to join them.

We moved everyone during the daylight when there was less chance of Scarletti being able to track us then. He didn't have a human servant so he had no eyes and ears during the day light hours.

Bane, Riot, and I supervised the vampires getting into their coffins and then nailing them shut. Bane made them all nervous and some of them refused to get into their coffins until we reassured them that he was not Wrath. I guess they were worried that Demon would suddenly decide to rip open the coffins and execute everyone.

Once the other vampires settled in for the coming day, we tried to get Tanith to get into her coffin so that we could seal it. She refused, demanding to speak to Demon. Bane swore and then turned to Riot. "Get him," he said shortly.

Riot returned with him a few minutes later. Demon strode into the room. "What is the problem?" he demanded.

Tanith smiled at him and then, she stepped into his arms and kissed him on the mouth, her hands sliding into his hair and pulling him closer. She drew back, still smiling. "There. That is all I needed." she purred.

It took Demon a second to pull himself together. "You called me down here for that?"

Tanith laughed. "Tell me it wasn't worth it."

Demon turned around and went back upstairs without speaking. Tanith was still smiling when she got into the coffin and pulled the lid down. I picked up my hammer and put in a nail. I glanced up at Bane and saw that he was holding his hammer in his hand like a weapon, staring at the lid.

"Don't do it, Bane." I said.

He glanced at me and then picked up a nail, hammering it into the coffin with a little more force than necessary, probably imagining that he was driving through her heart.

Once we finished sealing the vampires in their coffins, the other Deadlies came to help us carry them up the back stairs from the basement to our two vans waiting in the backyard. There were enough coffins that it would require more than one trip to get all the vampires to their temporary home at Serkan's place.

Bane and I shoved the last coffin into one of the vans and Demon closed the back doors. He turned away and I saw his expression change. "What the hell are you doing?" he yelled at someone.

I looked over my shoulder and saw Kit strolling toward us from the basement. Demon looked at us. "I thought you said that they were all sealed in their coffins ready to go?" he said through gritted teeth.

Before we could speak, Kit joined us. "I am going to ride with Tanith's coffin."

"You should have said something before." Demon told her. "She's already inside one of the vans. If you had told us earlier and got into your coffin before we started loading, we could have accommodated you. Now, it's too late."

"Oh, I am not travelling in a coffin." Kit told him. "I will ride in the passenger seat."

Bane and I looked from her to Demon. His expression was cold. "You are not. Go downstairs and get into a coffin."

We looked at Kit. She crossed her arms over her chest. "No."

Bane and I sucked in our breath and looked at Demon again. He took a deep breath, as if to get enough air to yell, but his voice was calm when he spoke. "Kit, it would be better if you would travel in the coffin. Someone might recognize you."

"Look, Demon, unless you are planning to force me into a coffin, I suggest that we get this show on the road. I promise that once we get to Serkan's house, I will remain with Tanith so that you are not burdened with my company longer than absolutely necessary," she said sarcastically.

"It isn't that," he told her. "Scarletti may have someone watching us. If that person sees you riding around in the van in broad daylight, knowing what you are, it could make things dangerous for you."

Kit stared at him, her arms uncrossed. "Oh. Well, I suppose I can understand that, but as you say, it is too late now."

"I suppose it is." Demon said. "By the way, does Tanith know about this ability of yours?"

"You mean does she know that I got it from you? No."

"Does she know about it, period?"

"No. If she ever concludes that we were lovers, she will kill me. She is rather jealous. Although, I could assure her that I was the only one who was in love. That might make her feel better." Kit said dryly.

Demon stared at Kit and then, abruptly, he turned and climbed into the driver's seat of his van, slamming the door closed.

"I'd better get in there." Bane said reluctantly.

"No," Kit said. "Since I am the one who pissed him off I'll ride up front with him." She opened the passenger side door and got in.

I looked at Bane. He shrugged, helplessly and then got into the back with Tanith's coffin, there not being enough room in the rental for all of them. I moved around to the driver side door. Demon was staring straight ahead, grimly. I tapped on the window. He rolled it down and leaned out. "Good luck with Maia." he said. "I'll call to check on you later."

"Okay." I looked passed him to Kit. "Good luck to you, too."

"Thank you." they both said at once and then scowled at each other.

I stepped back as Demon started the van and drove out of the yard. Riot and Kaz came out a few minutes later with Onyx. They hopped into the second a van and drove away. Morgana and Serkan pulled out of the driveway in his car a few minutes later.

I returned to the house to get Maia. I went upstairs to the room she had been sleeping in when she first came. Though she had slept in my room the previous night, all of her clothes were still in the guest room. She looked up as I came in. "I am running out of clothes." she told me.

"Borrow some of Morgana's." I suggested.

"I don't think I would like walking around in black leather all day."

I grinned. "I wouldn't mind."

"I know you wouldn't." She smiled back. "But, in this heat, I would keel over within an hour."

"Well, there is a washer and dryer where we're going." I told her. "You have enough for a week stay, don't you?"

"Well, yes," she admitted. "But, it would only take a second for us to stop at my apartment."

"Scarletti could have someone watching it, Maia. I am not going to take that chance."

She sighed and closed her suitcase. "Okay, I guess I'll make do."

Just in case I slipped one of Morgana's black leather halter tops and pants into Maia's suitcase when she went to the kitchen for something.

I carried Maia's suitcase to the car. Our destination was an old two-storey Victorian house about a fifteen-minute drive from our place. Maia parked Demon's car in the driveway and stared up at the yellow brick house. "Wow." she murmured, her eyes alight with admiration. "This is some house."

I smiled. "You like it?"

"I love it! It's like something out of a book!" she exclaimed.

I had to laugh. "Wait until you meet the owner. She's like no character you'll ever meet between the pages of a novel, I guarantee."

We walked up to the front porch together. She stood behind me while I rang the doorbell. A short, curvaceous woman with a long blond ponytail, wearing a tight black tank top and denim short shorts answered the door. Her skin appeared to be that of a normal human. Her red-brown eyes lit up when she saw us and her skin returned to its natural daemon-red colouring. She looked about my age so I'm sure anyone would have been shocked when she greeted me with "Dev! My precious little boy!" in a thick British accent and embraced me enthusiastically.

I heard Maia choking back a laugh and grimaced. "Hi, Mom."

My mother beamed at me and then at Maia. "Well, luv," she said to me. "Aren't you going to introduce us?"

"Mom, may I introduce Maia Severn. Maia, this is my mother, Maggie."

"Welcome, Maia. Dev talks about you *all* the time!" my mother told her.

Maia gave me a sidelong look. I blushed. "Not *all* the time." I mumbled.

"Don't you believe him, luv," my mother declared. "He's shy."

I glared at Maia as she tried to choke back a laugh. Grinning, Maia extended her hand politely. "It's so nice to meet you, Mrs. Xander."

"My dear girl, please call me Maggie!" My mother embraced Maia as enthusiastically as she had me. Maia gaped at me, confounded. I gave her a smug grin. Sometimes, I forget how overwhelming my mother can be. Maia didn't quite know what to do with my mother. A lot of people had that problem; not the least of those had been my father. Maybe I'm just biased, but there isn't a sweeter, gentler, kinder woman on Earth.

"Um…Dev?" Maia gasped.

"Mom, let up. She can't breathe." I said, laughing outright now. Maia glared at me over my mother's shoulder.

"Don't be silly, Dev." Mom said. "Of course she can breathe." My mother released her abruptly and Maia sucked in air. "See?"

"Well, then! Don't just stand there gaping like two fish!" my mother went on. "Come in!" We followed her into the house and I closed the door behind us.

"I have your rooms ready!" Mom announced as she bustled up the stairs.

"Your mother's British?" Maia asked as we started up the stairs.

I shook my head. "Nope, my father was British. I guess Maggie picked up the accent from him and just never lost it. She is Norwegian. *Old* Norwegian, I think."

"You think?"

"It's been so long that I doubt even my mother remembers anymore. All I know is that her father was some Norse god."

"Your grandfather is a Norse god?" Maia squeaked. "Which one is he?"

I shrugged. "Mom said his name was Balder. He died a long time ago so I never met him. Another god killed him in a jealous rage."

"Balder, the Fairest of the gods," Maia murmured.

"You've heard of him?" I asked surprised.

Maia hesitated. "Well," she began. "I do know a thing or two about gods."

"Like what—wait a minute!" I stopped short on the stairs. "Mom, did you say *rooms*?"

My mother turned back halfway up the stairs. "Well, of course! You can't stay in the same room, Dev! You aren't married!"

I gaped at her. Surely, she understood how ridiculous that sounded coming from her. "You have to be joking! You're a *succubus!*"

"I know that, luv, but Maia is human," my mother pointed out as if I didn't know that. "They have a very different point of view about premarital sex."

I rolled my eyes. "Mom, we aren't living in Puritan times anymore."

"Thank goodness!" Mom shuddered. "But, really, Dev, what would Maia's mother say?"

Maia cleared her throat. "Actually, Mrs. Xander—er—Maggie, since we're making confessions about our families, I should tell you that my mother is well aware of my relationship with Dev."

I gaped at Maia. "*She is?*"

Maia nodded. "She wanted to know why I wouldn't marry Mike so I had to tell her all about you."

"What exactly did you tell her?"

"I told her that I was in love with a Deadly."

Oh, boy. "How did she take it?"

Maia grinned. "Better than you think obviously. You're already cringing." Her expression turned serious. "She's okay with it, Dev. She knew about the Deadlies long before I became involved with you."

I was amazed. "How could she possibly know who we are?"

"She's a supernatural, Dev. She's a witch."

I still couldn't believe that Maia's mother was a witch. I had known Maia for years and I'd had no clue that she was the offspring of a supernatural. To top it off, her mother wasn't just any supernatural, she was Ceridwen, half-sorceress and half-goddess. Maia's father had been mortal, like mine. When I asked about her parents, many years ago, she told me that her father was dead but she had never mentioned her mother. Now it turned out that her mother was alive and probably as old as my own mother was.

"Are you okay with this?" Maia whispered. We were sitting at the counter in the kitchen sipping cold soft drinks while my mother held an enthusiastic conversation over the phone with Maia's mother.

"Well," I whispered back. "On the pro side, you're not mortal so I won't ever have to worry about you dying."

"Dev, that's so sweet!"

"And due to your mother being a goddess and therefore liberal in her notions about sex, my mother is going to let us share a bed after all."

She rolled her eyes. "What's on the con side?"

"If we ever get into an argument, your mother will turn me into a toad."

Maia began to laugh and my mother beamed at us. "Maia," she announced. "Your mother says to tell you that any man who makes you laugh like that is one that you should hold onto."

Maia smiled at me. "I always do what my mother tells me," she remarked turning on her stool to wrap her arms around my neck. She lifted her lips to mine.

"You're such a good daughter." I told her and kissed her.

CHAPTER TWENTY-FIVE

I WENT OUT TO the car and brought in the luggage while Maia assisted my mother in the kitchen making dinner, which was an oddity in itself. Maggie had picked up one of the human traditions that stated that guests did not help in preparing, serving, or cleaning up after a meal unless they were a family member. For some reason, when Maia offered, my mother took her up on it. I didn't ask why. I had a suspicion that the answer might make me panicky.

While I was putting the bags in our bedroom, the phone rang. Seconds later, I heard my mother call out to me. "It's Fechín, luv!"

I picked up the extension in the bedroom. "Hey, Fechín."

"Everything all right there?"

"Yeah, no problem," I said. "What about you? Everyone settled?"

"Yes." he said flatly. Then he changed the subject back. "No sign of Scarletti?"

"It's still too early for him to be up and about."

"What about Cooper?"

"Cooper? I didn't see—"

"The house and perimeter checked out then?"

It took me a minute to figure out what he was getting at. "Oh, shit. I mean, um...sure," I stammered.

There was a brief pause and then I heard Demon sigh. "Dev, check out the house and perimeter."

"Okay," I said meekly.

"And call me tomorrow morning at seven and let me know that you and Maia are still okay."

"Aw, you're worried about us. That's so sweet."

There was another pause. "Get some sleep, Dev. You're hallucinating."

I grinned. "Good night, Fechín."

Demon hung up and I sat down to relax for a few minutes. Demon was right. I was a bit tired.

I must have dozed off because the next thing I knew, Mom was shaking me and telling me that dinner was ready. I followed her into the dining room. Maia was waiting for us with a table so loaded down with food I couldn't see the tablecloth.

"Holy shit, Mom!" I gasped. "Were you expecting all of the Deadlies?"

"Dev, language!" Mom reprimanded me. "I haven't cooked for you in a long time, but I remember how you eat. I was worried that I didn't have *enough*."

Maia laughed and we sat down to eat.

Usually, I would have had no trouble packing away a third or even a fourth plate of food, but after about two bites from my first plate, I started yawning and couldn't seem to stop.

"For goodness sake, luv," my mother said. "What is the matter with you?"

My eyes snapped opened and I realized that I had dropped my fork on the floor and my hand was in my mashed potatoes and gravy.

"He's exhausted." Maia explained. She reached out and pushed back a strand of hair that had fallen in my eyes. "I don't think he has slept very well in the last two days."

Mom gave me one of her looks that told me I was in for a maternal lecture. "Dev, you should have gone right to bed!" she scolded.

"I'm fine, Mom." I assured her and yawned. My eyes drifted shut again. "Just give me a minute."

"Maia, put this boy to bed while I go and make some coffee. You and I can have nice long chat over dessert."

I heard a chair scrape back from the table and opened my eyes. My mother was gone and Maia was beside my chair, holding out her hand to me. "Come on, Dev."

"Really, Maia, I'm okay. I just need a cup of Mom's coffee. Believe me I'll be awake for days after a cup of that stuff."

"You're tired, Dev. You don't need coffee. You need bed. Let's go." she said firmly.

Obediently, I took her hand and allowed her to lead me up the stairs to our bedroom. I collapsed into bed and Maia covered me up. As she started to leave, I caught her hand and pulled her down on top of me. "I'm not *that* tired." I said, smiling.

Maia smiled back and kissed me on the cheek. "Good night, Dev." she said gently disentangling herself from my arms and getting up.

"But, I brought that leather outfit along." I protested as my eyes closed and I don't remember another damned thing until the next morning.

I awoke to find myself alone in the bed again. I was sure that Maia had been there at some point because I could still feel where her warm body had pressed against mine. I sighed. So much for my plans for the morning. I tossed back the blankets and sat up. Then, I caught sight of the clock.

Nine-thirty.

"Shit!"

I yanked on my pants and raced down the stairs barefoot. I screeched to a halt in the kitchen. Maia and Mom were sitting at the kitchen island sipping coffee. They looked up in alarm. "Dev, what is it?" Maia gasped.

"I'm late!" I told her. "Damn it! Demon is going to kill me!"

"What are you late for?" Mom asked, puzzled. She immediately started to pour out a cup of coffee that was so strong that it practically oozed out of the coffeepot. She frowned into the mug and then grimaced and dumped the contents into the sink. "I'll make a fresh pot."

"I was supposed to call him two and a half hours ago!" I snatched up the phone. I glanced at the two women. "You might want to leave." I told them grimly. "I don't want you to hear the language that he's going to use when he answers."

"He called already." Maia told me.

I paused in mid-dial with the phone in my hand and winced. "Aw, shit. What did he say?"

"Dev, *language!*" my mother scolded.

Maia turned her head and tried to hide her smile. She failed miserably. I glared at her. "Why yes, I am getting a lecture from my mommy. What of it?" I demanded.

Maia burst into laughter and then put her hand on mine as she leaned in to give me kiss. She drew back still smiling. "I told Fechín that you were asleep," she explained. "He wasn't angry."

"If you are trying to shield my delicate sensibilities, save it," I told her. "What did he really say? Or can't you repeat it?"

She laughed. "He said that he overslept."

"*Demon* overslept?" I said incredulously.

"Well, the poor boy hasn't slept in days," my mother said as she scooped some coffee grounds into a filter. I'm no judge but it looked like *a lot* of coffee. "After all, you overslept too."

I shook my head. "You don't understand. I'm Sloth. They expect me to oversleep. Demon *never* oversleeps. Half the time we can't even convince him to go to bed when he has already been up for days."

Maia's eyes twinkled. "He did say that they forced him to bed about five o'clock this morning."

I gaped at her. "Who had the nerve to try *that*?"

"It sounds as though they ganged up on him. Riot and Kaz dragged him up the stairs and tossed him into the bed. Bane sat on him to keep him there."

I paused and let that image sink in. "Are they in little pieces all over the house?" I asked, grinning.

Maia smiled back. "I heard them yelling at him in the background so I am assuming that they're still alive—pissed off, but alive."

Hmm. This was interesting. Now I was eager to talk to Demon to find out what revenge he had exacted. It was always fun when it was happening to someone else. I waited until after breakfast however and then, armed with a cup of Mom's lethal coffee, I wandered into the den to make the call.

"Hello!" Demon's voice snarled after the second ring.

Uh oh. "Hello, Fechín?"

"Oh. Uh no, Dev, it's me."

Oh, man. If *Bane* was answering the phone like that, maybe I didn't want to talk to Demon after all. "Maia said you had some excitement over there last night." I began cautiously as I sat down behind the desk.

"You have no idea." Bane replied dryly.

"What happened?" I took a sip of coffee and immediately wrinkled my nose, wishing I had added some milk to water it down some.

"Well for starters," Bane said. "After her Highness woke up she decided that she was not going to stay at the safe house."

Her Highness? "Tanith," I said as the light went on.

"Right."

"Why didn't she want to stay at the safe house?"

"Well, partly because her host wasn't treating her with the respect she felt was due to her."

I could just imagine Serkan's reaction to that. "He is her equal."

"That does not seem to matter to Tanith. I guess they got into it as soon as she woke up. She threw a tantrum when she discovered that Fechín wasn't staying there too. He told her to shut up and sit down."

"I'll bet that went over real well."

"You have no idea. But Tanith refused to stay in the house with him after that." Bane gave a short laugh. "She called Fechín shortly after nightfall and demanded to come back to our house."

"And he said..."

"He told her no. He reminded her that our house is not safe. He also reminded her that since she is attempting to take over Hadrian's kiss it would not be prudent for her to be running around Blackridge making herself a target."

"He didn't say it like that."

"No. He told her that she was an idiot and if Hadrian found her he would take her head off and spit on her body."

"Gross, but it is a good point."

Bane snorted. "For all the good it did him. She is as stubborn as he is. She absolutely refused to stay and finally he got fed up and told her that she could either accept the protection that she had been offered or she could bloody well take care of herself." He paused. "She hung up on him."

"*She hung up on him?*" I gasped. "She's crazy!"

"I thought so."

"So did she leave?"

"Well, about an hour later, Fechín started to worry. You know what he's like. He was pacing and swearing."

"That is never a good sign." Demon only curses when he is under a lot of stress and is seconds away from losing control. It usually ends with him trashing a room.

"Anyway, he called her back." Bane said. "She was still there, apparently getting ready to leave."

I snorted. "She probably had no intention of leaving. She was just messing with him."

"That was my thought too. Usually he doesn't play those games, but one minute he was telling her it is his way or the highway and the next, he has worked himself into a panic over her safety."

"Is it her safety that he's concerned about or Kit's?"

"That is the problem. I am not sure." Bane said gloomily. "I can tell that he is attracted to Kit. I don't mind that so much. I like her. However, I can tell that he is attracted to Tanith also. *That* worries me."

"Me too," I agreed. "So are they still at the safe house?"

"No. He told her that she could stay with us. We went back and brought everyone back about two o'clock this morning."

"You're kidding!" I gasped. "It's not like him to cave in! Where the hell is he anyway?"

"He was still cursing when he got up this morning and since we couldn't send him to the catacombs with our guests, I sent him out to the backyard. The last time I saw him, he was snapping tree branches into firewood. Oh, here he comes. By the way, I would not use the term "cave in" when you are speaking to him."

"I don't think I *want* to talk to him if he's pissed off." I pointed out, tapping my fingers on the desktop.

Demon came on the line. "Did you check the grounds again?" he asked without preamble.

"Good morning to you too."

"Good morning. Did you check the grounds?"

"Not yet. First, I want to know what you did to your brother in return for sitting on you."

"Call me back after you check the grounds and I'll tell you. Bye, Dev."

He hung up. I turned to find Maia standing in the doorway. "Is everything okay?" she asked.

"Yes." I opened my arms and Maia sat on my lap, smiling. She kissed my forehead. "Not exactly what I was looking for, but that will do for now."

She kissed my mouth then. It was slow and sweet. When she lifted her head, she looked happy and slightly dazed. I imagine I had much the same expression on my face. "Where's my mother?" I asked.

"She's in the kitchen."

"Damn."

"Why?"

I ran my hand over her hip. "I had lecherous plans for this morning and I was thwarted." I told her.

She giggled and then sucked in her breath sharply as my hand drifted along her side up to her left breast. "You can still be lecherous. I like it when you're lecherous."

"I know." I grinned. "I really don't want my mother to hear how much you like it."

"She won't. I can be quiet," she suggested.

"No, you *can't.*" I grinned pointedly. "That is why Riot was banging on the bedroom door the other night telling us to give it a rest."

She blushed. "I could *try* to be quiet. Think of it as practice for when we go home." she said.

I laughed. "I wouldn't want you to try to be quiet. I like it when you..." I leaned forward and whispered in her ear.

Fifteen minutes later, we were naked and I was flat on my back on the desk. Maia was straddling my legs and grinning down at me. She leaned down and gently kissed me. "You see? *I* was quiet," she teased.

I groaned. "I notice my mother has the radio in the kitchen cranked." I replied. "When did that happen?"

"Not sure." Maia admitted. "It could have been when we overturned the chair or maybe when we knocked all the books off the shelf when we were—"

"Stop!" I placed my fingers on her lips. "You realize that you're taking advantage of me in my mother's house."

Maia laughed and snuggled against my chest. "Absolutely."

I wrapped my arms around her. "Just checking."

CHAPTER TWENTY-SIX

YOU MAY NOT BELIEVE this, but I bore easily. It isn't that I was bored hanging out with my mother and Maia, but I'm used to a busy household. At home, there is always an execution, a hunt, or some other crisis going on. My mother lives a somewhat normal human life for a succubus. I was finding a bit dull after a couple of days.

By the third day, Mom and Maia got tired of watching me pace and my mother sent me out to the garden to work off some excess energy. This was very brave of her considering that I don't know my aster from a hole in the ground. Mom came outside about an hour later and to her credit, she didn't even wince when she saw the damage I'd wrought on her precious garden. Instead, she sighed and demanded to know what I was doing to her to asters. That is how I learned that an aster is a flower and not a weed.

I was helping Mom replace the flowers when Maia came out and waved at me. Mom looked over at her and then back at me. "Go on, luv. I'll take care of this."

In other words, "get your destructive self away from my damned garden." Sheepishly, I got to my feet and went into the house where Maia was waiting in the kitchen. She looked worried.

"What is it?" I asked as I went to wash my hands in the sink.

"I just got a call from an informant," she told me. "It was the same one who called to tell us about the rogues in the bar."

I wiped my hands off on a kitchen towel and tossed it on the counter. "Yes?"

Maia picked up the towel and draped it over a bar under the sink. "What the hell is that?" I asked, pointing.

"A towel bar." she informed me. Then when she realized that I seriously had no clue what she was talking about, she gaped at me. "You guys have these in the bathrooms at your house. Don't you know what they're for?"

I shrugged. "I thought it was a wall-handle to help me haul my ass off the floor when I slip and fall after a shower."

"You are supposed to hang your wet towels on so that they dry!"

"Oh. I guess that's why they keep breaking away from the wall."

She put her hands on her hips. "*Anyway*," she went on, returning to the more important and less volatile subject. "My informant called and said he had some information for Fechín."

"He's got information about Scarletti?"

"No, it's about the rogue sovereign."

"Does your informant know who the sovereign is?"

"So he says."

"And he *wants* to meet with the Deadlies?" I blurted incredulously. I found that hard to believe. Maia's informants only talked to her under the agreement that she did not give their names to the Enforcers. "Is he a nut?" I asked suspiciously.

"He doesn't actually want to meet with you personally." she admitted. "But he's a solid informant, Dev. He did come forward with the information about the rogues."

"How is he planning to give us this information without meeting with us?"

"He wants me to be the go-between."

"Oh no," I shook my head vehemently. "No way in hell."

"Dev, it's the only way and so far, it's your only lead."

"Why can't he give this information over the phone?" I demanded.

"He's afraid that someone is watching him and tapping his phone."

I snorted. "That is supposed to encourage us to let you go there? We are not going to take chances with your safety, Maia. *I* am not going to take the chance."

"That's very sweet, Dev, but surely we can come up with something that will satisfy everyone," she pleaded.

I thought about that. "Let me talk to Demon and I'll see what I can do, but I am not promising anything." I told her.

Demon had checked in with me a few times over the last few days. They had been out hunting Scarletti and, though I had forgotten about it, I was sure Demon had been keeping an ear to the ground for information about the rogue sovereign. So far, he'd had no luck. I hoped that was about to change.

I gave him the message from Maia's informant and his request that Maia act as a go-between. "No." Demon said.

I sighed. "I can't say that I'm surprised. I told her that you wouldn't go for it."

"I don't like it, Dev." Demon said. His mind must have been running along the same suspicious lines as mine was. "If this information is so important, then why won't the informant meet with us in person?"

"You're an Enforcer and you have to ask that?" I asked incredulously.

"He could just give her the information over the phone."

"I thought of that too, but this guy is completely paranoid. He thinks that people are spying on him. Look, Fechín, I don't like it either, but we have to trust that she knows what she's doing. After all, this is her informant. I'm assuming that she knows him well enough to know whether or not he would set her up."

Demon was quiet for a moment. Finally, he said, "Very well, tell Maia that we agree to the meet but under two conditions. First, it will be during the day and second, one of us will accompany her to the meeting."

"I want to be the one to accompany her." I said immediately.

"I assumed you would." he replied dryly. "It's fine with me. I know you will kill anything that threatens her so she will be as safe with you as she would be with anyone else."

"Thanks."

"Call me back when Maia has a time and place."

He hung up. I went back to the kitchen and relayed the message to Maia. "I'll see what I can do." she said, flipping open her cell phone.

A few minutes later, she hung up and frowned, puzzled.

"What?" I asked. "He didn't agree to the arrangements?"

"I didn't get a chance to ask. He just backed out," she said slowly. "He suddenly got the wind up about something and said it was off."

"You think that the rogue sovereign somehow found out what he was up to and threatened him?"

"But, it's the middle of the day." she pointed out. "How would a vampire find out and be able call him within the last twenty minutes?"

"If this is a sovereign then he or she probably has a human servant." I said.

I called Demon back and told him what had happened. "You're probably right about the servant." He was quiet for a minute and then, he growled, "This makes me wonder where Tanith's human servant is."

"I forgot about that! What was her name?"

"Dagmar something." He went silent again. Then, he said, "Perhaps I should ask Tanith exactly where her servant is. It is a little strange that she has not tried to contact her."

"It looks like Tanith goes back on the suspect list." I said.

"She was never really off it." he replied.

I was very uneasy about the whole thing though I wasn't sure what it was that I suspected. "If Tanith hasn't tried to contact her servant, how does the servant know how to get in touch with her?"

"Perhaps it isn't a servant. It could just as well be a beschermer, one that can walk during the day." Demon said grimly.

"Are you accusing Kit now?" I demanded. "Do you really believe that she take part in rogue activity?"

He sighed. "Hell, Dev, I don't know."

"Well, you should!" I snapped. "Really, Fechín, you're so busy trying to keep her at bay that you aren't looking at this fairly."

"We really don't know her."

"The hell we don't!" I yelled at him. "Damn it, Fechín! She was a friend. You can talk about her as if she is a rogue all you want but I heard you the night she was dying! You were desperate! You love—" I broke off, horrified by the discovery.

"Fechín," I went on in a quieter tone. "I'm sorry. I didn't realize."

For a minute he didn't speak. "Let us drop this subject," he said at last.

"Okay," I said gently. "But, don't you think that you ought to tell her that you love her?"

He was silent again. "If she is involved with the rogues I cannot afford to love her."

"You don't really believe that she is one of them."

"I hope not because I don't think I can kill her." he said abruptly and hung up.

Slowly, I replaced the receiver. That was a more candid admission than I thought I would ever get from Demon. Now that I had it, I didn't know what to do about it. I knew that I couldn't fix this for him. It was something that he would have to figure out for himself. But, would it be before or after he had destroyed any chance of happiness that he might have with Kit?

No sooner had I hung up the phone than I heard Maia hollering from the kitchen. "Um, Dev? Could you please step in here for a moment?"

The panic in her voice had me bursting into the kitchen, blade drawn, in less than three seconds. The cause of her alarm was immediately apparent.

There was a daemon in the kitchen.

He was a bit shorter than I was and stockier. His skin was deep red, but his shaggy hair was blond and his eyes were brown. He would have looked like a daemon version of my father had he not been wearing blue, red and yellow coloured surfboarder shorts and an unbuttoned Hawaiian shirt. He looked from Maia to me with the bewildered, hurt expression of a dog that doesn't understand why his master is scolding him.

"Yo, bro," he said to me. "I just walked in and this strange chick started yelling at me."

I sighed. "This isn't a strange chick. This is Maia Severn, my girlfriend." I turned to her and saw her smiling. I guess she liked the girlfriend part. It did sound nice. I smiled back reassuringly. "Maia, I'd like you to meet my younger brother, Damien."

"Big D." my brother corrected, giving her the "radical, dude" sign.

I rolled my eyes. "*Geez.*"

Maia looked at me as I banged my head against the kitchen counter. "You have a brother?"

"Yes." I groaned. Maia sipped her coffee to hide her smile as I lifted my head from the counter to glare at my brother. "You're not still on that kick, are you? The eighties are over."

"The eighties are never gonna be over, dude!" Damien declared. "The eighties are forever! The eighties are like *immortal,* man!"

I shuddered at the thought of eternal parachute pants and leather jackets covered in zippers. "Frozen in time by ten million pounds of hair gel," I told him sarcastically.

Maia choked and spit coffee on the counter. I pounded her lightly on the back with one hand and mopped up the coffee with the other.

Damien looked from me to her. "Bro." he remarked.

Damien went back outside to "hang" with Mom. I finished cleaning up the coffee and Maia poured herself another cup. She made a few attempts to drink it, but kept having to wait until the fits of giggles had passed. Finally, she gave up. "So," she began, shoving the cup to one side. "You have a brother."

"Yeah," I said, continuing to clean.

"You never told me about him."

"His name is Damien."

"I figured out that much from the introduction," she said wryly. "Any other siblings I should know about?"

"This one is more than enough." I muttered, dropping the wad of paper towels in the garbage can under the sink with the "towel bar." "What is it you want to know about him, Maia?"

She shrugged. "Tell me everything about your family. We know each other so well in every other point, except that one."

"Wow, you don't ask for much, do you?"

"Come on, Dev."

"It's just that I don't like talking about it." I admitted. "My father was a "god-fearing" human, yet he fell in love with a succubus. I doubt Maggie ever told him that was what she was, but he knew that she was not human. When I was born with wings, he flipped. He figured that his god was punishing me for his sins. Of course my mother's choice of a name for me didn't help."

"What was the name?"

I pretended not to hear the question. Like Riot, I am not fond of my daemon name. "My father left us right after I was born." I went on "I didn't even meet him until I was four years old. I guess he thought it was the only way to atone. He couldn't stay away from Maggie though. He loved her too much. Damien was a last ditch effort on my parents part to reconcile. It didn't work out. Take one look at Damien and you can see why. He is more daemon than I am even with the black wings. Maggie tried to give Damien as human a name as possible. She had learned her lesson with me, but it still didn't make any difference. My father just couldn't cope."

"My mother never really understood the whole "god" thing. The only gods and goddesses she knew were her father and his family." I replied. "Maggie tried to convince him that any god worthy of the name would never command a man to stop caring for the children he created no matter what they looked like."

"Good for her!"

"She tried. I will give her that, but he didn't listen to her. We never saw him again. Damien never even got to meet his own father." I paused, the familiar surge of jealousy and anger flooding back. "He moved to another village and remarried. I had several half-siblings. I never met them though. He was too ashamed of us. He died when I had just passed my thirtieth birthday."

"He must have been quite young."

"He was fifty-one."

Maia clutched her coffee cup in her hands, staring at me and blinking back tears. "I'm so sorry, Dev."

I shrugged and kissed her on the top of her head. "It was a long time ago, Maia."

"He made a terrible mistake," she said. "You are a wonderful man and he should have been proud of you."

I smiled slightly. "Thank you."

Maia lifted the cup to her lips and took a sip. "So, what is your daemon name?" she asked by way of changing the subject.

"I'll never tell."

"I'll ask your mother."

"That's dirty pool." I hesitated and then sighed. "Okay, but you have to promise never to call me by this name."

She made an "X" over her heart. "Cross my heart."

I rolled my eyes. "Oh, boy. I cannot tell you how that inspires confidence."

"Don't be sarcastic, Dev, and don't change the subject."

"What was the subject?"

Maia turned toward the screen door. "Oh, Maggie!" she called out.

"Okay, okay!" I groaned. "Geez, woman, you're stubborn!"

Maia took another sip of coffee. "I prefer the term determined."

"Darkflame," I grimaced.

She looked up and blinked. "Excuse me?"

"My daemon name is Darkflame." I told her, my teeth gritted.

Maia's mouth dropped open and I winced. "That is so *cool!*" she gasped.

"No, it isn't!" I groaned. "It sucks!"

"Are you kidding me? I *love* that name!"

"Maia!" I said, alarmed by her dreamy expression. "You promised!"

"If I ever have a baby I might just use it since you don't want it."

"Not for *my* kid you won't!"

She grinned. "Were you planning to have children with me, Dev?" she teased, batting her eyelashes at me.

I could feel the blood draining out of my face. My skin was probably completely white. Maia laughed. "It isn't funny!" I exclaimed, frustrated.

"Okay, okay. I'm sorry. I won't tease you anymore and I promise not to call you Darkflame even though it *is* a totally cool name." She got up from the stool and kissed me with enough heat to make my skin turn almost as red as Damien's. "But you owe me."

I scooped her into my arms and headed for the stairs. "How can I ever repay you?"

She wound her arms around my neck. "I'm sure you'll think of something."

My brother stayed to dinner and to my surprise, he wasn't a total doofus. He could actually carry on a relatively normal, intelligent conversation when he wanted. He didn't mention the eighties once. He had heard about the rogue sovereign though.

"Do guys have any idea who it is?" Damien asked.

I shook my head. "We have a few suspects and two of them are women. But, there is no evidence connecting any of them to the murders of humans."

"You mean the dead humans they found at the zoo last week?" Damien asked. "I thought the human cops said that they snuck into the lions' cages and got eaten. I thought it was a little strange that ten humans crawled into a lion's cage and that two lions could eat ten people in only twelve hours but maybe they were small humans."

"Hold it!" I gasped. "Back up! What's this?"

Damien told me about the report from the Blackridge six o'clock news about eight days ago. It appeared that the person who feeds the lions arrived to find a mass of decimated bodies in the lions' cage. At the time, they were not sure how many, but eventually they discovered that there were ten adults. The cops decided that they had been out drinking (obviously...I mean what sober person is going to get into a cage with a lion?), and the lions killed and ate them. I was with Damien. Two lions were not going to eat that many people in less than twelve hours. It turns out that it was not the first time either. According to Damien, five human bodies turned up in the hyenas' cage a month earlier. The newspapers claimed that it was a variation on the game of chicken, but it was too coincidental for me. No wonder we never heard about any vampire victims. Demon was right. Something had been eating them.

"How the hell could we have missed that?" I wondered aloud.

Damien shrugged. "It was in all the newspapers."

"I'd better call Demon." I said rising from the dinner table. I paused. "Hey, thanks for the tip, Damien."

He beamed at me. "No prob, bro."

I phoned Demon and Hex answered. She said that he wasn't there. He and the others were out hunting. I left a message and then called his cell phone next and left a message there too. I returned to the dinner table in time for dessert, coffee and a deep discussion with my brother about the reasons why ten people would get into the lions' cage and under what circumstances two lions might be persuaded to eat them all or at least chew them up enough to hide the real cause of death. I have to give Mom and Maia credit. They sat there sipping their coffee, listening to us, and their only response to our gruesome discussion was a wrinkled nose or putting the fork down in the middle of a bite.

By the time Damien left us at eight o'clock that evening, I admitted to my mother that I was duly impressed with how grown up he seemed. Mom was amused. "He's been grown up for several centuries, Dev."

"He always seems so immature. You know, with the whole "the eighties are immortal, dude" crap."

Mom smiled and set her wine glass on the tray she had used to serve us our after dinner drinks. "You think that way because you're his big brother. Just because you aren't interested doesn't mean that your brother's interest is immature."

"Mom," I said pointedly. "It's the *eighties*."

She laughed and rose from the sofa. "Well then, my mistake."

I rolled my eyes. "Okay, okay. Being interested in the eighties doesn't mean that Damien is immature, just weird."

My mother didn't respond to that. She picked up the tray and left the room, shaking her head. I looked at Maia. "Am I wrong on this?"

"No." she said. "Your brother's weird, but I still like him."

I smiled. "Actually, I do, too."

The phone rang beside me. I checked the caller ID, but there was no number on the display. That meant only one thing to me. I called out to Mom that I'd get it. "This is Dev." I answered.

"Dev. Fechín. Tell me what's going on."

I repeated the story that Damien had told me about the lions and added the tidbit about the hyenas too.

"Hmm," Demon remarked. "That was right around the time when we were out of town for a few weeks."

Then I remembered. "We were hunting that hellhound. We didn't get back until two days after the last victims were found."

"Yes. If the rogue activity started then, perhaps the timing was not coincidental."

"Was Tanith in town then?" I asked.

"I don't know." Demon said thoughtfully. "However, I will certainly ask her. I will also call the Satana ME and find out what he knows. There must be some kind of autopsy report on them. He will probably have access to it. Now, is there any news from the informant?"

"He hasn't changed his mind about giving us his information if that's what you mean." I frowned. There was a lot of noise going on in the background. "Where the hell are you? What's with all the static?"

"I was tracking down a lead on Scarletti," he told me. "I am on the motorcycle."

"You're driving a motorcycle while talking on your cell phone? Damn, Fechín, that's dangerous!"

He snorted. "I'm a Deadly, for crying out loud, Dev! It's not like I can die!"

"You mean, unlike the other people on the road with you." I asked dryly.

"Okay, okay. I'm pulling in the driveway anyway."

"Hey, did you happen to ask Tanith about her human servant?"

"Not yet."

"Why not?"

"I left before she was up for the night."

"You could have asked Kit."

"She would not tell me."

"Why not?" I asked again.

"Her loyalty is to Tanith, not me."

I shook my head. "I am not so sure of that."

Demon gave a low growl. "This just gets more and more frustrating," he said.

"All we have are questions and no answers. Why would anyone torch Tanith's house? If I was trying to kill her, I would make certain that she was in it."

"It may not have been meant to kill her." I suggested. "Maybe it was just a warning."

"How is it that both Hadrian and Tanith's people have been involved in the rogue activity yet neither of them is the rogue sovereign?"

"Are you so sure that neither of them is the rogue sovereign? And I thought Scarletti torched Tanith's house."

"But *why*, Dev? What reason would he have for torching it *without her in it*? That is what makes this so puzzling. He may have set the warehouse fire but we have no proof that Scarletti set the fire at Tanith's house. No, something else is going on here. I feel the fire at Tanith's house is somehow connected to the rogues but I cannot see how." He was silent for a minute. "It is weird, isn't it?"

"What is?" I asked. "I mean, specifically?"

"Some of Hadrian's people are involved in the rogue activity, but so are some of Tanith's. So one or the other *must* be in control of the rogues."

"Perhaps they are in it together." I suggested.

"How is that possible unless Tanith plans to kill Darkmoon in order to take her place as Hadrian's mate?" Demon asked. "There have not been any attempts on Darkmoon's life or she would be running to us screaming her head off."

"Or she would take matters into her own hands and torch Tanith's place."

"Again, she would make certain that Tanith was in it first. Hold on a minute while I get the front door open." I waited. Then Demon said, "Besides, Tanith has been telling everyone, even her own people, that *I* am her mate."

"It could be a ruse."

"Maybe." he growled in frustration.

"Demon, try to calm down." I urged. "Getting all wound up isn't going to help you solve this."

"Damn it, there isn't time to relax, Dev! They are murdering innocent humans! The longer this takes to solve, the more humans who will die." He sighed. "Are you sure that Maia will not give you the informant's name?"

"She can't, Fechín." I reminded him. "If she gives us his name and any of her other informants find out, they'll never trust her again and we'll lose a valuable source of information."

"Okay. You're right." He paused. "Look, ask her to call him one more time and try to talk him into meeting with us."

"All right," I agreed.

"Hey, Dev?"

"Yeah?"

"We miss you and Maia. It's not the same here without the whole team."

I smiled. "Yeah, we miss you guys too."

"Listen, Dev—hold on a minute. What is it, Bane?" Demon must have put his hand over the receiver because all I heard was a muffled conversation. In a second or two, Demon was back. "Dev, we have a problem."

Alarmed by the urgency in his tone, I sat up straight. Maia did the same, watching me intently. "What's wrong?" I asked.

"We need the name of that informant and we need it now!" Demon told me.

"Why? What's happened?"

"Tanith and her people are gone."

"Gone where?" I gasped.

"I don't know. We were all out hunting Scarletti," he groaned. "They have disappeared, Dev."

Maia made a frantic phone call to her informant. He didn't answer his phone. It occurred to us as it had to the others, that if Tanith was the rogue sovereign then it was probable that she knew about Maia's informant. Whoever he was, he might now be in danger.

I called Demon back and explained that the informant was not answering his phone or his pager. He had news for me too. "I called the Satana's medical examiner about those bodies. I wanted to see if he had any contacts in the human ME's office." Demon told me.

"What did he say?"

"He said that there was very little blood in the lions' cage and hardly any on the lions or in their stomachs. There was a lot of human meat, and flesh and bone but no blood."

"As if someone had drained them of blood before throwing them in with the lions," I suggested. "The humans didn't think that was odd at all?"

"Perhaps they did, but the last thing they would suspect would be a vampire. This was certainly not done by a human."

I didn't think so either.

"Is there any news from Maia's informant?" Demon went on.

Maia had made the difficult decision to give Demon the informant's name if only to save his life. "I know where Blacktooth Scummer lives." Demon said. I heard the motorcycle starting up over the phone. "I have already sent the others on ahead to pick up you and Maia. They should be arriving any time. I will meet you at Scummer's apartment."

Before I could protest, he disconnected. I hung up and looked at Maia, waiting nervously to find out what was happening.

"What do we do now?" she asked.

I explained that the others were coming to get us and that Demon would meet us at Scummer's place. "You don't have to come though."

"Demon said that I was supposed to come too."

"I don't want you endangered, Maia. Scarletti is still out there looking for you."

She laid her hand on my arm. "Dev, Blacktooth is one of my sources. I just handed him over to the Enforcers. I know you are not going over there to hurt him, but I feel that I should be there if only to reassure him."

I agreed, but I didn't like it. "If you're going," I told her. "You're going armed." I handed her one of my smaller daggers. "Here, let's attach it to your belt." A minute later, I stepped back, glad that she had it, but far from satisfied with the situation.

On impulse, I pulled her into my arms and kissed her hard. Maia responded with the same air of desperation and fear that I was feeling. We finally parted and stared at each other.

"Marry me." I blurted.

"Okay." She agreed breathlessly.

I kissed her again. Suddenly, headlights swept the front windows and tires crunched over the gravel. I peeked out the window. "They're here." I said grimly. Maia's face was pale but she wore the same grim and determined expression.

"Let's go." I said and reached for her hand.

She took it and we left the house together.

CHAPTER TWENTY-SEVEN

BANE LOCKED UP ALL four tires as he screeched to a halt in the parking space next to Demon's black Ninja. The rest of us staggered out of the van on weak knees as Bane swung out of the driver's seat, grinning from ear to ear. Riot collapsed at Demon's feet and stared up at him with accusing eyes. "What did we ever do to you?" he demanded.

Demon gave his brother a look of disgust. "You're signing up for driver's ed. classes as soon as we finish talking to Scummer!"

Bane stuck his tongue out at Demon. "Which apartment is his?" Demon asked Maia, choosing to ignore his brother's immature behaviour.

"It's on the fifth floor," she said. "5A. Demon, I really think that I should come up with you. If Blacktooth got my messages, then he knows you're coming. He's going be anxious enough as it is without you guys showing up on his doorstep without me."

"Just let us check the place out first, Maia." Demon said. "If we are walking into a trap, we do not want you walking into it with us. We will survive it." I was glad that he left out the part that she would not. "I will send Dev out if everything is clear, okay?"

"Stay with Maia." Demon said to Kaz. "Kill anything that doesn't identify itself first."

217

"Got it." Kaz climbed back into the van and slid the passenger side door closed.

"I'm not sure I like the idea of leaving her out here." I protested.

"Do you prefer the idea of us running into a gang of rogue vampires in the stairwell with Maia playing target? She is only semi-immortal, Dev."

I glanced back over my shoulder at the van. "We could keep her behind us."

"So, you think someone couldn't sneak up behind us?" Demon replied. "It's too risky. We don't know what we are walking into yet."

"Hell, we're taking a big risk having her here after dark!" I reminded him. "Or have you forgotten that Scarletti is looking for her?"

"I have not forgotten and Kaz is with her."

"We should have left her with my mother." I said gloomily.

"We could not leave her with your mom. Scarletti knows that she was there."

I stopped walking. My stomach plummeted into my boots. "*What*? How?"

"Don't shriek. You sound like a girl."

"Oh, now that hurts, Fechín. What the hell do you mean he knew where she was?"

"Daedalus came to the house." Demon said. "He was waiting when Bane and Riot got back. He was worried because Todd Cooper never came back to his apartment and he found out that he had not been to work in a few days. Also some of the department's phone tapping equipment is missing."

"Oh shit."

"Daedalus thought that Scarletti might have taken control of Cooper again and that they might be tracking Maia through the telephone."

"Fechín, my mother is still there by herself!"

"Serkan went to get her. He will not let anything happen to Maggie."

I took a deep breath and tried to will away the urge to be sick. "Thanks."

"Scarletti may still come here." Demon led us into the building. He stopped in the foyer. "If Maia's cell phone has GPS on it then he might be able to track her. Do you happen to know if she has GPS?"

Oh, shit. I nodded. "We insisted on it, remember? We were worried that someone might use her to get to us and we thought we'd be able to find her using her cell phone." It had never occurred to me that the bad guys could use it to their advantage too.

I stopped in the foyer. "Fechín, I can't do this. I can't leave her."

Demon studied me for a second and then nodded. "Okay, here is what is going to happen." he said. "Bane, you and Riot are going upstairs to check on the informant. The rest of us are going back to wait with Kaz and Maia at the van. Clear the apartment quickly and then call me. We will bring Maia in as quickly as possible. In the meantime, the rest of us are keeping an eye on that van until Bane gives us the signal."

"Thanks." I said as we turned back.

Demon patted my shoulder. "Don't worry, Dev. Let's go back to the van."

Suddenly, we heard a loud bang from outside and something that sounded like fingernails on metal. We burst out of the building in time to see a vampire on top of the van, hauling Maia out by her throat. Her hands clutched his as she tried to pry herself loose. He had peeled the roof back like an orange. Kaz was climbing out after him. It took me a second to recognize Mike Scarletti.

I had seen this kind of vampire before. The wasted body and the paler than pale skin made it evident that he had not fed in days. Black hair hung in thin, greasy strands against its face. Two dark sunken eyes glared at us as we started to run toward the van. These kinds of vampires were desperate and they tended to drain their victims.

And he had Maia.

Kaz had no blade in his hand, but there was something pointed stuck up through the roof from inside the van. I guess Kaz had done what Demon told him and tried to kill whatever didn't identify itself first. Unfortunately, he had missed. Kaz was not about to let Scarletti take Maia without a fight, however. He grabbed for the vampire's ankle, but Scarletti kicked Kaz in the head and Kaz fell backward into the van. Scarletti jumped down on the opposite side of the van, out of our sight as we ran forward.

"Get him!" Demon yelled. He and Bane went around the front of the van while the rest of us circled the back.

It was too late. A second later, a car flew backward out of the parking space on the driver's side. We all had to jump back out of the way, the car narrowly missing us, and I fell over Onyx. I scrambled to my feet as the car spun around and in that brief moment, I recognized Todd Cooper as the driver. Maia was in the back seat struggling with Scarletti.

Demon grabbed the back bumper but Cooper threw the car into drive and fishtailed on his way out of the driveway, tires squealing. It threw Demon off. He rolled and came to his feet in one motion. "Go! Go! Go!" Demon yelled as he ran for the bike. I was right behind him.

The motorcycle roared to life and I jumped onto the back of it as Demon blazed out of the parking lot after Scarletti. Demon went over the curb in an attempt to cut the car off, tossing me like a salad on the back. I clung frantically to the bike's seat trying to stay on and wishing the damned thing had a sissy bar. I kept my eyes on the vehicle ahead. I was terrified that Demon would lose Scarletti who already had a hell of a head start.

In spite of my fear that we were going end up as speed bumps on the road I urged him to drive faster. "*Stand on it!*" I yelled in Demon's ear.

"I am going as fast as I can!" he yelled back.

I heard a horrible screech and glanced behind us. The others were in the van chasing us. The rest of the roof ripped away. I watched the metal roof clattering across the pavement, sparks flying.

"I hope there was no one behind them!" I hollered. "Can't this piece of shit go any faster? Scarletti's getting away!"

"He is not going to get away!" Demon argued.

"Try cursing at it!" I suggested. "Maybe the foul language will convince it to go faster!"

"Hang on!" Demon yelled back. "Corner!" He veered away from Cooper's car. The van roared past us as we continued down a side street going 150.

"What the hell are you doing?" I yelled. "We're going to lose them!"

"Trust me!" he shouted back.

He took another corner, still doing 150. I know because I was staring intently at the speedometer. Suddenly he started to slow down and came to a stop, blocking the road.

"What are you waiting for?" I asked.

"That." he said pointing.

I looked up. Cooper's car was heading directly for us. "Uh, Demon? Is he going to stop?" I asked.

"Brace yourself." Demon replied.

"Brace—" I repeated and then realized what he meant. "Oh, shit." I squeezed my eyes shut waiting for the impact.

Suddenly, I heard the squeal of tires and I barely had time to grab onto Demon before he took off after the car. The van pulled in behind us. Cooper's car made another sharp left down a side street.

"What is he trying to do?" I demanded. "He's driving in circles!"

"He is attempting to get downtown." Demon called back. "We don't want him going that way. There are too many innocent people around."

"He probably thinks we won't execute him in a public place!" I shouted.

"He's wrong, but I would rather not have an audience," he replied. "So we're going to try to drive them out of town."

A bug smacked me in the forehead. I was starting to understand why people wore helmets with face shields. "How are we going to do that?" I demanded.

"Trust me," he said again as we squealed around another corner.

Cooper's car turned right at the other end of the street and headed toward us again. He spotted us and tried to make a right. The van suddenly appeared at that corner, blocking him. At the last second, Cooper wrenched the wheel and made a left. We took off down another side street. Every turn Cooper made, there we were blocking his exits, methodically forcing him away from Blackridge.

As soon as we hit the city limits, Cooper hit the accelerator, pushing the car as fast as it could go without falling to pieces. Demon sped up as well. I checked the speedometer again. I couldn't see the needle anymore.

Two miles outside of town, Cooper swung the car down a gravel side road. It was a foolish thing to do. That side road ended at a field. Demon glanced back at me. His hair whipped around his face, nearly obscuring his eyes. "Ditch the coat and get ready!"

Obediently, I shed my jacket. The wind ruffled my feathers and pulled at my wings. We were finally starting to catch up. The bike could go far faster than Cooper's car. As we drew closer, the headlights from the bike shone into the back seat. I couldn't see Maia but I could see her feet as she kicked at Scarletti. He was leaning over her, snarling, with his fangs bared. Her hand, curved like a wolf's claw, came up and swiped at him. He reared back for the moment, but she couldn't hold him off indefinitely. He was stronger than she was and he finally yanked her up, twisting her head back and baring her throat even as she started to shift into werewolf form. Then suddenly, Cooper lost control of the car on the gravel and it began to fishtail wildly.

Demon looked back at me over his shoulder. Our gazes connected. "This is your execution, Dev!" he yelled. Then his voice lowered to a hiss. "Take the bastard's head."

In response, I opened my wings out just enough so that I could wrench my weapons from their sheaths on my back. I rose to my feet, standing on the seat

221

of the bike, keeping low with my wings folded until Demon gave the signal. *"Take him!"*

Using the wind from the speed of the bike, I opened my wings all the way and launched myself into the air as Demon ducked his head giving me lots of space. I soared over him and landed on top of the car just as it fishtailed again. I fell to my knees, still clutching the blades in my hands. In one motion, I jammed both blades through the roof of the car. The car went out of control sending me flying off. I slammed into a tree.

Seconds later, I heard the van screech to a halt and the next thing I knew Kaz, Riot, and Morgana were standing over me, their faces tight with concern. "Dev," Riot gasped. "Are you all right?"

Onyx rushed up at that moment, his expression one of admiration. *"That* was bloody *awesome!"* he said fervently.

"Maia!" I started to leap to my feet and then hissed in pain, sinking back to the ground clutching my arm to my chest.

"What's wrong?" Kaz demanded. He leaned over me again. That was when I noticed his black eye.

"I think my arm is broken or something. What the hell happened to your face?"

He grimaced and touched his left eye gingerly. "That's where Scarletti nailed me."

"Help me up." I said.

Kaz and Riot gently assisted me to my feet as a large dark wolf flew out of the back door of the car and promptly turned back into Maia. She ran to me and threw her arms around my waist. She was sobbing hysterically. "I killed him! I killed him!"

"You killed him?" I peered over her head into the car. The small dagger that I had given to Maia was stuck in Scarletti's gut. There were also big chunks of flesh missing from Scarletti's arms and big claw mark marred his face. It appeared that she had gotten him right across the eyes and nose. Those injuries he probably would have recovered from, but Scarletti was also pinned to the back of the seat with a blade through his chest. The other blade had gone straight through the top of Scarletti's skull. There was no recovering from that.

"It looks like you went wolf on him." I said to her.

Her eyes shifted away from mine. "I did and I stabbed him too."

"However, judging from the big sword through his skull I think I can safely suggest that *that* probably had more to do with his death than the couple of little nibbles you took out of his arm." I told her.

"Oh, Dev!" Maia gave a laugh that turned into a sob. She leaned her forehead against my chest and hugged me tightly.

"Ow!" I announced.

She drew back, abruptly. "What is it?"

"He broke his arm when he slammed into the tree." Kaz told her.

Maia gaped up at me and tears filled her eyes again. "Oh god, Dev!" She buried her face in her hands.

"Hey. Don't cry." I said gently, stroking her hair. She looked up at me and my fingers skimmed over her chin and neck. "I'm a Deadly. I'll be healed before you can say Sloth." That is when I saw the blood seeping through my fingers. "What happened? I didn't nick you with the blades, did I?"

"No." she said, touching her fingers to her neck. "I stabbed him when he bit me and then he let me go just before the blades came through the roof."

I gaped at her. "He bit you?" I tilted her head to look at her neck. Two fang puncture wounds oozed blood. "He bit you! That sonofabitch bit you!"

I leapt into the back seat of the car, yanked the dagger out of his gut, and proceeded to stab him into mincemeat. It didn't matter that he was already dead and couldn't feel it. I was beyond reason by that point. I heard Maia screaming and felt hands pulling me from the car. My arm shrieked in protest so I let them drag me away. Kaz and Riot released me as Bane snatched the dagger from my hand. Maia wrapped her arms around my waist again. I held her tightly, breathing hard more from fear and anger than from exertion.

"Damn him!" I snarled. *"Damn him to hell!"*

"Don't, Dev!" Maia sobbed against my chest. "Please, I can't stand anymore!"

Feeling guilty that I had upset her, I stroked her back gently and took a deep breath to try to calm myself down. "Okay. I'm sorry. Where's Fechín?" I demanded, looking around. I hadn't seen him since I had launched myself from the back of his motorcycle.

"There." Onyx pointed.

I looked back at the car. I'd forgotten about the driver but Demon had not. He was sitting in the front seat talking to Todd Cooper.

"That sonofabitch!" I started for the car again but Maia held me back.

"Dev, please." she whispered. "Hold me, please. Just hold me."

"You're injured, you idiot!" Bane reminded me sharply. "What are you going to do? Beat his ass with one arm? Let Demon handle Cooper."

I drew Maia back to me and held her tightly against me with my one good arm. Kaz, Riot, Bane, Morgana, and Onyx moved in closer to us and we stood huddled together, watching Demon and Cooper. Cooper was staring at Demon with wide eyes as he spoke. With each word, Todd seemed to grow paler and paler. Finally, Demon pointed at Scarletti and Cooper looked over his shoulder into the backseat. The next second, he was stumbling out of the car. He fell to his knees in the dirt and retched up possibly every meal he had eaten for the last week.

When Cooper had finished tossing up his guts, he staggered to his feet on shaky legs. Demon grasped him under the arm and hauled him up. Cooper looked at all of us with wild, terrified eyes. "Oh my god, I'm sorry. I'm sorry," he moaned.

"You think saying *I'm sorry* makes up for—" I burst out angrily. Maia touched my cheek to stop me. I didn't say anything more but Demon wisely kept Cooper out of my reach.

"If I were you, Cooper," Demon said coolly as he extracted his cell phone from his coat pocket. "I would abandon this car."

Cooper needed no further encouragement. He started running like hell for Blackridge and never looked back. Kaz looked at Demon. "Were you planning to make him run all the way back to Blackridge?"

Demon shrugged. "It's not that far. Besides, I don't really care if he gets a leg cramp, do you?"

Kaz didn't smile. "I hope the bastard drops dead of a heart attack."

"From the look on his face when he saw the body," Riot said. "I'm surprised that he didn't."

"Don't be too hard on him." Demon replied. "When I got in the car and started talking to him, he didn't respond. I thought he was in shock at first but that wasn't it."

"He was hypnotized?" Bane asked.

Demon nodded. "It took me five minutes just to break through Scarletti's hold on him."

"I thought that would have been broken as soon as Scarletti died." Bane said.

"It doesn't work that way. Most human servants go catatonic when their vampire master dies and they never come out of it."

"If he was Scarletti's servant," Onyx frowned. "Then he was a willing participant in all of this and you just let him go?"

Demon shook his head. "One doesn't have to be willing to be made a servant, Onyx. It makes it easier, but since Cooper was hypnotized then chances are that he resisted and it was the only way Scarletti could get Cooper to help him." He glanced toward Cooper's retreating figure. "He's lucky that Scarletti's hold over him was not very strong. Some human servants end up in mental hospitals after their master dies."

"How nice for him," I sneered. "I'd really hate to see him suffer."

Demon looked at me. "Dev, I know how you must feel, but—" He broke off with a sigh. "Look, let's just get moving and start the clean up before someone comes along." He flipped open his cell phone and glanced up as he hit a speed dial button. "Kaz, retrieve the bike, please. Morgana, take Maia and Dev home while the rest of us finish up here. Call Daedalus on the way home and tell him to send some officers to help us."

"Okay, Demon." Morgana said and started to lead Maia away.

I stood my ground. "I want to help with the clean up."

Demon barely glanced at me. "You are on the injured list right now. Go home."

"I'll heal."

"Not in the next thirty seconds you won't."

"Someone still needs to check on Scummer."

"We can take care of that later." He stared off into space for a moment. "I have a bad feeling about him. I don't think an hour or two is going to make much difference now."

"You think he is dead." I said lowering my voice and glancing over my shoulder to make sure that Maia had not heard us.

Demon reached out and touched my uninjured shoulder. His tone was compassionate. "Listen, Dev, don't worry about this. Just go home and take care of Maia. She needs you right now more than we do. You have done your part; now let us take care of the rest."

I glanced back at Maia, standing next to Morgana, shaking and pale. I looked back at Demon and nodded. "Okay." I walked toward the two women and led Maia over to the van. As I helped her into it, I heard Demon speaking to whoever had answered the phone.

"Nightscare, this is Fechín," he said. "Tonight, dinner is on us."

LaVergne, TN USA
07 December 2010
207637LV00001B/37/P

9 781450 271677